I0588739

EUREKA

KAYLA SPAIN

EUREKA

KAYLA SPAIN

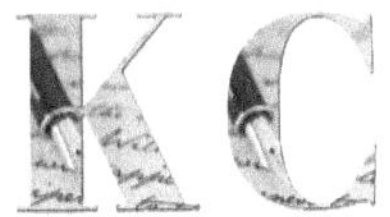

Title: Eureka
First published in 2025 by Kani Consultants, Newcastle, Australia.
Copyright © 2025 Kayla Spain.

A catalogue record for this work is available from the National Library of Australia

Cover and illustrations designed by Lea Deering
Published by Kani Consultants www.kaniconsultants.com.au

Typeface: Times New Roman 12 point

ISBN: 978-0-6450773-4-6   Eureka (paperback)

Author: Spain, Kayla
Subjects: Fiction / General, modern, nursing home, elderly, juvenile, assisted suicide, drugs, drama, romance, fantasy, action, adventure, saga,

CHAPTER ONE

"The court finds the defendant, Frances Louise Hadfield, guilty. You are hereby sentenced to six months' community service in a location not less than one hundred kilometres from the plaintiff. Court dismissed."

As the crack of the judge's gavel echoed through the almost empty courtroom, Frankie shook her head in frustration.

"Fucking typical," she muttered to herself. It wasn't the first time she'd been betrayed by the people closest to her. Far from it. This was her lot in life, and today's events confirmed it.

"What now?" Frankie asked the woman in a suit sitting next to her.

"Well, now, you'll need to decide where you'd like to serve your hours. Then, we'll need to find you a workplace and somewhere to live. Come back to my office and we'll go through it."

Back at the legal practice, the lawyer printed out a map and placed it on the desk in front of Frankie.

"Right, this circle here is a one-hundred-kilometre radius from Melbourne, so you'll need to choose a location outside that. Why don't you take this home with you and have a think about where you'd like to go. We just need to have your decision for the court by Monday."

"Awesome, can't wait," said Frankie sarcastically. "So many wonderful places to choose from, how will I ever pick one?"

The lawyer leaned back in her chair, removing her glasses. "Look, I know this is hard Frances …"

"Frankie," she interrupted bluntly.

"Frankie. I know it's hard, and I know that arseholes win all the time when it comes to the law, but you've got to learn how to outsmart them. If you hang around with vipers, you're going to get bitten."

"So, what, you're like my mum now?" spat Frankie, snatching the map from the desk and storming out of the room.

"Monday, Frankie!" shouted the lawyer after her.

"What fucking ever!" Frankie yelled back.

Frankie marched out of the building, her head hung low, her long black hair swinging across her face. She was angry. Angrier than usual. *That fucking bastard,* she thought. *After all the things I've done for him. Double-crossing mother fucker. He'll fucking pay for this.*

Weaving through the bustling crowds on the street, she made her way down the stairs to the platform at Flinders Street Station. She boarded the next train to Springdale and leant against the doors, staring out at the blur of passing scenery, wondering what the hell she was going to do. She imagined forcing the doors open and throwing herself in front of an oncoming train. Problem solved. It seemed her whole life was one big problem to solve. One big problem with no solution.

Her daydream was interrupted by people congregating around her, preparing to get off at the next stop. She wondered where they were all going. Were they going home to a loving family? Were they going home to eat a lonely microwave dinner on their own? Were they going to the park to sleep on a bench tonight? So many people, so many stories. It made her feel more alone than ever.

Arriving at Springdale Station, Frankie got off the train and wandered slowly to her house. A shitty house in a shitty suburb. A place where no-one looked after anything, mainly because no-one owned any of it. A place where you had to look out for yourself, because no-one else would. Everyone was too busy trying to take something from someone else. She hated this place and everyone in it.

"At least I'll get the fuck away from these losers for six months," Frankie muttered to herself as she swung through the broken screen door of her house.

Her Aunty Isobel shouted at her from the filthy kitchen. "Frankie! Where were you? I couldn't find you anywhere!"

"I had an appointment Izzy – sorry! What do you want?"

"Don't worry about it now, I needed some durries, so I had to make Alan go and get them. You're so unreliable. I never know where you are!"

"Sorry Aunt Izzy! I have things to do you know. You're not the only one with …"

Crack! A massive punch to the side of Frankie's face sent her crashing to the floor.

"Fuck! What the …"

Again, another vicious blow struck her head. Dazed and confused, Frankie squinted up to see her cousin, Alan, standing over her. His sweaty, red face and bloodshot eyes were seething with rage, his fist clenched above her face, almost begging her to utter another word.

"I suggest you apologise to your cousin for having to do your jobs!" spouted Isobel with a smug look on her face, her fat arms crossed against her fat chest.

"Sorry," Frankie whimpered, dragging herself across the floor and wiping the blood from her mouth. She slowly pulled herself to her feet, staggered down the hallway to her bedroom and closed the door. She flopped on her bed, desperately trying to stifle any thoughts of her parents, but this time she couldn't. This had been one of the worst days ever and she couldn't fight it any longer. She hugged her pillow and began to sob.

Opening her bedside drawer, she took out her fix-it pills, quickly swallowing four. *Only fifteen minutes* she thought, and she continued to sob for those fifteen minutes.

Six hours passed before Frankie stirred from her drug-induced slumber. The room was dark, apart from the streetlight shining through the window. She peered at her phone to see it was just after eleven. She hurriedly stuffed all her belongings into her only suitcase. Pressing her ear up to the door, she listened for voices. Everything was quiet. Slowly and silently, she opened it and tiptoed through the house, carefully dodging the maze of empty beer cans strewn all over the floor. As she stepped through the broken screen door and onto the dimly lit street, something inside her knew that she would never again set foot in this house. *Good fucking riddance,* she thought. And off she went. To see the lawyer. She only had ten hours to kill.

The walk to the train station took longer than usual. Not only was Frankie lugging all her worldly possessions, but she was also nursing a throbbing, swollen face and a headache from hell. Luckily, she managed to catch the last train into Melbourne. It was much safer to loiter around the city with the other zombies than to be stuck at Springdale Station for the night.

After finding an empty bench under a streetlight just outside Flinders Street Station, Frankie took out the crumpled map she'd snatched from the lawyer's office.

"Right," she muttered to herself. "Where shall we serve our sentence Frances Louise Hadfield? Bumfuckville perhaps?"

Glancing around to see if anyone had noticed her rambling to herself, her only companions were the local hobos sleeping on their sheets of cardboard, covered in old blankets. As she looked at them, she felt a strange comfort. She realised there was still some leeway left before she finally hit rock bottom.

"There!" Frankie stabbed the map with her finger. "That's where we're going!"

She stuffed the map back into her pocket and curled up on the bench using her suitcase for a pillow, trying to ignore the enormous thumping pain in her head.

The sound of traffic woke Frankie with a start, surprising her that she'd managed to get any sleep at all.

Commuters were streaming out of the station like an army of ants, many of them staring at her as they passed. *Haven't they ever seen a person with a fucking suitcase before?* she thought, annoyed also by the stiffness in her neck from sleeping on her suitcase. Her aching face quickly made her realise why people were noticing her. She immediately put on her sunglasses and pulled her hair forward to hide her face.

The time was just after seven so she only had to fill in another couple of hours before she could see the lawyer. She slowly stretched, picked up her suitcase and joined the morning bustle, making her way down to McDonalds to use the bathroom.

Catching her reflection in the mirror, Frankie let out a gasp of horror. The damage to her face was much worse than she expected. Tears started to well in her eyes, so she blinked them away, frantically stuffing down the myriad of emotions which were bubbling to the surface.

Now wasn't the time for reflection or self-pity. She just needed to get this shit done.

She gently washed her face, brushed her hair, took several deep breaths, and walked out to buy herself a much-needed large dose of caffeine.

Wandering down to the river, Frankie sat under a tree and drank her coffee, staring blankly out at the sunlit ripples on the water. She laid on the grass and closed her eyes, lulled off to sleep by the constant hum of the passing pedestrians.

The sound of kids squealing shocked Frankie from her semi-consciousness. It took her a moment to remember where she was. She checked the time. It was five to nine. *Finally.*

She gathered her belongings and made her way up to Collins Street.

"Yes, can I help you?" asked the well-dressed receptionist on the twenty-third floor, looking Frankie up and down with a condescending smirk.

"You can start by pulling your head out of your arse!" snapped Frankie, as she stomped off to find her own way to the office.

"Excuse me! You can't just go in there without an appointment!" squawked the receptionist.

Frankie lifted her arm, giving her the finger before turning the corner and entering the lawyer's office.

"Frankie!" The lawyer was obviously surprised to see her standing there.

"Sorry Miss Hooper, I tried to" whimpered the receptionist who had chased Frankie down the hallway.

"It's fine Sophie, I can see her now."

Frankie put her hand on her hip and smiled sarcastically at the receptionist, who was trying her best to appear unruffled before strutting off.

"She needs a good root," muttered Frankie.

"So, Frankie, take a seat. Can I get you a water or a coffee or something?"

"No thanks." Frankie pulled out a chair and sat down.

The lawyer leant forward, staring at her. "Frankie! What the hell happened to you? Are you okay?"

"My fucking *family* happened to me," answered Frankie, hanging her head and pulling her hair across her face.

"Do you want me to call someone? The police?"

"Fuck no!" barked Frankie. "Let's just get this done already! I've decided where I want to go. Ballarat."

"Oh, the *golden* city. Okay, why Ballarat?"

"Why not? It's the only place I remember. I used to go there on holidays when I was a kid."

"With your *family*?" quizzed the lawyer with a concerned look.

"No, not them. My parents. They're gone now."

"Oh, I'm so sorry. So, this other *family* of yours, who" she pointed to Frankie's face.

"I don't want to talk about it okay? Just *leave* it!" she snapped.

"Okay, fine," said the lawyer, holding her hands in the air. "Well, right then, let's see what we can get organised, Frankie!" She typed on her computer, printed out a list and handed it to Frankie. "These are all the government subsidised accommodation options in Ballarat that currently have vacancies."

"Do any of them have a pool?" asked Frankie sarcastically.

"If they did, I probably wouldn't swim in it!" quipped the lawyer, instantly looking embarrassed as Frankie glared at her. She quickly changed the subject.

"So, what sort of community service work would you be interested in? There are a few different options. You could work for the Salvation Army or the Samaritans, you could help out at a soup kitchen, or a youth centre, or an old people's home, or"

"Old people's home," interrupted Frankie. She didn't really know why that choice appealed to her but decided to go with it.

"Okay, great. Let's see which ones would be willing to take you." She again typed on her computer while Frankie stared out the window. She could see people in other high-rise office buildings and wondered if anyone else was in her situation, meeting with their lawyer to organise their own banishment from the city.

"Here you go, Frankie. This is a list of all the retirement homes in Ballarat which are approved for the government's relocation program. You don't have to choose now; you can wait until you get there. You'll need to have a supervisor at the home who'll sign off on your attendance and conduct, report once a week and send it through to the Department. You'll also receive a fortnightly government allowance, but out of that you'll need to pay all your expenses, including your rent. Got any questions?"

"What about transport? I don't have a car."

"Here's a Myki card – it's got a hundred dollars' credit on it. Use this to get down there; bus or train; up to you. I'd suggest choosing your accommodation close to where you'll be working. That'll save you some money. You'll have a week to get everything organised; all the details are in your paperwork. I've also put in my business card. If you need anything, please give me a call and I'll help in any way I can."

She handed Frankie an envelope and grabbed her gently by the hand. "Good luck, Frankie. I really hope this works out for you. I know things probably don't feel too hopeful at the moment, but you know what they say about a change being as good as a holiday."

"Yeah, well, it can't be any worse than this shithole." She turned and walked out of the office, suitcase in tow, blowing a kiss to Sophie on the way out.

Frankie made her way to Southern Cross Station to wait for the next train to Ballarat. *Golden City here we come. Golden City my arse,* she thought, but the events of the past day had left her with very few options. Oddly, it made her feel better knowing that she had no choice but to leave. At least that was one less decision she had to worry about.

CHAPTER
TWO

"Next stop, Ballarat Station." The announcement interrupted Frankie's dream in which she was trying to ride a bike up a hill, but the pedals wouldn't work. She was relieved to wake up. She hated that dream. Almost as much as the falling from the sky one. Yawning, she looked at her phone. It was almost midday. She'd planned on choosing her workplace and accommodation on the train, but she was so exhausted that the clattering and rocking of the train had sent her off to sleep.

Her stomach rumbled.

Shit, she thought, *I haven't eaten anything for two days. No wonder I feel sick.* She lifted her suitcase down from the overhead rack as the train was pulling into the station. Stepping onto the platform, a flood of memories washed over her. She hadn't been here since her last holiday with her parents. They'd always caught the train here, and Frankie instantly recalled as a kid what a huge, exciting adventure it was.

She slowly walked through the concourse, soaking in the surroundings. The old majestic architecture of the station seemed familiar, as did the feeling of stepping back in time. A bittersweet sensation of nostalgia suddenly knotted itself in her stomach, which she quickly dismissed before heading out in search of a cheap meal.

As she wandered up the main street, the smell of bacon wafting from a café quickly got her attention. She took a seat at one of the rickety tables on the cobblestone footpath and picked up the menu. Almost immediately, a cheery middle-aged woman in a red and white checked apron appeared, carrying a bottle of water and a glass.

"Hello love! How are you today? Here's some water. Are you ready to order or do you need a minute?"

"Morning," answered Frankie "Yep. I'd like bacon and poached eggs and a large cappuccino please."

"No worries – coming right up!"

Frankie was glad to see a friendly face after all the hostility she'd endured recently. As she waited for her meal, she began to read over her list of housing options.

"Here we are – bacon and eggs and your coffee!" Frankie's mouth started to water at the sight of her very generous plate of food, complete with baked beans and sourdough toast slathered in butter.

"Thank you." She looked up at the waitress to reveal her technicolour shiner emerging from the side of her sunglasses.

"Oh dear! What happened to you? Are you ok?"

"I'm fine," answered Frankie, pulling her hair forward and waving her hand to imply it was nothing to worry about. "I'm actually new to the area, and I'm trying to figure out my way around."

She pointed to the list in front of her, diverting the conversation away from her blatantly obvious injury.

"Ooh, well, I can help you with that love! I'll let you eat your meal in peace first though!" She patted Frankie gently on the arm and went back inside.

Frankie consumed everything on her plate and enjoyed every morsel. She sat back in her chair slowly finishing her coffee, feeling very satisfied and ready to take on the next part of her journey.

"Well, someone was hungry!" laughed the waitress, collecting her empty plate.

Frankie nodded, rubbing her stomach. "That was great."

"Let me get rid of these, and I'll be back in a jif."

She returned with Frankie's bill and sat down in the chair opposite her.

"So, what can I do to help you find your way around?"

"Well, I have a list of places here, but I have no idea where any of them are, or what the areas are like, so do you reckon you could have a look for me and—"

Before she could finish her sentence, the waitress had taken the list and was scanning it with a serious look on her face. "Well, if it were *my* choice, I'd definitely go with the Lake Wendouree one – it's lovely out there. You've got the lake, and the gardens. Lots of beautiful homes out there too. And it's *safe,*" she emphasised, looking Frankie directly in the eye.

"But then again," the waitress continued, "the young ones love it in town. There's lots to do and you've got all the pubs and restaurants, if that's your thing. It's a good place to meet people. Maybe you could take a stroll and have a look? Just follow this road and it will take you straight into the heart of town. These ones here… do you mind?" she asked, pulling her pen from her apron to write on the list.

"No – go for it." replied Frankie.

"These ones here," she said, drawing asterisks next to several listings "are all in town, all in walking distance of here. If it was me, I'd choose one of these or the one at Wendouree. I'd probably give the other suburbs a miss. A bit harder to get around without a car. I'm guessing you don't have a car?" she said with a smile, looking at Frankie's suitcase.

"No, I don't. Not yet anyway. I actually like the sound of the ones in town. Thanks for that. I'll go check them out." Frankie stood up and rummaged through her wallet to pay the waitress.

"Thanks love – you have a good day. Hope to see you again some time… and good luck!" and with a wave she flitted off to serve another customer.

Frankie made her way along the street, her suitcase in tow, feeling much more cheerful with a full stomach and a plan of attack. She took her time, enjoying the sunshine and admiring all the beautiful old buildings. At that moment, she almost felt like she didn't have a worry in the world.

She noticed the people on the streets seemed different here; much more relaxed. They were all going about their day without that look of desperation on their faces. Unlike the mindless drones of the Melbourne rat race. *I reckon I might like it here,* she thought. *It'll be like six months of chill time. Time away from Melbourne and...* Her thoughts were jolted straight back to the scumbags in her life and instantly she felt the familiar black cloud closing in around her.

"Right! Let's find these places," she muttered to herself, pushing away all thoughts of Melbourne and the people there.

Frankie wandered the streets for the next two hours, checking out all the inner-city options on her list, trying to visualise what it would be like to live in each one. She finally decided on one which, although not the nicest looking place from the outside, was in an area that seemed to have a good vibe about it.

There were shops and restaurants nearby and an old Irish pub around the corner. A lover of Guinness, she'd already imagined herself there, propped up on a bar stool drinking a pint of her favourite black brew.

"Learmonth House" she read on the old brick façade of the building as she climbed the stairs, taking a deep breath to calm the nerves which were now beginning to surface. She pressed the old brown Bakelite doorbell and waited. The door opened with a creak and she was greeted by the smiling face of a woman in her fifties, her silver-grey hair pulled up into a bun.

"Hello, can I help you?" asked the woman in a soft voice.

"Oh hi," answered Frankie, "I'm hoping you might have a vacancy here for me - I have paperwork here." Frankie fumbled around in her pocket to retrieve the folded papers, handing them to the woman. "I'm on a government program, and well, the paperwork will explain everything."

"Come on in," smiled the woman, leading Frankie down the hallway into the office at the end. "Please, have a seat. I'm Ruth. I manage this place, well, try to anyway," she said with a chuckle. Frankie instantly felt at ease with her. She liked people with a sense of humour.

"I'm Frankie, um, Frances. I'm on a community service program," Frankie squirmed in her seat, "but I'm not a criminal!"

"It's okay, Frankie," laughed Ruth, grabbing her hand gently. "It's not the Spanish inquisition here, no need to feel nervous. We've all got our stories to tell. And I'll bet you have a few of your own."

Frankie instantly felt awkward and pulled her hair over her bruised face. "Don't worry, I've seen much worse than that." Ruth continued, "We have people come to stay here for all sorts of reasons. Some are recovering addicts, some are escaping from abusive relationships and have nowhere else to go, some are just regular folk who can't afford anything else. But we're all just one big family here, warts and all." Ruth smiled and quickly looked at Frankie's paperwork.

"You're very welcome here, Frankie. I'll just need to let you know the rules first. We have a curfew here – everyone has to be inside by ten pm each night. The front door is locked at ten and if you miss the deadline, you won't be able to get back in until six am the next morning. There are no drugs or alcohol allowed in the building, for obvious reasons. If you want to go out and drink, that's your business, as long as you don't disturb anyone else when you get back. Breakfast is served each morning in the dining room between six thirty and eight, and dinner each evening between six and seven thirty. You just need to organise your own lunch. Rent is a hundred and eighty dollars per week, paid up front, which includes the meals. We have wifi here, there's a TV room and a games room, and there's a laundry out the back. I think that's about it, but I'm always buzzing around somewhere so you only have to ask."

"I'll take it!" blurted Frankie nervously, "Please."

"Great. Come on, I'll show you your room."

On the way, Ruth showed Frankie the dining room; a huge old room with high ornate ceilings and dark timber floorboards, which would have been magnificent back in its day. The lounge room was next, with old red velvet lounges and a table in the middle filled with books. There was a big flat screen TV on the wall, which looked totally out of place, but which also reassured Frankie that she hadn't been caught in a time warp back to the eighteen hundreds.

Ruth led the way up a creaky old staircase with carved wooden handrails and worn red carpet.

"All the bedrooms and bathrooms are up here Frankie. You'll need to share the bathroom with some of the others, so if you can leave it clean and tidy, it makes life easier for everyone."

Frankie stuck her head in and saw the old pink bathtub with the shower above and a white shower curtain. The tiles on the wall were also pink and the floor was covered in a patchwork of black and white tiles. It instantly reminded her of her grandma's bathroom; even the smell of it was familiar. She didn't remember a lot about her grandma, but she definitely remembered her bathroom.

"This is you, Frankie – I hope you'll be comfortable here."

Ruth opened the door to the last room at the end of the hallway. Inside was a single bed with a yellow chenille bedspread, a small white dressing table with a round mirror and two wooden wardrobes. Frankie walked over to the window and looked out.

The room was at the front of the building, so she could see straight out onto the street below.

"It's fine, Ruth – thanks."

"I'll let you settle in, Frankie. Here's your room key. Come and see me later and we'll sort out your first week's rent. If you need anything, just let me know. See you at dinner. You'll get to meet the others then. They're not a bad bunch."

And with a kind smile, Ruth closed the door.

Frankie flopped on the bed, relieved that she finally had somewhere to call home for the next six months. *I hope they're not all a bunch of weirdos.* Then again, who was she to judge? She'd just had an AVO issued against her by a lying scumbag drug dealer and been beaten up by her alcoholic cousin. *I'm probably the biggest fucking weirdo here.* She started unpacking her clothes into the mothball scented wardrobes. She took particular care to hide her bag of contraband out of sight in one of her jacket pockets.

From outside her window Frankie could hear the hum of the traffic and a sudden loud burst of laughter from a passing group of people. She looked out to see two young couples wobbling up the footpath, laughing and joking with each other. They'd obviously been enjoying a few lunchtime drinks. *What the hell, unpacking can wait.*

She ventured back out and down around the corner to the green-tiled Irish pub with "Liam O'Connor's" emblazoned in huge gold letters above the door. "Nice to meet you Liam – I'm sure we'll be great friends," she muttered to herself as she walked inside and ordered herself a pint of Guinness at the bar. Frankie took a seat at a table next to the window as the smiling barman brought over her drink.

Looking out at the passing parade, she felt calm and relaxed. The slower change of pace was more enjoyable than she'd imagined, and the people here seemed so much friendlier than the cold-hearted Melbourne natives she'd been accustomed to. *Christ*

– they even pour their Guinness slowly and bring it over to you!

As she sat enjoying her beer, she took out her list of retirement homes. One of the names on the list instantly stood out. It was a home called 'Golden Leaves' at Lake Wendouree. *That's the place that waitress was talking about,* thought Frankie, smirking to herself as she wondered why anyone would choose such a terrible name for an old people's home. *Golden Leaves – all waiting to drop off the tree no doubt.* She googled it and liked what she saw on their website. It was surrounded by trees and situated right on the lake. It was also less than five kilometres away, making it easily within walking distance from Learmonth House. Frankie swigged down the rest of her pint before going to find a chemist to buy something to cover the bruises on her face. The last thing she needed was to play twenty questions with all her new housemates at dinner.

After a satisfying hot shower in her new pink bathroom, her hair wrapped in a towel, Frankie laid on her bed and recounted the events of the day. It felt like days ago since she'd left Melbourne, but it had only been a few hours. She wondered what it would be like working with old people. *I hope I don't have to clean up shit all day.*

Sitting at the dressing table she looked in the mirror. "Jesus!" she shouted. Her face had gone from red to purple with a hint of green.

"Fuck you Alan, you piece of shit! I hope you rot in hell you fucking loser!"

Frankie spent the next thirty minutes awkwardly applying the concealer she'd bought from the chemist, which hid her bruising surprisingly well, considering she had almost zero experience in applying makeup. She got dressed, dried her hair and headed downstairs for dinner.

As she came down the old staircase, Frankie could hear the clattering of pots and pans coming from the kitchen. Several of the residents were already sitting at their tables eating. Ruth was bringing platters of food to the table at the side of the room when she noticed Frankie.

"Hi Frankie. Everyone – this is our new guest Frankie – please make her feel at home."

Frankie gave a self-conscious wave to everyone as they all said hello and stared at her. She quickly headed for the buffet table and dished herself up a plate of food. For the next hour she sat listening and chatting to the others. Frankie had always thought life had dealt her a shit hand, but after hearing some of the conversations that night over dinner, she walked away feeling like Paris Hilton. For the first time she could ever remember, she was actually grateful to be herself. And later, for the first time in a long time, she drifted off to sleep with a calm feeling of peace.

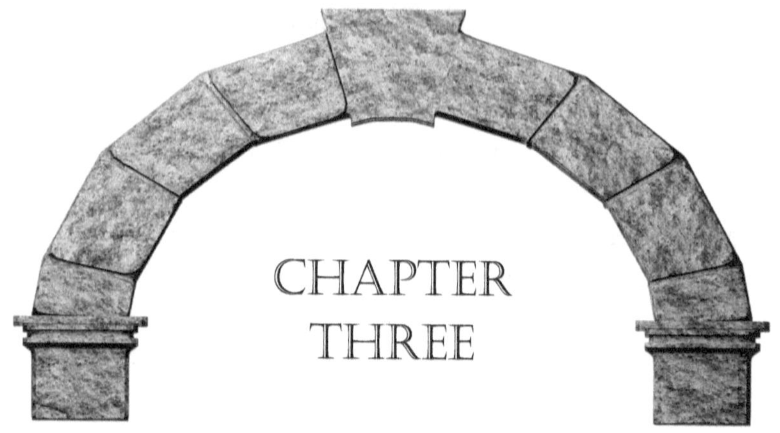

CHAPTER THREE

"Hello, how can I help you?" beamed the young attractive receptionist from behind her desk.

Frankie wondered why it was that all receptionists seem to have this annoyingly fake cheerfulness. If there was one thing she couldn't stand, it was fakers. Or liars. Just like her boyfriend. No, make that *ex*-boyfriend.

"I'm Frances Hadfield. I've got an appointment at ten. I rang earlier."

"Oh yes, I remember. Take a seat and I'll let them know you're here. I'm Clare by the way," she chirped with a smile before disappearing behind swinging doors.

Frankie nodded and took a seat in the sunlit room on one of the plush lounges, next to a coffee table complete with a huge vase of flowers and home decorating magazines. *Looks more like a fancy hotel,* she thought to herself, expecting something far darker and dingier.

She stared through the tall glass windows which surrounded the entire room. Outside were perfectly manicured lawns with lots of tall trees and flower gardens that could have been featured in any of the magazines on the coffee table. She could see some of the old people wandering around the grounds, some with walkers, some in wheelchairs, some alone and some with staff members.

Oh god, she thought, *if I ever get like that, I want someone to put a bullet…*

"Frances, hi!"

A tall, slim middle-aged woman breezed in wearing a crisp white coat, her hand outstretched to greet Frankie.

"I'm Maggie Fletcher. I'm the Facility Manager here. I hear you're interested in joining us?"

"Yes, I am," Frankie answered, fumbling around in her bag to find her paperwork.

"Follow me, Frances. We'll go and talk in my office."

"Frankie. You can call me Frankie."

"Sure, Frankie," smiled Maggie as she led the way up the corridor to her office. It too was a stylish sunlit room looking out onto the lush green landscape.

"Have a seat."

Frankie sat on the edge of her chair, documents in hand, anxious to get the interrogation session over with.

"Here, have some water," said Maggie as she poured from a tall glass decanter. "So, you're from Melbourne. What brings you to Ballarat?"

Frankie took a sip from her water and sat the documents on the desk in front of Maggie.

"Well, as I said on the phone, I'm on a community service program, so I had to go somewhere at least one hundred kilometres from Melbourne. So, I guessed here is as good as anywhere."

Frankie wasn't sure how that answer would come across, but she didn't really care – she was just being honest.

"It's a great town here, Frankie, I'm sure you'll really like it. The staff here are a great bunch of people, and we have some lovely residents. They each have their own problems but our number one priority here is making them all feel at home. There are two different types of care we offer here. Assisted living is for the ones who can do a lot of things for themselves, such as washing and dressing themselves, getting their own meals, getting around mostly on their own. They just need help with things like housework, laundry, and getting them to appointments. They also have medical services on hand twenty-four seven in case they need it. The other type of care we offer is nursing home care. They need constant care and are unable to look after themselves. Some are more able than others, but they need around the clock supervision. What's your background Frankie? Why did you choose Golden Leaves?"

"Well, the last few years I've actually been doing courier work, but I thought a change might be good." Frankie hoped Maggie didn't ask *what* she was actually couriering, so she didn't have to lie. "I was also told this area was nice so that's why I chose this place."

"Yes, it's one of the nicer facilities in Ballarat. I'm sure we'll find plenty for you to do. We're always glad of extra hands around the place. The residents here do a lot of activities, so I'm sure you could help out with that. We'll put you on a two-week trial and see how you go. Anyway, I won't bore you with all of the details. I'll let Rob do that. He's our Head Nurse and he'll be your supervisor, so he can run you through all the fine print and let you know what you'll be doing."

Maggie picked up her phone and called Rob, who appeared in the doorway almost immediately.

"Frankie – this is Robert Turner. Rob, this is Frankie. She's going to be with us for a while, well, hopefully anyway!"

Frankie was surprised by how young he was. She expected the Head Nurse to be someone old and frumpy, but he looked like he was about thirty, maybe younger. Except for the coat he was wearing, he looked nothing like a nurse. He had shoulder length hair pulled back and reminded her of someone you might see in a pair of overalls rather than a medical coat.

"Great to meet you, Frankie! Is that short for something?"

Robert said with a grin and a big firm handshake. Frankie was relieved by the handshake. Her father had always told her to never trust a man with a piss weak handshake.

"Hi Robert. Yep, it's short for Frances."

"Alright then, come with me and I'll show you around the prison!" he joked, clicking his heels together and saluting at Maggie.

"Oh God, Rob, don't scare her off already!" laughed Maggie. "If you need anything at all, Frankie, just let me know. This bloke should be able to help you, but I'm always here as well."

"Thanks Maggie," replied Frankie, having absolutely no idea what to expect next. And with that, Robert strode out of Maggie's office and down the hallway, Frankie racing to keep up.

"So, Frankie, where you from?" asked Robert glancing at her as they walked down the hallway.

"Melbourne".

"Uh huh. Next question, the obvious one – what the bloody hell are you doing here?"

Frankie laughed out loud, surprised by Robert's straight to the point question. "What do you mean?"

"Well, why would a young woman from Melbourne want to come and work at a retirement home in Ballarat?"

"Because I'm on a court order so I had to move somewhere at least a hundred kilometres away. Not sure why I chose Ballarat, maybe 'cause I used to come here as a kid."

"And the work? Why a retirement home?"

"Why not?" shrugged Frankie.

"Good point!" grinned Robert as they made their way to the end of the corridor and through some glass doors. "Well, hopefully this place won't be too boring for you! Don't expect Melbourne nightlife here. After all, the residents have to be in bed by ten!"

He laughed and gently elbowed Frankie. *God what a dork*, thought Frankie, but at least he was upbeat, even if he was corny.

They spent the next hour looking around the whole facility. It surprised Frankie to see how modern the place was, and how content the old people seemed, even if they had no idea who they were. They all seemed to love Robert, probably because he spent most of his time joking with them.

She couldn't help feeling sorry for them though, poor old things, stuck in here and left to die. They looked through the accommodation of the property and Robert explained the different types of care they offered. He introduced Frankie to some of the residents, even ones who were just lying there, oblivious to anything that was going on. She also met a lot of the staff who ranged from nurses and carers to cleaners and cooks. Her head was spinning afterwards. There was so much to look at and take in, much of it confronting and disturbing.

"And that concludes our grand tour of Golden Leaves Estate," said Robert as he gestured like a waiter for Frankie to take a seat in the dining room. "Would you like a coffee?"

"That'd be great, thanks." replied Frankie, relieved that she could finally sit down and rest her brain.

Robert returned with the drinks. "So, what's your impression of the place, Frankie?"

"It's a nice place, the rooms are great, and the gardens are beautiful," Frankie paused, "but it's just…"

"The residents, right?"

"I just feel sorry for them, that's all."

"Well, there's absolutely no reason to feel sorry for them. They live better than I do. I don't have anyone to cook my meals or wash my clothes or drive me places! They're living a life of luxury. They even get to colour in and play bingo! Can you believe it?"

It seemed to Frankie that Robert would find a way to clown around even if the world was going to end. Which was obviously why he was working here. The perfect person to help everyone pretend that their life was happy and meaningful in some way.

Even the ones who were lying there dribbling and shitting their pants.

"You get used to it, Frankie", said Robert on a serious note. "It gets easier after a while. And someone has to look after the old buggers. It's pretty rewarding, actually. Anyway, it'd be great to have you help out around here. I hope we haven't scared you off."

"Not yet. When do I start?"

"Great. Tomorrow! Get here around eight-thirty and I'll be ready with your internment papers and ball and chain!"

Frankie flinched and froze for a moment. How was she supposed to take that last comment? Was he calling her a criminal? She stood up abruptly and quickly slung her bag over her shoulder.

"Great!" she said in a deliberately loud voice. "See you then Robert!" And with a flick of her hair, she stomped out of the dining room with her head in the air.

I'm no fucking criminal, she thought as she strutted angrily out of the grounds. *You wanna see criminal? Try looking at the fucking arsehole who put me here in the first place!*

She chose not to catch the bus back to Learmonth House. She needed the walk to diffuse some of the anger that had ignited like a wildfire inside her. Instead of going straight home, she decided to go and visit Liam instead.

Stepping inside the pub, the smell of burgers and steaks wafted in the air and reminded her how hungry she was. She ordered herself a meal and went to the bar for a drink.

The same barman was there and greeted her with a smile. "Guinness?"

"Yes please" Frankie smiled back and went over to the same table by the window she'd sat at the day before. *Ha, I'm almost a local already.* The barman brought over her pint.

"You new around here?" he asked, grabbing some empty glasses from the next table.

"Yep, I'm from Melbourne. Just staying here for a few months."

"You chose the right pub," he said with a grin. "Best Guinness around."

"I don't doubt it," replied Frankie, taking her first sip.

"Just so you know, we've got live music here Fridays and Saturdays and trivia on Wednesdays. It usually gets pretty packed on the weekend, so it's a good place to meet up with people. Lots of young ones come here. By the way, I'm Tom. I'm the publican here."

"Hi Tom. I'm Frankie. I'm sure I'll be back for more of these," she said, holding up her beer.

"Cheers. Enjoy." said Tom as he took his glasses and returned to the bar.

Frankie sat, going over everything she'd seen that morning. Her head was swirling with thoughts about the home and all the people in it. It was horrendous seeing some of the old people lying there like vegetables, unable to do anything for themselves. She didn't see the point in it all, prolonging life like that. Even though she'd probably chosen the wrong work, she decided she'd wait out the two-week trial and see how it went. Hopefully she wouldn't murder Robert the comedian nurse during those two weeks. Or that annoying receptionist Clare. The waitress interrupted her thoughts with a big chicken parmigiana which she ate way too quickly, washed down with her silky pint of Guinness.

Tom gave her a wave as she left the pub and went to find the local Vinnie's. The uniform at Golden Leaves was black pants and "comfortable" shoes, as Robert had put it. Daggy was more the word that sprang to her mind. Obviously, her ripped jeans and boots weren't going to be good enough for Golden Leaves standards. She found what she needed and headed back to Learmonth House.

As she walked down the hallway past the lounge room, a group of housemates were having a raucous game of cards. One of them spotted her and yelled out to her to join them, which she politely declined. As she climbed the stairs, she met Ruth halfway.

"Hi Frankie. How did you sleep last night? I hope you were comfortable."

"Yep, fine thanks. The traffic woke me up a bit but I'm sure I'll get used to it."

"I see you managed to dodge the big poker game downstairs?"

"Yeah – maybe another time."

"Oh, there'll be plenty of other times. They're games mad that bunch! They're always playing something, always trying to beat each other. It's pretty funny to watch. They've got a big whiteboard out the back with all their scores on it. You'd swear it's the Olympics! Anyway, see you at dinner?"

"See you then," replied Frankie, the thought of eating making her feel sick after wolfing down her lunch at Liam's. She got to her room and collapsed on her bed, rubbing her bloated stomach. She could still hear the card game going on downstairs, with a big roar at the end of each hand, followed by yells of objections.

At dinner that night, the card playing group were still bantering with each other about their game, boisterously accusing each other of cheating and underhanded tactics.

"Who won the poker game?" interrupted Ruth from the buffet table.

"I did!" yelled Pete with a big toothless grin, raising both his arms in the air. "And on Saturday I'll be winning the Roses!"

This again started the others off on a barrage of bickering.

"You play for roses?" asked Frankie, confused.

"Roses chocolates," laughed Ruth. "Give me real roses any day, but who can afford *them*?"

"Hey Frankie, wanna be in the sports club?" asked Pete. "It's only two bucks a week and you get a chance at winning the Roses!"

"Sure! What other games do you play?" asked Frankie, which started almost everyone in the room talking over each other, louder and louder, all trying to answer her question. After several minutes of constant babble, she'd gotten all the answers she needed.

"So, croquet, hey? Count me in on that one. But I played hockey in high school, so you better watch out!"

Once again, the noise erupted. Frankie laughed at how easily you could set these guys off. This was going to be fun. She agreed she'd be part of the sports club and that she'd put her name down on 'the board' for upcoming games. Frankie totally enjoyed dinner that night. It was fun being part of a group of misfits and outcasts and no hopers, because none of them expected anything from you. You could be whatever the hell you wanted, and no-one gave a flying fuck.

CHAPTER FOUR

These shoes really are comfortable! thought Frankie as she entered the grounds of Golden Leaves after her long morning walk. *Shit, I hope I'm not turning into an old fart.*

"Good morning!" chirped annoying Clare. "How are you today? It's great you'll be working here with us! Here's your vest. Rob said he'll meet you here at eight thirty."

"Morning!" sang Frankie back loudly, sarcastically imitating Clare's tone, which went straight over Clare's head. Reluctantly she put on her light blue vest which had 'trainee' written in big white letters across the back.

"These are stylish," she joked to Clare.

"They'd be nicer if they were pink." Clare giggled.

Frankie rolled her eyes and took a seat to wait for Robert, the comedian.

Through the doors he bowled. "Morning Frankie! Welcome to your first day! So, you've met Clare our gatekeeper, I take it?"

"Yep, we met yesterday." *What is it with all these jail references he keeps banging on with?*

"Come on, let's get you organised. I've got a special job lined up for you. Follow me."

They walked out into the grounds and over to the assisted living units. As they got to the open door of Unit four Robert knocked.

"Knock, knock! Avon calling! Anyone home?"

"Come in if you're good looking," came the reply from inside.

"You'd better go in, Frankie, I'll wait out here," laughed Robert as they went inside. "Joan! I've got someone very special for you to meet. This is our new addition, Frankie. Frankie, this is Joan."

Joan was sitting in a wheelchair in the middle of the lounge room, looking like she was ready to go to a ball. She wore a long flowing brightly coloured dress which was adorned with intricate beadwork, and her tanned, manicured hands were covered in what looked like very expensive diamond jewellery. Her white-grey hair was immaculately pulled back into a neat bun to show off her perfectly applied makeup and diamond stud earrings. Even her shoes were covered in brightly coloured stones and tassels and looked like they'd come from a designer boutique. The only thing that gave even the slightest hint that she was an old lady in a retirement home was her wheelchair.

"Nice to meet you, Joan." said Frankie, trying not to let on how absolutely gobsmacked she was. She suddenly felt very self-conscious about her poorly applied concealer, her messy ponytail and her comfortable shoes. Not to mention her light blue trainee vest.

Joan put her hand out to grab Frankie's hand. "You too dear!" smiled Joan. "You're not here to steal my boyfriend, are you?" she said, giving Robert a wink.

"You know you'll always be my number one girl," said Robert as he gave her a kiss on the cheek.

"I swear if it wasn't for young Robert here, I'd be in the nuthouse by now."

"But you *are* in the nuthouse Joan!" Robert leaned over to Frankie, pretending to whisper. "See how bad she is? She doesn't even know where she is!"

"Oh, stop it," chuckled Joan, slapping him on the hand, clearly loving the attention.

"So, Joan, I thought Frankie might be able to help you get things organised here. I'm sure you could find plenty of jobs to keep her busy and off the streets."

There it is again! Frankie was about ready to punch old Punch & Judy in the face.

"I'll leave you two to get acquainted, and I won't be far away if you need me. Frankie, I'll see you at lunchtime in the dining room – around twelve thirty? Have a nice morning ladies." And off he went on his merry, minstrel way.

"Frankie – that's an unusual name. Is that your real name dear?"

"No, it's Frances, but I prefer Frankie."

"Oh, Frances is such a pretty name. A pretty name for a pretty girl."

Frankie felt her face glowing red under Joan's intense stare and tried to change the subject. "So, what jobs are you needing help with?"

Joan's smile instantly vanished as she pointed over at the stack of unfolded boxes leaning against the wall. "Packing."

"Packing? Are you moving somewhere?"

"Not if I can help it."

Frankie suddenly sensed she'd been thrown into a deep end of some sort.

She looked around at Joan's unit and everything was as immaculate and well looked after as the lady herself. There were framed photos on every wall and beautiful vases and ornaments on display shelves. She'd obviously gone to great lengths to decorate, as it was one of the nicest homes Frankie had ever seen. This was one stylish woman.

"Your home is beautiful," said Frankie, being completely honest, but also hoping a compliment would lift her mood. It did the exact opposite. Joan burst into tears, hiding her face in her hands. Frankie frantically looked around for tissues, finding some on the kitchen bench.

"I'm sorry. Are you okay?" said Frankie, nervously waving the tissues in front of Joan, feeling totally useless and embarrassed.

"Oh, it's not you Frances," blubbered Joan as she wiped her eyes and nose. "They want to put me into the nursing home."

And with that Joan started sobbing. Really sobbing. It was like she'd just been told someone had died. Frankie had no idea what to do. She wasn't good at personal interactions, especially awkward ones. She crouched down beside Joan's wheelchair and rested her hand on Joan's arm. She could feel the tears welling up in her own eyes just watching this poor woman so distraught.

"I'm sorry dear, it's hardly a good first impression. You just caught me at a bad time," sniffled Joan, patting Frankie's hand with her own.

"Would you like me to make you a cuppa?" said Frankie, finally thinking of something she could do that might be helpful.

"Yes, that would be lovely. White tea with one sugar for me, please. It's all on the kitchen bench. Make one for yourself as well."

Frankie made the tea and Joan suggested they go and sit outside in the fresh air.

The pathways meandered in all directions through the lawns and gardens, and they found a shady spot under one of the beautiful big gum trees.

Frankie sat in silence, taking in the fresh air and tranquil surroundings. The last thing she wanted to do was talk about anything that would upset Joan again, so she decided she'd let Joan do the talking instead.

"So, Frances, tell me about yourself. Where did you grow up?"

"In Melbourne. Footscray. I lived there till I was fifteen, then I moved to Springdale to live with my Aunty."

"Didn't you get on with your parents?"

"Mum and Dad were killed in a car crash. I didn't have any other family, so I had to move to my aunty's place. She's my godmother. More like a devil mother."

"Oh dear, I'm so sorry. That must have been an awful time for you. Do you have brothers and sisters?"

"Nope. Mum was actually lucky to survive having me. The doctors told her if she had any more, it'd kill her. I always wanted a sister; I've got friends, but I don't really see them anymore."

Frankie realised she was starting to sound pathetic, but she was determined to keep Joan off the subject of moving.

"Is that why you moved to Ballarat? For a sea change, or should I say a tree change?"

"Um…not exactly. I was made to come here. Well, not here, but somewhere a hundred kilometres from Melbourne."

She took a deep breath. "I had an AVO issued against me, so I didn't have a choice." Frankie didn't even bother trying to convince Joan of her innocence. She was sick of thinking about it. It just made her angry.

"Well, you don't look too dangerous to me Frances!" A smile returned to her face. "Sometimes the bastards deserve it."

Frankie laughed out loud; surprised Joan had just actually sworn. "And if there's one thing I've learnt in my life, it's that you can't let the bastards get you down."

"Hear, hear!" said Frankie. She was starting to really like this woman. She had spirit. "So… what's happening with you Joan?" Frankie asked, bracing herself for another flood of tears.

"I've got Alzheimer's. I was diagnosed with it about two years ago. I've been good – I forget things occasionally but who doesn't? A few weeks ago, I fell asleep with something in the oven, and now they want to lock me up in the nursing home like some kind of invalid!" Tears started to well up in Joan's eyes, but now she seemed angry. "I don't want to go! If I can't live here in my unit, then I'd rather be dead. What kind of life would it be stuck in that place with people feeding you and dressing you and changing your nappy? No. I'm not going. They'll have to drag me kicking and screaming."

"So, have you told them you don't want to go?"

"Oh yes, they know. But they treat me like I'm some kind of moron instead of a human being. They say it's the best thing for me. What would *they* know about what's best for me? The best thing for me is to let me live here in my own home without someone poking and prodding at me twenty-four hours a day. Either that or let me die. This disease will kill me anyway, so what's the point?"

Frankie agreed totally with what Joan was saying. What *was* the point? Why keep people alive so they can lie around waiting to die? It made no sense. But she wasn't going to encourage her. Joan was already wound up enough. And packing was now totally out of the question.

"Feel like going for a walk, Joan? I haven't really been around the grounds properly, and I'd like to have a look at the lake."

"Sounds wonderful, Frances. Let's grab some bread for the ducks."

Joan was truly in her element during those next few hours. She took great delight in showing Frankie around the grounds, telling her all about everything from the types of trees and flowers to the names of her favourite ducks. She rattled off an inventory of every resident and their reason for being there. She introduced Frankie to everyone they passed, as though Frankie was her personal assistant. Joan was like the lord mayoress of Golden Leaves and clearly loved being the centre of attention.

It was lunch time when they got back to Joan's unit.

"So, I'll see you after lunch I guess, Joan?"

"Sounds good, Frances. I really enjoyed our walk."

Frankie spotted Robert sitting at a table in the dining room and pulled up a chair next to him, glaring at him.

"Hi Frankie. How'd it go with—"

"Why didn't you tell me?" demanded Frankie, trying to control her anger and not raise her voice. "Talk about throw me under the bus!"

"You mean the whole moving thing?"

"*Yes,* I mean the whole, *whole* thing! That poor woman is distraught about it and you send me over to make her pack?"

She flounced back in her chair and crossed her arms in annoyance.

Robert looked at her with a smirk and then let out a snorting laugh, which just made Frankie even angrier.

"It's okay, Frankie. Sorry. I just thought it'd be better for you to get acquainted without any pre-conceived opinions."

"Having to move is hardly an opinion! It sounds to me like her opinions don't even count! She doesn't want to move!"

"Yes, I know. The problem for Joan is that she doesn't really have much choice. She's got Alzheimer's and—"

"Yes, I know" snapped Frankie, "she told me all that."

"And… it's not your run of the mill Alzheimer's. It's progressing really quickly. A few weeks ago, one of the groundsmen found her down by the lake first thing in the morning. She'd wheeled herself down there and she'd been there all night. She doesn't remember it at all. She has days when she can't tell you what day it is or where she is, but then the next day she's right as rain. She almost burnt her unit down not so long ago 'cause she'd put a pie in the oven and then forgot about it."

"She told me she fell asleep."

"No, she didn't fall asleep. She decided to go for a stroll. Lucky we've got smoke alarms. Look, I know she doesn't want to move, but it's getting to the stage where it's unsafe for her to be living on her own. The doctors gave her a scan two weeks ago and the lesions in her brain are almost double what they were a year ago."

"That's fucked."

"Yep. It is. But, unfortunately, it's our job to keep her safe, even if it means making her do things she doesn't want to do."

"That's even more fucked." And with that Frankie got up and walked out. She'd lost her appetite.

Robert came out and sat on the bench next to Frankie as she stared into the distance.

"Here, I brought you a sandwich." They sat in silence for a few minutes. "Frankie, I know it's hard seeing the harsh reality of some of these people's lives. I remember when I first started, I wanted to throw it all in after the first week. But after a while you realise that even though you can't change anything about their disease, you can help to distract them and make them feel a bit better in other ways. Why do you think I go around carrying on like a dickhead?"

"Because you're a dickhead?" Frankie paused. "*Kidding*."

"Well, yes, partly. Thanks for pointing that out. It makes them laugh. Plus, it makes *me* feel better. It's almost like a bit of an escape from reality. But it helps. You should try it Cranky Frankie!"

Robert laughed and put his arms up, pretending to block an incoming punch to the face. Frankie half smiled then pretended to punch him.

"How about you call it a day for today and have an early mark? I'll let Joan know you'll be back in the morning. Okay?"

"Okay"

Frankie picked up her sandwich and started walking. She wasn't sure where she was heading but it didn't matter. As long it was away from here. *Cranky Frankie. Pffffttt. Good one, comedian Robert. Comedian dickhead Robert.* She had to admit though, it was pretty true. She *was* cranky.

CHAPTER FIVE

"Morning Frankie," trilled annoying Clare like clockwork next morning. "Rob said to tell you to meet him over at the AL units."

"AL?"

"Oh sorry," giggled Clare, "Assisted Living units. It's through those doors and—"

"Yep, I know where they are. Have a great day, Clare!" replied Frankie, once again mimicking Clare's sing-song voice. Approaching the units, she could see all the residents gathering outside.

"Morning Frankie. How you feeling today?" asked Robert, waving as he walked over to her.

"Yeah, fine thanks. What's going on?"

"Excursion day. We do one every month. It's usually on a Friday, but I thought we'd do it a day early. It's supposed to rain tomorrow, plus, I thought it might be a good chance for you to see some of the fun things we do here to make up for all the cruelty." Robert grinned at Frankie.

"Okay, so what do you want me to do?" she asked, ignoring his smart-arsed comment.

"You can help me round up all the troops! We need to get them over there." He pointed to the minibus parked at the entrance to the main building.

Frankie noticed Joan waving to her from outside her unit, so she walked over to say hello. Joan was again dressed in a colourful, extravagant long dress, complete with matching jewellery. She wore a big blue flower in her hair and a beaded Oroton handbag was sitting on her lap.

"Wow, you look nice, Joan."

"Oh, thank you Frances. I'm so glad you're here. I thought I might've scared you off when you didn't come back yesterday."

"No, I just felt a bit sick that was all," lied Frankie.

The procession to the bus got underway. A line of oldies – some with walking sticks, some with walkers and others like Joan, in wheelchairs slowly trundled down the path. Robert led the way in fine form, telling his corny jokes and making them laugh. Frankie dawdled towards the back like a father duck, trying to make herself useful in some way, but not really knowing how.

Trying to make small talk, she asked a few of them where they were going, but no-one seemed to know. Finally gathered around the minibus, Frankie helped them climb into their seats while Robert packed all their walkers and wheelchairs into the back. It must have taken about thirty minutes to get everyone in and buckled up. *Bloody hell*, thought Frankie, *I hope we're going somewhere good after all this!*

She looked around from the front passenger seat to see a big sea of smiling faces. They were all laughing and chatting to each other, clearly excited to be going on their excursion. Frankie felt an unexpected and overwhelming surge of happiness spring up inside her. Maybe this was what Robert was talking about. Maybe all this really did make a difference.

"Okay folks, this is your captain speaking. Please keep your arms and legs inside the cabin at all times. There is no smoking allowed and please make sure your seat belts are kept fastened in case of unexpected turbulence. Frankie's not driving though, so that shouldn't be a problem."

Frankie laughed and slapped Robert across the arm. A barrage of laughter from the passengers followed, along with animated banter.

"So, who can guess where we're going?" continued Robert.

The suggestions came thick and fast, louder and louder, ranging from the beach to the park, to the moon and back. It was bedlam inside the bus. The racket was something you'd expect from a belligerent bunch of schoolkids, but they were all having a great time and Robert was also clearly enjoying every minute of it.

"Well, you're all wrong. First stop – the museum!" Robert's announcement was met with some enthusiastic approval, and some pretend grumbling.

"Before anyone complains, just remember, it's important to learn new things and keep the old grey matter working. There'll be a quiz on the way home!"

A loud "Boooooooooo!" rang out from the back.

"It's not all bad news though," he continued. "We'll be going to the RSL for lunch and then, if you all behave, we'll be going to… the lolly factory!"

The cheers were almost deafening. It occurred to Frankie that Robert should be on a stage with the way he could control a crowd. He looked over at Frankie and they both laughed.

The bus arrived at the museum and Frankie helped Robert to get everyone out of the bus and inside. A smiling tour guide was waiting to greet them and take them on their trip back in time to learn about the history of Ballarat. The tour centred around the one thing Ballarat was most famous for – gold. The story was told of the Eureka Stockade and what life was like in the colonies of the goldfields. There were impressive gold exhibits ranging from actual gold nuggets to jewellery made by some of the gold diggers who'd been lucky enough to strike it rich.

Frankie noticed that Joan was particularly taken by the gold jewellery on display in the glass cases.

"I don't think it's for sale, but I can distract them while you make a run for it," Frankie whispered in Joan's ear, making her laugh.

Even though a museum was the last place Frankie would ever choose to visit, she found herself captivated by the stories of life on the goldfields. *What a shit existence,* she thought, *gold or no gold.*

After the tour ended, they all shuffled their way back onto the bus, booklets in hand, chattering to each other about what they'd seen. Something about the museum felt familiar to Frankie and it made her wonder whether her parents had taken her there as a kid. She immediately distracted herself, stopping another sad trip down memory lane.

"What's next?" she asked Robert.

"Something to stop this infernal babbling," he said, smiling at her. "Right, who's hungry?" he shouted.

"*Me!*" they all yelled as the bus pulled out to make its way to the RSL.

Frankie got to know some of the residents over lunch and listen to some of their long-winded stories. Little did they know, she'd already been given the lowdown from Joan about most of them, just a different version. It was funny to hear the other side of their stories. Robert was in his element, telling corny jokes and making them all laugh, no doubt helped along by the wine and beer they had with their lunch.

Back onto the bus they piled, ready for the highlight of the day. "What do you reckon, Frankie?" said Robert loudly, "Do you think they've behaved themselves today? Do you think they deserve a trip to the lolly factory?"

"Hmm…" said Frankie "I think *they* have, but I'm not sure about *you!*" The bus erupted in a commotion of laughter, and Robert played straight into it, making theatrical objections, pretending to be greatly offended. It reminded Frankie of being on a pub crawl bus after about the fifth stop. It was actually pretty funny.

They arrived at the lolly factory for their final stop.

"Before we all go in, just a reminder that this bus has a two-tonne weight limit, so if you can keep that in mind, that would be greatly appreciated. Oh, and in case you're wondering, my favourite lollies are Fantales." Frankie looked at him and shook her head. "What!" said Robert with a stupid grin on his face.

Inside the lolly factory was amazing. The walls were filled with every kind of lolly you could imagine. It was like Willy Wonka's chocolate factory. You could spend hours there and still not see everything. Frankie grabbed a trolley to carry it all and helped everyone reach what they wanted from the shelves. It was pretty clear to her how the saying 'like a kid in a candy shop' came about. They were like a bunch of old kids, shuffling their way along the aisles, staring up at the multitude of choices, almost mesmerised.

After what seemed like an eternity, they all made their way back to the bus with their bagfuls of loot.

"Has anyone here still got their own teeth?" yelled Robert as he packed everything in the back of the bus. A few hands went up. "Well, not for long!"

The ride home was considerably quieter thanks to the post-lunch slump. It had been a long day for them all and some were nodding off.

"Has everyone had a good day?" asked Robert. Most of them muttered "yes", but not with much gusto. "Sorry, did someone say something? Did you have a good day?"

"*Yes!*" they all yelled.

"Glad to hear it! Now, as promised it's time for the quiz!" A loud moan came from the back of the bus. "Who can tell me what year the Eureka Stockade riot took place?"

"1854" came a quick reply.

"Frankie – is that correct?"

"How would I – ugh," said Frankie as she grabbed the booklet off the dash and looked it up. "Yes, that's correct."

'Well done! Next question – what colour is the Eureka flag?"

"Blue!" "Blue and white!" came the replies. Robert looked over at Frankie.

"Correct," said Frankie, rolling her eyes.

"And what does the word Eureka mean?" asked Robert.

"Woohooooooo!" yelled someone. They all laughed.

"Not exactly, but it should mean that. Anyone else?"

"Look what I found!" yelled someone else.

"Ooh very close. Frankie?"

"I don't know!" snapped Frankie, getting sick of the game.

"It actually means '*I found it*' in ancient Greek. Pretty cool, hey?"

"Yeah, cool," said Frankie sarcastically.

They arrived back at the home and slowly got all the passengers off the bus. They each collected their stash of lollies and headed back to their units, exhausted but happy.

"How did you enjoy that, Frankie? A bit better than yesterday?" asked Robert.

"Yeah, it was good actually. They all loved it, didn't they. It was good to see them all having a laugh."

"Yeah, they love getting out. It's a massive mission with all their gear, but it's worth it. Anyway, thanks for helping out today."

"I didn't do much."

"You did more than you realise."

Robert looked at his watch. "It's after three, so you can go now if you want. Not much point in hanging round. I'll see you tomorrow?"

"Okay, thanks. See you tomorrow. Oh, almost forgot." Frankie reached into her plastic bag from the lolly shop and threw a bag of Fantales to Robert.

"You *do* listen to what I say! I knew it!" he laughed.

"Sometimes," answered Frankie. "See you tomorrow."

Back at Learmonth House, Frankie decided to check out the sports club whiteboard. She went out the back through the laundry area into another large room. There were old cupboards along the walls filled with old board games and books. In the middle of the room was an old ping pong table which had obviously been out in the weather at some point. It was warped and the edges were peeling off. On the far wall was the whiteboard. The scrawl on it looked more like a scientific equation than a scoreboard. Frankie added her name to the bottom of the list and wandered outside to check out the yard. Ruth was out there hanging some tablecloths on the line.

"Hi Ruth"

"Oh, hi Frankie," said Ruth, looking around from behind the washing. "How was your day?"

Frankie stood chatting to Ruth and telling her all about her new job at the home. She told her how much the oldies had enjoyed their excursion day and where they'd taken them.

"I used to be a disability carer before I came to Learmonth House. I loved it, but this job came up which was perfect for me, being on my own."

"So, you've never been married?"

"Oh yes, I was married a long time ago. Patrick was his name. Beautiful man. He died at 38. Cancer."

"Oh no, that's horrible. You poor thing." Frankie knew exactly how it felt to lose someone you love.

"Fancy a cuppa?" asked Ruth, grabbing her laundry basket.

"Love one." answered Frankie. She sensed that Ruth wanted someone to talk to, and she probably didn't get much chance with the others that lived there.

They both sat in the kitchen sharing stories and telling each other about their lives. They sat there for over an hour, talking and laughing, like a pair of best friends. Frankie couldn't remember the last time she'd ever had such an open, honest, comfortable conversation with anybody. They were polar opposites in so many ways, yet they got along like they'd known each other their whole lives. Ruth was old enough to be Frankie's mother but she felt she could tell her pretty much anything. Which she did. Every last sordid detail of how she got here, and the arsehole who put her here. Ruth didn't even seem to bat an eyelid. She'd obviously been through the wringer herself yet had managed to somehow stay so caring and kind. She'd spent her life giving up everything to care for others. Frankie couldn't help but admire Ruth. She was like a powerhouse of strength disguised as a gentle angel.

"Oh God, look at the time! I had no idea we'd been talking so long!" laughed Ruth, getting up from her chair and clearing away the cups. She grabbed Frankie by both hands. "I really loved our chat, Frankie. We'll have to do this more often!"

"Count me in," said Frankie with a smile. "I'll see you at dinner."

Frankie went up to her room with a feeling of contentment after their heart to heart. She laid on her bed and stared at the ceiling, going over and over their conversation in her head. It was like a breath of fresh air to have someone to talk to. Someone she trusted. At that moment Frankie realised she'd just had one of the best days in a very, very long time.

CHAPTER SIX

The sound of heavy rain against the window woke Frankie early. Rubbing her eyes, she got up to look out. It was pouring down and she could see people with umbrellas running along the footpath and cars ploughing slowly through the built-up water over the road.

"There goes my walk," muttered Frankie to herself. She got dressed for work and went downstairs to have a cuppa with Ruth before the breakfast rush.

"Hope you can swim," laughed Ruth as she poured Frankie a cup of coffee.

"Thanks. I'll be bussing it today."

Ruth pointed out to the hallway where Pete was pacing up and down. She whispered to Frankie "He's been there since six. He's worried about tomorrow."

"Tomorrow?" whispered Frankie back.

"Sports Day"

Frankie started laughing, covering her mouth to stop the sound. Not able to help herself, she walked out into the hallway.

"Hey Pete! How are you? Not sure if you noticed, but I put my name down on the sports board!"

"Yeah, I know Frankie, I saw it. I'm just a bit worried about this weather, you know? It's the croquet comp tomorrow, and if it rains, then we'll have to cancel it. Then we'll have to wait till next week, and that'll throw out all the stats. I just hope it stops in time. I'll have to check the ground too and make sure it's not too boggy. If it's too muddy the ball doesn't move properly, you know?"

"Could you move the comp to Sunday, Pete?"

"No, no, no. Saturday's sport day. It can't be on Sunday. Saturday's always sports day."

"Well, it's okay Pete, I saw on the forecast that it's supposed to stop raining later. I'm sure it'll all work out for tomorrow."

"Oh, good. That's good. That's what we need. It needs to stop raining."

"Come on Pete," said Ruth waving him over. "Time for breakfast."

"Anyway Pete," teased Frankie some more. "Don't get too excited cause *I'm* going to win the croquet comp! I can already taste the Roses in my mouth!"

"Aaaahhhhhh," said Pete with his toothless grin. "We'll see about that!"

Frankie arrived at Golden Leaves dripping wet from the waist down. Even the short walk from the bus stop was enough to nearly drown her. She stumbled through the front doors to be once again greeted by annoying Clare's cheery welcome.

"Morning Frankie! Ooooh – you're soaking!"

"No kidding!" snapped Frankie, wrestling with her dripping umbrella.

For the first time, Clare shut up and put her head down.

"Did Robert say where I have to meet him today?"

"No, I haven't seen him yet, but I'm sure he won't be too far away. Have a great day, Frankie!"

Frankie had never met anyone as hard to offend as annoying Clare. She couldn't work out if Clare was a truly happy, chirpy person or just a dumb bimbo. Whatever she was, at least she was consistent. Frankie walked through the hallway and found Robert sitting with Maggie at a table in the dining room.

"Hey Frankie," smiled Robert, looking at her wet clothes. "Did you swim over today?"

"Just about," replied Frankie, biting her tongue because Maggie was there.

"Have a seat Frankie," said Maggie, pulling out a chair. "We're just going through your paperwork to look at what we need to do."

Frankie instantly felt a pang of guilt rush through her. She'd almost forgotten the real reason she was here.

"Rob tells me you're doing a great job and that you're very popular with all the residents. How are you liking it?"

"It's good. Yesterday was fun. They all seemed to have a great time on their excursion."

"I don't doubt it," said Maggie, looking at Robert. It was obviously common knowledge that any outing Robert was involved with would include fun.

"Frankie was the perfect co-pilot." laughed Robert. "She helped me keep them all under control, especially at the lolly factory. Plus, she's a great quizmaster."

"Sounds great," smiled Maggie as she got up from her chair. "Anyway, I'll leave you to it. Just sit down with Frankie at the end of the day and fill out her report and we'll be good to go. Have a good day guys."

"Thanks for that." Frankie said to Robert once Maggie was out of earshot.

"For what?"

"For giving me a good rap."

"I just told her the truth, that's all."

"Hmmm, yeah right, which version?"

"My version. Do I get more Fantales now?" he laughed.

It crossed Frankie's mind that Robert hadn't asked about her AVO. Surely, he was curious about what she'd done to have that slapped on her. Especially a one-hundred kilometre one. She wasn't going to volunteer that information though, not unless he asked.

It humoured her to imagine him guessing what she'd done to deserve such a punishment. Maybe she was some dangerous villain with a murderous streak? Maybe she was a stalker? Maybe she was blackmailing someone's husband?

Robert interrupted her train of thought. "I was thinking because of the weather, how would you feel about spending some time with Joan today, and maybe seeing if you can coax her into getting used to the idea of moving?"

"So, you want me to con her? I already know that answer."

"Con her? No. More like soften her a bit."

"Soften her? What am I – some kind of thug? *Here I am Joan – I'm here to soften you up!*" said Frankie in a gangster voice, punching her fist into her other hand.

Robert laughed out loud. "Hey, that might actually work! It scared *me!*"

"Oh, I'm scary alright!" said Frankie, staring straight at Robert, playing on her previous thought that he had no idea what she was capable of.

"Yes. You are. But seriously though, maybe just spend some time with her and see where she's at. We're in the position now that we don't have much time before we'll have to move her, so we want to do it with as little trauma as possible."

"For you."

"For *her,* Frankie." Robert frowned. He seemed like he was getting annoyed. Frankie knew he wanted the best for Joan. Her last comment was bitchy and mean.

"Okay. Sure. I'll go and spend some time with her. I'll catch you later."

"Thanks." Robert got up and left without his usual comedy routine.

Looks like I've managed to piss him off, Frankie thought to herself as she grabbed her umbrella and headed out into the rain to Unit four.

Joan opened the door and greeted Frankie with a surprised smile on her face. "Oh Frances – hello dear! I thought you'd be hiding away today out of this torrential rain."

"Just thought I'd come for a visit – is that okay?"

"Of course it is! Come in, come in! You're saturated! Would you like some dry clothes to put on?"

"No, I'm fine thanks. I'll dry off soon enough."

Frankie had visions of herself waltzing around the room in one of Joan's flowing gowns, jewellery dripping from every limb.

"I'm just sorting through some things," said Joan as she went into the lounge room. There, on the table was more gold jewellery than Frankie had ever seen in her life. It must have been worth tens of thousands of dollars, if not more.

"Whoa!" uttered Frankie, unable to hide her astonishment. "I've never seen so much jewellery!"

Joan laughed as though it was a pile of rocks sitting on the table. "When we were at the museum yesterday, it reminded me that I needed to have a bit of a tidy up. I haven't seen some of this stuff in years!"

Stuff? thought Frankie, gobsmacked. *How much money does this woman have?* "You could start your own museum with this!"

"Well, there you go – after I'm dead, you can be the curator!" laughed Joan. "How about a cuppa dear?"

"Sure." Frankie made the tea and coffee while Joan started reminiscing about her jewellery. She told Frankie the story behind each piece; where she'd been in the world, and who had given it to her. Most of it had been given to her by her late husband Ernie. The jewellery was like her life story, the thing that she accumulated wherever she went, like other people might collect magnets or coasters. It baffled Frankie how this woman sitting here telling her the story behind a twenty-year-old bracelet could suddenly wander off and sleep next to a lake, totally oblivious.

"So, tell me about Ernie. How did you meet him?"

"Oh, now there's a story! We met on Broadway in New York in sixty-seven. Or was it sixty-eight? One of those. Anyway, I was dancing in one of the big shows over there. Cabaret. Have you heard of it?" Frankie shook her head. "Oh, it was a huge success. Well, after the show ended, everyone went out to celebrate. Dancers, singers, executives, stagehands, everyone. I was sitting at a table with some of the other girls, and up walks this handsome man and looks straight at me. Me! It was the producer! He asked if he could buy me a drink, and the rest is history. He told me that I had the best legs on Broadway. He swept me off my feet and we got married three months later."

"Wow, that sounds like a fairy tale."

"It was. Our lives were blessed that's for sure. We fell in love over fifty years ago and stayed in love until the day he died. He was a great man. Not perfect mind you, but a good, kind, strong man. He always took care of me no matter what. He was my rock. And handsome! He looked like Neil Mason – you know, the actor? Here, I'll show you."

Joan went into the bedroom and came out with some photo albums on her lap. The first album was full of black and white photos of her and Ernie in their showbiz days. Joan pointed out some famous faces; some Frankie knew, others she didn't. There were photos of Joan in her glamourous Broadway shows, surrounded by lines of beautiful dancing girls in beautiful costumes.

"You really *did* have great legs!" said Frankie, amazed by what she was seeing.

"Yes, I did back then. Until they let me down. All that dancing ended up giving me arthritis. It's pretty common among dancers, but that's the price we paid to be on Broadway."

"So, you can't walk at all?"

"Oh yes, I can walk when I have to. I have a walker, but the damn thing keeps getting caught on my dresses, so it's easier to be in a chair to get around."

"Who's that?" asked Frankie, pointing to a baby Joan was holding in one of the photos.

"That's our son, Daniel. He's about eighteen months old there, I think. We took him everywhere with us. Everyone loved him. He's a choreographer now. He does a lot of the big shows and works on movies too."

"So, where's he now? Do you see him much?"

"No. I only see him when his conscience gets the better of him. Sometimes birthdays and occasionally Mother's Day, if I'm lucky. He used to live in Melbourne, but he moved to Sydney not long after he put me in here. Probably so he doesn't have to visit me as much."

"So does he ring you at least?"

"He sometimes rings on Sunday evenings to tell me how busy he is and how he can't talk long because he's got looming deadlines."

Frankie took a deep breath before she asked her next question. "So… does he know they want you to move?"

"Ha! It's probably his idea! He probably can't wait until I'm a dribbling vegetable – then he won't have to visit me at all! Well, I've got news for him and all of them – I won't be leaving here unless I'm in a box!"

Frankie was surprised how much bitterness Joan had towards her son, but he did sound like an absolute arsehole. What kind of person would put their mother in a retirement home and leave her to rot like that? Surely something else had gone on to ruin their relationship. Frankie was intrigued.

"So, were you close to Daniel when he was young?"

"Oh yes, we were very close. He was such a beautiful, happy little boy. All he wanted to do was become an actor. So, we sent him to NIDA, but he hooked up with a bunch of deadbeats who were more interested in drugs and alcohol than they were in acting. He threw it all away, right down the toilet. He got mixed up in some pretty serious stuff and it nearly cost him his life."

"So, what happened?"

Joan closed the photo album and stared at Frankie.

"Well, he wanted to come home, but Ernie wouldn't let him. He told him he'd help him, but he wouldn't be welcome back home until he cleaned up his act. It broke my heart, but Ernie insisted it was the right thing to do. Tough love. Daniel never forgave his father for that. And I don't think he ever forgave me either. It did the trick though. Daniel went to rehab and got clean and now, years later he's got an amazing career and lives in a beautiful home overlooking Sydney Harbour."

"He doesn't have you though."

Frankie couldn't understand anyone throwing away their relationship with their mother. What a tragic waste. She would give absolutely anything to have her mum back again.

"Well, anyway, it doesn't matter anymore. I've done what I came here to do. Brought my son into the world and lived a wonderful life with a wonderful man. I can't complain. Now I just need an escape plan. My time is up and it's time to exit stage left. Time to meet up with Ernie again." Joan paused. "Do you think you could help me, Frances?"

"What?" asked Frankie, uneasy about what Joan was saying to her. "What do you mean?"

"I need someone to help me. I've asked every doctor I've seen to let me die, but they've all told me that it's out of the question."

"Are you serious?"

"Deadly serious, dear. Pun intended. I'll cut my wrists if I have to. If they think I'm going to let them put me into that nursing home to be some kind of science project, they're wrong. Will you help me?"

Frankie couldn't believe what Joan was asking. She wanted her to help her die. What the fuck! She didn't sign up for this. "But how could I help you? I'd go to jail. I'm in enough trouble already. Isn't it legal now to let people die if they've got terminal diseases?"

"Yes, but only if you've got less than six months to live. And even then, there are so many hoops to jump through that by the time that day comes, I won't even know my own name! I know it's a huge thing to ask Frances, but I'm running out of time. Surely, I could just take some pills or something. I really don't want to cut my wrists. It would be disgusting and painful and I'd probably mess it up. Is there anything at all you could do to help me?"

The desperation on Joan's face was heartbreaking. To see this proud woman begging someone to end her life was unbearable. What a cruel way to end your time on earth – locked away in a nursing home, day by day losing everything you once valued, until you withered away to nothing. This world was fucked up. It was all wrong. None of it made sense. Surely people's lives belong to them, not some rich arsehole in a white coat who drives home to his happy family in his BMW.

The more Frankie thought about it, the angrier she got.

"It's a lot to take in, Joan. I can totally see where you're coming from, but I really don't know if there's anything I'd be able to do."

Joan took Frankie by the hand and looked at her with tears in her eyes.

"I'm begging you dear. Please help me."

It was all too much for Frankie. She broke down sobbing and hugged Joan, rocking back and forth. A flood of emotions washed over her. Love, hate, grief, fear, rage, resentment, all rolled into one huge swirling black mass.

Joan had tripped a switch in her and she was smashed head on with a lifetime of emotions that until now she'd managed to stuff away in the dark depths of her soul. Suddenly she was back there. Holding the phone. Hearing those words. Frozen, unable to move or speak. Her world ended that day and she'd been living in oblivion ever since.

When Frankie finally emerged from the blackout of her traumatic memories, she found herself crouched in front of Joan, her head on

Joan's chest. Joan was hugging her and telling her everything was going to be alright. Embarrassed and disoriented, Frankie jumped up and went to get some tissues to wipe her face.

"Sorry about that," she spluttered, blowing her nose.

"It's okay, Frances. I think you needed to get that out. You must really miss them."

"Every day," whimpered Frankie as yet more tears began to fall, despite her best efforts to control herself.

"Life can be such a bitch at times. To some more than others. But you know what I've always found dear? If you've got someone who loves you by your side, all those hurts are shared, so they don't hurt as much. I know I haven't known you for long, but it seems to me that you're trying to take on the world single-handedly. I'm sure there's a horde of young men out there who'd be proud to have such a beautiful young woman as yourself beside them."

"Don't know about that," sniffled Frankie "I've got shit taste in men."

"I think you just need to realise your own worth Frances. Stop hiding yourself away. Come here."

Frankie walked over to Joan and sat down next to her. Joan pulled Frankie's hair away from her puffy, red face. "You can start by showing the world this beautiful face."

"Ha," laughed Frankie as she blew her nose to avoid the compliment. "I might go and get some fresh air, I think. I'll come back after lunch if that's okay?"

"Certainly dear. I'll be here."

Frankie went out into the rain and wandered down to the lake. She felt like she'd been hit by a truck. Never had she experienced such a profound torrent of emotion. It was like a lightning bolt had come from nowhere and struck her right to her very core.

But strangely, she felt lighter.

Like she was in a daze.

Like she was high on drugs.

She sat on a bench under her umbrella and stared out at the water, trying to make sense of what had just happened.

What a fucking weird day.

She had an inexplicable feeling in the pit of her stomach that somehow, everything had just changed.

CHAPTER SEVEN

Frankie slowly made her way back to Joan's unit, feeling much calmer after her long break by the lake.

"How was your walk?" asked Joan, sitting at her table, still sorting through her jewellery.

"Good – I feel heaps better. How's your sorting going?"

"Almost done. I found this one." Joan picked up a beautiful fine gold necklace with a small enamel bluebird charm hanging from it. "I want you to have it, Frances."

"Oh no, I couldn't take" Joan put her finger up to her mouth to shush Frankie.

"Please, take it. Don't worry, it's not expensive. Ernie gave this to me a long time ago when I was going through a hard time of my own. He told me it was a bluebird of happiness. I never wear it, so I'd love you to have it."

"Thank you. It's lovely, Joan." Frankie took the necklace and put it around her neck. It had been a long time since anyone had given her a gift, especially a thoughtful gift like this.

"I'd also like to apologise for throwing all that at you earlier, dear. I realise it must have been a bit of a shock."

"Well, yep, it took me by surprise, I guess. But I totally get it. I'd be exactly the same. I've always thought that there's no way I'm going to a home. I don't see the point."

Frankie realised what she'd just said. "Sorry, I don't mean—"

"Don't be! It's true! There *is* no point! I'm not scared of dying – we all have to do it. So why not now rather than later? It should be my choice."

"Exactly!" said Frankie.

Joan and Frankie spent the rest of the afternoon drinking cups of tea and coffee and telling each other about their lives. Frankie was surprised by how switched-on Joan seemed and how she recalled such intricate details of her past. Then she remembered what Robert had told her. Joan had forgotten about almost burning down her unit. She'd also forgotten about spending the night down by the lake. Maybe all the stories were just another figment of Joan's imagination.

"So, Joan," said Frankie, not quite sure how to broach the subject, "what happens with Alzheimer's. I mean, what does it do to you?"

"Well, it all started because I couldn't remember who the prime minister was. The doctor asks you all these questions when you have your check-up and for the life of me, I couldn't remember. I've also had a couple of things happen lately that I just don't remember at all. They gave me a scan and told me it's getting worse a lot quicker than they expected. It's killing my brain. Like a lot of the other poor devils in this place."

"So, what you were talking about before, how do you know it's what you really want and it's not the Alzheimer's making you think that way?"

"I can prove it to you Frances. Ask me a question. Any question. I can prove that my mind is still sound and I'm able to make decisions."

Frankie asked her lots of questions, more to amuse them both than to test Joan's mental capacity. "You'd be great at trivia!" laughed Frankie. "Maybe I can ask you a question every time I see you, so I know you're okay."

"I found it!" said Joan suddenly.

"Found what?" asked Frankie.

"Eureka" replied Joan. "It means '*I found it*'. In ancient Greek. How's that for a memory?"

Pretty fucking amazing, thought Frankie. Even she didn't remember that.

"Eureka it is!"

"So, Frances, can you at least think about what I asked you before? I know it's a lot to ask, but like I said, my time is running out. I have plenty of money and—"

"*Stop!*" yelled Frankie, startling Joan into silence mid-sentence. "You won't be paying me *anything*! I don't even know if I can help you! But… I promise that I'll think about it."

"Promise?"

"I promise." Frankie leaned over and gave Joan a kiss on the cheek. "Thanks again for my bluebird. I'll see you Monday. Have a nice weekend, Joan."

"You too, dear. Thanks for your company today."

Frankie made her way down to the dining room to fill in her weekly report with Robert. He wasn't there so she made herself a cup of coffee and took a seat at one of the tables. He walked in a short time later and slapped down a folder in front of him. He was obviously still not in the greatest of moods.

"So, how'd it go with Joan today?" he asked with a serious look on his face.

"Yeah good, I softened her up a bit and told her we'd be sending the boys round if she doesn't start towing the line."

She looked at Robert with a grin on her face. He was trying hard to keep a straight face.

"Very funny," he said in a monotone voice. "Well anyway, let's get this report done so I can send it off and we can both get out of here."

He opened the folder and took out the paperwork.

"So, has the participant met the following criteria? Attendance – satisfactory or unsatisfactory?"

"Satisfactory," Frankie chimed in. Robert didn't answer but just ticked the box.

"Behaviour," said Robert pausing with his pen above the paper. Frankie didn't know whether he was joking or not. "Hmmmmm… satisfactory, I guess."

"Appearance – satisfactory. Sorry Frankie, there's no box for excellent."

Robert let out a belly laugh and elbowed her. Frankie pretended to be pissed off that he'd strung her along with his sulking act, but she was actually relieved. Her nerves were frayed after her day with Joan, and she just wanted a bit of peace and quiet.

Robert finished the report and they both signed it at the bottom. "So, what's on for you this weekend, Frankie? Big night out on the town?"

"Doubt it. I'll probably just go and have a few beers at Liam's."

"Oh." There was a bit of a pause and for once Robert seemed lost for words. "Okay. Sounds like fun. Is he a friend of yours?"

Frankie realised what was going on and decided to put Robert on the receiving end of a joke for once.

"Yep. I've only known him a few days, but we get along so well. I feel so comfortable there and his cooking is to die for."

"He's already cooked for you?"

"Yep. I always leave there feeling *really* satisfied."

"Okay, that's too much information now."

"You should try it some time."

"Try what?" said Robert, his face turning bright red. Frankie was enjoying making him squirm.

"Liam's cooking!"

"I think three's a crowd, actually."

"Oh, there'll be heaps more than three of us there."

Robert looked at Frankie like she was speaking Swahili.

She burst out laughing, so pleased with herself that she'd managed to fluster him.

"Liam O'Connor's!"

Robert sat there for a second. "Oh, the pub?"

"Yes, the pub!" laughed Frankie. "I'm staying just round the corner, so it's my new local."

"That's my mate's pub!"

"Tom?"

"Yes! You know him? Geez Frankie you really don't waste any time do you!"

"No, I've only been here a few days and already I know your mates and I'm having an affair with Liam. By the way, Tom pours an amazing Guinness."

"That I know!" Robert nodded. "Hey, I might see you there later for a drink. I end up there most weekends at some point. It's pretty popular with the locals."

"Yep, and there's live music there Fridays and"

"Saturdays," said Robert shaking his head. "See you later then?"

"Not if I see you first."

The rain outside had slowed to a spit, and Frankie was glad she'd be able to walk home. She had a lot to process. She could almost taste the Guinness in her mouth. She guessed she'd be having a few more than usual tonight after the crazy mixed-up day she'd had.

Back at Learmonth House Frankie ran herself a hot bath. She laid there soaking, staring at the pink walls, reliving her intensely weird day with Joan. Thinking about what Joan had asked her to do, all sorts of unwelcome scenarios started racing through her mind. She saw Joan sitting there in her wheelchair with a kitchen knife, sawing through her wrists, her beautiful dress covered in blood. It made her feel sick to her stomach.

Maybe there *was* a way she could help Joan. But how? Surely an overdose would be the best option. But what drug would you use?

How much would you need? Would it be painless? Joan seemed intent on killing herself regardless, so what would be so wrong about helping her do it with dignity?

Hundreds of questions and images were spinning around and around in Frankie's head like a mouse on a wheel. She dunked her head under the water, trying to wash them all away. She got out of the bath. *Enough of this shit. I need a beer.*

Wrapped in a towel, she went back to her room and sat in front of the mirror. The bruising on her face was finally starting to fade, unlike her hatred for Alan. That was something that would never disappear. Not ever.

Her eyes drifted to the beautiful little bluebird perched around her neck. She was becoming quite fond of Joan and wondered what she would have been like when she was young. She looked drop dead gorgeous in the photos, and probably would have been a real firecracker as well. No wonder Ernie fell in love with her.

It made Frankie realise how pathetically sad her life was, getting nothing but shit thrown at her from all angles. Christian treated her like garbage, and she had the AVO to prove it. She suddenly felt the overwhelming urge to get drunk.

As she dried her hair and got dressed, she recalled what Joan had said to her about hiding herself away. She pulled her hair back, turning her head from side to side to look at her profile.

What the hell she thought.

She tied her hair up in a high bun, the ends cascading down over her face. She also changed the top she was wearing to one she'd bought on a whim but had never worn; one that showed off her figure and made her stand out rather than blend in.

As she looked in the mirror again, she smiled at a totally different person.

She pulled on her boots and headed downstairs for dinner.

"Hey Ruth," said Frankie as she walked into the dining room. Ruth was still setting up for dinner.

"Frankie! Hi. Look at you – you look great! I love your hair!"

"Just thought I'd do something different with it for a change. I think I'm a bit early for dinner."

"That's okay, it's just about ready. Are you going out tonight?"

"Yeah, I'm just gonna go to the pub for a while. After the day I've had I need a drink! How was your day?"

"Good. I think Pete's worn a hole in the carpet in the hallway, but the gods are smiling on us with the weather. Tomorrow's supposed to be fine."

"Oh, that's right – the croquet comp!"

"Bring your earmuffs," laughed Ruth.

Frankie quickly ate her dinner before most of the others arrived. She wasn't in the mood for all their endless banter, and the pub was calling her. She waved goodbye to Ruth and headed out.

Liam's was a lot livelier than she'd seen it before. Groups of people were crowded around the tables, many of them in tradie hi-vis clothes, having their well-earned Friday afternoon drinks.

There were two extra people working behind the bar with Tom, all of them with a line of customers waiting to be served. Tom spotted Frankie, gave her a wave, and pointed over towards her regular table.

She peered through the crowd to see Robert sitting at her table with two pints of Guinness in front of him.

"Saved you a seat," smiled Robert, handing her a beer.

"Thanks. Perfect timing." She took a long swig of her Guinness. "God, I needed that."

"Rough day with the insurgent, huh? By the way, I love your hair like that."

"Um, yeah, thanks" she said, trying to act unsurprised by how different Robert looked. He was dressed in jeans and a light blue polo shirt and had an amazingly good build. She'd never seen him in anything other than his nurse's uniform, so this was definitely an improvement.

"Did you just get here?"

"About ten minutes ago. Tom told me where you sit, so I grabbed the table. Lucky you got here when you did or I would have drunk your beer too."

Frankie couldn't help but wonder what Robert and Tom would have said about her.

"So, do you know all these people?" asked Frankie, looking around at the crowd.

"Yeah, some of them. I play cricket with a few of the guys over there." He caught one guy's eye who yelled out "Hey Robbie!", causing the others to look over, raising their glasses and giving him a cheer. Frankie guessed they were cheering him because he was sitting with her, making her feel a bit embarrassed.

"So, cricket hey? I've got a big croquet match coming up tomorrow." Robert nearly spat out his mouthful of beer.

"Croquet?" he laughed. "What the… where?"

"Oh, don't laugh. It's deadly serious. We're playing for the Roses. At my local sports club."

"Don't you mean the ashes? Which sports club?"

Frankie laughed. "Where I'm staying. They play different games for a box of Roses chocolates."

"Well, what the bloody hell are you doing here? You should be at home getting an early night!" laughed Robert.

"Don't worry, I'm working on my arm strength. Cheers!" said Frankie as she clinked Robert's glass and sculled the rest of her beer. "I'll get the next one."

She grabbed their empty glasses and headed over to line up at the bar. Tom put up two fingers. "Two more?"

"Yes please" said Frankie, putting the empty glasses on the bar and waiting for Tom to pour two more.

Walking back to the table, Frankie felt unusually self-conscious. Probably from the fact she had her hair pulled up and was wearing figure hugging clothes.

"So, Frankie, tell me about you. How come you decided to come here?"

Here it comes, thought Frankie, but it was something she knew she couldn't avoid so she just wanted to get it over with. She took a deep breath.

"Well… I've lived in Melbourne my whole life. My parents were killed in a car crash ten years ago and I went to live with my aunty. I got mixed up with a drug dealer who turned out to be a total fuckwit, he slapped an AVO on me, and here I am!"

Robert sat in stunned silence.

Frankie continued, "so, how come *you're* here?"

"Well… I grew up on a sheep farm in Mildura. I was studying viticulture 'cause I wanted to start up a vineyard. Then my girlfriend got killed in a horse-riding accident, so I moved to Ballarat and became a nurse!"

Now it was Frankie's turn to sit in stunned silence.

"Well," said Robert with a smile. "Glad we got all *that* out of the way!"

Frankie laughed as they clinked their glasses together.

"So, what did you do to him?" asked Robert.

"To who?"

"The fuckwit drug dealer."

"Nothing actually. He owed me money. A lot of money. About ten grand. I'd been driving for him for months and he still hadn't paid me. I kept asking and asking him for it, but he kept making excuses, so I turned up to his house with a baseball bat."

"*Ha!* I can just imagine that!" laughed Robert with a huge grin on his face. "Cranky Frankie on the loose. Did you hit him with it?"

"No! I wasn't going to hit him. I was just going to maybe smash something. I just wanted him to take me seriously and give me my money! But his stupid nosey neighbours rang the cops, and I ended up with an AVO."

"So, is he the one who hit you?"

"What?"

"Your eye. I noticed it when you were sitting on the bench the other day."

"Oh that. No, that was another fuckwit. My big fat loser cousin. Thank God I'm out of that shithole." Frankie could feel herself getting angry, so she diverted the conversation.

"So, tell me about your girlfriend."

Robert's demeanour instantly changed, and Frankie could tell he was still feeling the loss of her.

"Amy was her name. She was a gorgeous, fiery redhead with big brown eyes. We'd been going out for about four years. We used to talk about moving away and starting up a vineyard somewhere. On Valentine's Day I was going to ask her to marry me, but she died before I got the chance."

"Fuck," said Frankie, disturbed by Robert's story. "That's so sad. It's hard to get over losing people you love, hey."

"Almost impossible. I'm hopeless. I've been out with other girls, but even after six years, I still compare everyone to her."

"Maybe you're just not ready yet," said Frankie. "It took me years to finally realise that my parents weren't going to walk through the door and shout, *'We're back,'* like they'd been on holidays. I tell you what though, if there is such a thing as God, I'll be punching him in the face when I die."

Robert started laughing.

"I can see it now. Amy would have said something like that. She's probably up there punching him right now. Anyway Frankie, enough of the sad stuff. Let's talk about something good. Like the upcoming war of the Roses. Cheers!"

They both laughed and clinked their glasses together.

The crowd in the pub was growing and the band started to set up in the corner of the main bar. As everyone kept drinking, the noise level kept rising.

As Frankie and Robert continued swapping stories about their lives, Frankie realised Robert's comedian act she'd witnessed at work was masking a huge underlying sadness and loss. She also realised that her cold-hearted bitch act was probably masking the exact same thing. It made her feel strangely comfortable to be hanging out with someone as damaged as herself.

Suddenly, the Irish band started to play and the whole pub erupted in singing and dancing.

"Come on Frankie, let's jig!" shouted Robert over the noise.

"No, I don't..." but before she could object, Robert had grabbed her by the hand and dragged her out into the middle of the crowd. He had one arm around her waist and the other holding her hand, spinning her round one way, then the other, like a rag doll. It was exhausting but exhilarating being part of a rowdy drunken mob, all having the same wonderful, chaotic time.

After a few songs, breathless and sweating, they staggered back to their table, swigging down the rest of their drinks.

"Oh god, that was so much fun!" yelled Frankie. She was feeling euphoric, no doubt helped along by the previous four pints of Guinness. "Let's have another beer!"

While Robert was at the bar, Frankie thought about the upcoming croquet match and how excited Pete would be. Then she remembered the curfew. *Shit*! *The door's locked at ten"*. She looked at her phone. It was nine-thirty. Good! Time for one more.

"Here you go, Frances!" said Robert handing her beer to her.

"I just remembered, I'll have to be home by ten, 'cause they lock the doors. I'll have to go after this one."

"Aww," said Robert as he screwed up his face pretending to be sad. "You could just say you want to go, you know."

"I don't want to go!" said Frankie "I'd love to stay here all night drinking Guinness and getting thrown around the dance floor."

"You know, I've got an idea. You could...," whispered Robert.

"Could what?"

"You could stay at my place. I've got a spare room you know. Plus, I've got JD," he said, winking at Frankie.

"Thanks, but I probably should have an early one anyway. It is the war of the Roses, after all."

Frankie felt tempted to take Robert up on his offer, but decided against it. She'd seen Robert in a whole new light tonight and realised there was a lot more to him than she'd thought. She didn't want to end up having drunk sex with him like she'd done with other guys, despising herself the next day. Plus, she had to be able to face him at work. She couldn't believe she was being so sensible. It was so unlike her.

"No worries. Sporting honour must come first! I respect that in a woman!" he laughed. They finished their beers and Frankie picked up her bag to leave.

"I had a great night tonight," she said. "I'll see you Monday, I guess. I really need to talk to you about Joan. Maybe we could catch up at lunch time?"

"Sure thing, Frankie. I'll see you then. You know what?" he said, pointing at her with one eye closed, "You're a lot more fun than you pretend to be!"

"Thanks. I think."

Robert stood up, put his hand gently on the back of her neck and kissed her on the lips. It was a little bit longer than a kiss you'd expect from a friend and Frankie could feel her face starting to turn red.

"See ya, Frankie. Good luck tomorrow. Hope you kick their arses."

"See ya Monday, Robert. I'll bring the Roses to work. Have a good weekend."

Frankie walked away, glancing back at Robert on her way out. He was still standing up, watching her leave. She gave him a wave. What a day. What a night. What the fuck. She didn't have the brain power to think about one more thing. She was glad she was drunk.

At least she could go to bed and pass out so she could get away from her thoughts.

CHAPTER EIGHT

The blinding sun woke Frankie from her stupor. Her head was throbbing and her dry mouth tasted disgusting. She was still wearing her clothes from the night before. Her hair was still tied up and there was a wet patch of dribble on her pillow. She groaned and laid there trying to gather her thoughts. She recounted the events from the night before. The beers. The dancing. Robert.

Robert's kiss. *We were both drunk,* she told herself. *I'm sure he wouldn't have done it otherwise.*

She dragged her aching body out of bed and swallowed four Panadols, washing them down with as much water as she could stomach. The time was seven-thirty, so she changed her clothes and stumbled downstairs to catch the end of breakfast. Ruth was sitting at one of the tables drinking a cup of coffee and reading the paper.

"Morning Ruth," said Frankie in a husky voice.

"Morning Frankie. Good night?" she asked with a smirk.

"It was actually," she replied, pushing her unbrushed hair from her face. "It's a wonder you didn't hear the noise from here."

Frankie poured herself a bowl of cereal and slumped down at the table with Ruth.

"So, tell me all about it," said Ruth, putting down the paper and taking off her glasses.

"I just met up with one of the people from work and we had a few beers and watched the band."

"Who is he?"

"He? How do you know it's a he?" Frankie pushed away her bowl of cereal.

"Oh, I don't know, call it women's intuition."

"Well, his name's Robert. He's a nurse at the home. We're just friends. Well, we aren't even that really. We just work together. His mate runs the pub so he goes there anyway."

"Uh huh," said Ruth "So do you like him?"

"Robert? No! Like I said we just work together. He seems like a nice enough guy though. His girlfriend died so he's pretty screwed up from that. We're all screwed up from something though, right?"

"That's true. Sometimes it's nice to hear about other people's struggles. It helps bring people closer together." Ruth smiled at her.

What was Ruth getting at? Actually, she knew exactly what she was getting at, but Frankie wasn't ready to even think about that, let alone talk about it.

"What time's the big croquet match?"

"Ten am, *sharp*," laughed Ruth. "Pete's out there inspecting the pitch and getting everything set up."

"Good. That gives me time to have a shower and hopefully get rid of this hangover."

"Hang on a sec." Ruth went into the kitchen and returned with a tube of Berocca. "Here, have a couple of these. But don't tell Pete or I'll be in trouble for match fixing."

As Frankie stood under the shower soaking her throbbing head, she started thinking about Joan and their strange conversation the day before. The more she thought about it, the more she was leaning towards wanting to help her, even though that was insane. And illegal.

Just because something's insane and illegal, doesn't mean it's wrong.

Her mind drifted to Robert; the way he was spinning her around on the dance floor and how it felt when he kissed her. She hadn't experienced that feeling for a long time. But then again, so what? He kissed her. Big deal. It was just a peck. He probably kisses lots of girls. He probably takes girls home all the time too. He probably ended up taking someone home last night after she left.

Putting an end to her internal babbling, she decided to block Robert out of her head all together. She already had enough to think about after her talk with Joan. She got dressed, sculling down her Berocca before heading back downstairs for the croquet match.

Out in the yard, Pete was meticulously placing the croquet hoops in their positions.

"Hey Pete, how's the ground looking?"

"Hi Frankie. Yep, the ground's good. It's holding a bit of water, but it's playable. I'd rate it as heavy."

"So, what are the rules? I've never played before."

That was a question Frankie wished she'd never asked. It was like she'd flicked a switch in Pete's brain, setting him off on a rant like she'd never heard. He must have recited the entire croquet rule book to her in the space of a few minutes.

Ruth had come out into the yard and was standing there smiling at Frankie, waiting for Pete's tutorial to end. "I'm sure you'll get the hang of it once we get going." said Ruth. "Fancy a pre-match cuppa?"

"I'd kill for a coffee." They both went into the kitchen.

"So, tell me about your day yesterday," said Ruth as she handed Frankie her coffee. "You looked a bit frazzled when you got back."

"Oh God, what a day. Where do I start? One of the residents there – Joan's her name – well, she wants me to help her kill herself!"

"What? Why?" asked Ruth with a shocked look on her face, quickly getting up to close the kitchen door leading to the hallway.

"Well, she's got Alzheimer's, and they want to move her from her unit where she looks after herself into the nursing home part.

But she'd rather be dead, and I don't blame her. I hope someone'll kill *me* if I ever get like that." Frankie suddenly remembered Ruth's story about her husband dying. "Oh Ruth, sorry I"

"No. I agree, Frankie," said Ruth, obviously unoffended. "When Patrick was dying, it was almost impossible to keep his pain away. Here was this bloody disease eating him away before my very eyes, and there was not a goddamn thing I could do about it. It absolutely broke my heart."

Tears were welling up in Ruth's eyes. "If I could have put him out of his misery, I would have. I could tell by the way he looked at me in those final days that he just wanted to die. He didn't want to be like that."

Frankie hugged Ruth as she wiped away her tears. They sat together as Frankie told her all about her time with Joan; her stories and photographs, her jewellery and beautiful dresses, her relationship with her son and how she'd also lost a husband who she adored.

"So, what are you going to do?"

Frankie breathed a heavy sigh. "No idea. I'd love to help her, but what could I do without ending up in jail? Add that to my AVO, and they'd lock me up and throw away the key!"

"What about the new euthanasia laws? Maybe that's an option. I wish they were around when Patrick was dying."

"Apparently that's not an option. I might talk to Robert about it."

Her thoughts drifted back to Robert. And the kiss. Frankie contemplated telling Ruth about the night she'd had with Robert at the pub but decided against it. After what she'd just unloaded on her, poor Ruth had heard enough for one day. "Anyway, it must be getting close to croquet o'clock! Thanks Ruth, for listening to me bang on about this. It's been driving me crazy!"

"Any time," smiled Ruth. They both went out the back to join the others for the war of the Roses.

About a dozen housemates had gathered out in the yard for the croquet match. Pete was in all his glory; his old, dented whistle around his neck, announcing the rules of play to everyone. Most of them took no notice, too busy with their usual competitive banter. Frankie stood silently watching Pete, wondering what he would have been like if he hadn't been afflicted with his mental condition. Would he be married with kids? What would he have done for a living? Maybe he would have been a doctor. Or an electrician. Or a baker. Probably a professional sportsman, knowing Pete. As sad as it was, it was pretty clear that Pete's life still held value for him. He was unaware of not being 'normal'. He was just getting on with his life. He had a purpose.

That's it, thought Frankie. *That's the key to all of this. Without a purpose, your life has no meaning.* Even though it was obvious, she'd never really thought about life in that way. Joan was a woman who had lived such a full, vibrant life, about to be reduced to a miserable patient in a nursing home, with absolutely no purpose other than wanting to die. Joan's days were clearly numbered, thanks to her hideous disease. No-one could change that. But maybe, Frankie could help her to find some kind of purpose in her death. This was like a revelation to Frankie. Make her death *mean* something! She now understood exactly what she needed to do. She just had to work out a way to do it.

"Whooooooooaaaaaaahhhhhhh!"

Frankie's train of thought was interrupted by the loud roar following Ruth's amazing shot which cleared two hoops at once. Everyone was clapping and cheering.

Ruth took a bow and handed the mallet to Frankie.

"Here, your turn Frankie."

Frankie whacked the ball but it went way off course and hit the fence, causing an uproar of laughter. Her mind was a million miles away, just like her aim. The match lasted just over an hour, with Ruth winning the Roses, closely followed by Pete.

"You're pretty good!" said Frankie as they packed up the equipment.

"Years of practice," winked Ruth.

Frankie ran upstairs and returned with a bag of Fantales. "Here you go Pete," she said, tossing them to him. "I think you've earned these today."

Pete's face lit up with his signature toothless grin. Frankie loved that grin. It was contagious.

"Thanks Frankie. I love these. You know they have stories about movie stars on the wrappers?"

The mention of movie stars reminded Frankie of looking at all Joan's photos with her famous friends and Joan telling her about her husband's likeness to Neil Mason. Surely a woman who'd lived such a wonderful life deserved to go out on her own terms. Maybe she needed a last hurrah. A celebration. A recognition of some sort. Frankie felt a fire building inside her. Maybe this was *her* purpose. To help Joan. God knows she'd just been wandering aimlessly through life since her parents died, wasting her time with losers. Maybe this was the very thing she needed to get her mojo back. For *her* life to mean something.

Frankie spent the rest of the day in her room, her head buzzing with ideas of creative ways she could help Joan. She wrote page after page of notes, beginning with a list of the different ways you could help someone to die. From accidents to overdoses, her inventory was growing by the minute. Next to each one she wrote the pros and cons, making it overwhelmingly clear that the number one problem was going to be how to avoid going to jail for murder.

She researched euthanasia, reading about the types of drugs used and how they worked. She'd had some experience with drugs, but only the illegal ones. And from the stories she'd heard on the street, overdoses were anything but peaceful or pleasant. Maybe she'd talk to Robert. He was a nurse after all. Surely, he'd know all about these drugs and how to inject them. That was something

Frankie had never done, no matter how much Christian had tried to persuade her. She drew the line at needles. Just the sight of them made her feel like passing out.

It was at that moment she realised there was no way she could pull this off by herself. She'd need a partner in crime. Literally. Should she ask Robert? What would he say? Would he be on board, or would he betray her like everyone else? Would he get her sacked? Or maybe turn her in to the cops? Her mind started imagining all sorts of scenarios, most of them frightening. For now, she just needed to focus on one thing at a time. She'd worry about Robert later.

Needing a break from her swirling thoughts, Frankie went to her wardrobe and took the stash out of her coat pocket. *Far out, I haven't even thought about this stuff since I've been here,* she thought, feeling surprised and pleased with herself. She put a joint and a lighter in her pocket before going out for a walk.

Wandering through the streets, Frankie eventually made her way down to a quiet spot on the riverbank and sat on the grass. She lit her joint, drawing it in deeply as she stared out at the water. Slowly the chaotic fight going on inside her head started to mellow into peaceful tranquillity. She laid down on the grass, gazing up at the sky.

As the fluffy white clouds drifted past, she could see the image of a woman's face and started thinking about her parents. Back to the days when they brought her here on holidays. She wished she could remember it more. Maybe they sat on this very spot all those years ago. Maybe they walked down the same streets. Maybe they *did* visit that same museum. If only she'd known back then that the days with her parents were numbered, she would have appreciated them more. She would have told them how much she loved them. She wouldn't have been such a rebellious, headstrong little bitch.

Her thoughts drifted back to her mum standing in front of her, hands on her hips, yelling at Frankie *"Who do you think you are*

– the Queen of England?" while her father sat in his chair reading the paper, oblivious to the argument raging on around him. *"Oh Helen, don't worry about it. She's a teenager!"* he would say, after Frankie had said or done something to infuriate her mum.

She wished she'd been a better daughter. Wished she could have that time all over again. Wished she still had someone in her life who loved her so unconditionally. The pain of their loss was still as raw as the day it happened.

Then she noticed it. That feeling. It was back. The insidious beast lurking inside her soul, ready to devour her if she looked it in the eye. It was here, growling right in her face, making her dizzy and turning everything black. Frankie yelled in terror to try and escape its clutches.

A group of people suddenly appeared, standing over Frankie as she laid on the riverbank sobbing.

"Are you okay? What happened?" said one of the onlookers.

"I'm fine," blubbered Frankie, "I just need a minute." They continued to stand over her, staring.

"Are you sure you're okay?" asked another.

"I'm fine!" she snapped. Slowly, they all wandered away. Frankie felt like she was going to pass out or throw up. Or both.

"Fuck!" she yelled, wiping away her tears with one hand and hitting the ground with her other. *"Fuck! Fuck! Fuck!"*

She laid there on the riverbank, staring at the sky in stunned silence, tears running down her face and into her ears. Even though she thought about her parents constantly, all this talk about Joan dying had brought her grief thundering back to the surface. It was at that moment Frankie realised that Joan was going to be yet another loss she'd have to grieve.

CHAPTER NINE

Monday morning couldn't come quick enough. Frankie had spent a lot of time alone with her thoughts, and she needed a break from her internal rollercoaster.

"Good morning, Frankie!" For once she was truly glad to hear Clare's melodious greeting as she walked through the doors. "Oh, I *love* your hair like that! You look so different!"

"Thanks Clare. Have a good weekend?"

Clare told her all about the dreamy weekend away in the mountains which her boyfriend had surprised her with, and how delightfully romantic it was. Frankie smiled as she daydreamed about swapping places with Clare for a day. How fantastic it would be, being blissfully unaware and not having a care in the world.

Clare was still chattering as Robert walked in.

"Morning ladies. Clare, have you met the new Frankie? This is *fun* Frankie."

"I was just saying how I love her hair. She looks so pretty," chirped Clare. Frankie instantly felt awkward, hoping Robert wasn't going to start talking about their night together at the pub.

"So, what's on today?" Frankie asked as she started walking out, breaking up the little warm and fuzzy gathering. She led Robert into the dining room, and they sat down.

"Well?" asked Robert, staring at her.

"Well, what?" Frankie was nervous, not knowing what he was going to say next.

"Where are the Roses?"

"Oh," said Frankie, relieved. "I played like shit. I couldn't concentrate."

"Too much fun the night before?" Robert asked with a grin.

"Too much Guinness more like."

Frankie shut down the conversation before it could get personal.

"So, am I with Joan again today? I've been helping her sort through all her stuff."

"Yep, if you like. I'm in the clinic today so I probably won't be around much."

"I really need to talk to you about her, actually. In private."

Robert's smile disappeared. "Okay. I can meet you after work, otherwise it'll have to be tomorrow."

"After work's better. And not here."

"Okay. I'll see you in the carpark." Frankie nodded. "By the way," said Robert as he got up to leave, "Clare was right."

Frankie was relieved when Robert left the room, unable to see how embarrassed she was.

As expected, after knocking at Unit four, Joan answered the door, once again looking immaculate in a beautiful brightly coloured dress, with matching jewellery and shoes.

"Frances! I was hoping it was you. Come in, dear."

Frankie went in and sat down as Joan sat staring at her with a big grin on her face.

"What is it?" asked Frankie

"Your hair, Frances! You look so much better now I can see your lovely face."

Joan went into her bedroom and returned with a pink drawstring bag.

"Come over here, dear." Frankie sat in front of her as Joan started brushing her hair, pulling it up and carefully pinning it in

76

place. After about ten minutes, Joan asked her to turn around as she sat there studying her artwork, adjusting a few little bits.

"There," said Joan. "Go and have a look in the mirror."

Frankie went into the bathroom and couldn't believe what she saw. She looked like she'd just walked out of a movie. Not a hair was out of place.

"What do you think?" yelled Joan. Frankie walked out of the bathroom with her mouth open.

"It's amazing, Joan! Where did you learn to do hair like that?"

"My days on Broadway, dear. It was all part of the job. It also had to be perfect or we'd get strips torn off us. I remember many a poor girl running back to the dressing room in tears – me included. So, we all learnt very quickly." She looked at Frankie and sighed. "I remember being young and beautiful like you and taking it for granted. Make the most of it, Frances, because it doesn't last. Now, how about we do your makeup too?"

"I don't really like wearing makeup."

"Have you ever tried wearing it?"

"No."

"How do you know then until you try it?"

Frankie didn't have an answer for that.

"Come on, I'll show you."

They sat in front of Joan's bedroom mirror as Joan patiently taught her how to apply makeup, step by step. Frankie had never seen so much makeup. There were pots and pallets and creams and powders and lipsticks and brushes of all kinds. She felt like she was a canvas in a painter's studio and watched in amazement as Joan methodically transformed her face into a work of art. When she was finished, Frankie sat staring at her reflection in disbelief. Joan smiled, obviously pleased with the end result.

"Well? What do you think?"

"Oh my God!" said Frankie "I can't believe that's me! I look like someone else!"

"You look like you stepped out of a magazine. You could be a model, you know."

Frankie just sat there, turning her head from side to side, admiring herself in amazement.

"It's all about highlighting your positive features, dear. And you have plenty of those. Anyway, let's have a cuppa."

They sat and talked more about Joan's days on Broadway and all the things she'd learnt about looking glamourous. Frankie was astonished by how different you could look and feel with a bit of effort and the right equipment.

The look on Joan's face suddenly turned serious. "So, Frances, did you have a think over the weekend about our conversation?"

"Yes, I did. I did a lot of thinking actually. I'd like to help you Joan…

"But?" said Joan, looking worried.

"But I just need to figure out how. Well, I have an idea of how, but I mean without going to jail."

Joan looked relieved, a big smile beaming across her face. "Oh really? You're willing to help me?" She grabbed Frankie's hand as tears welled up in her eyes.

"Yes, I am. I totally understand how you feel, and I'd be exactly the same."

Joan grabbed Frankie and hugged her, sobbing and thanking her over and over. It reinforced to Frankie just how serious Joan was about this, and how much it meant to her.

"Oh, and by the way, I forgot. Eureka?"

"I found it!" spluttered Joan, laughing and crying at the same time.

Frankie told her about the research she'd done over the weekend on euthanasia and all the different scenarios. It felt very strange talking to Joan about choosing her own death as if she was choosing a new set of curtains. But, as Joan kept reminding her, once she was stuck in the nursing home, her options were gone.

At least this way, she still had a choice. But only if Frankie could pull it off.

"I'm going to talk to Robert about it." said Frankie. "He'd be the perfect person to help us. I'm going to ask him after work, so if I don't come back tomorrow, you know I've been sacked. Or locked up."

"Oh, I'm sure he wouldn't do that. Just use your feminine charms on him. Once he sees you looking like this, he'll do anything for you!" Joan laughed.

"I doubt it. He's still hung up on his old girlfriend."

"Oh, the one that died. Yes, he told me about her. Sounds like he loved her a lot. But he's still so young, Frances. He's got his whole life ahead of him, so it's about time he moved on. Maybe you're the person he's been waiting for."

"You've got it all figured out, haven't you Joan!" laughed Frankie. "You should write fairy tales."

"Yes, I can see it now" said Joan, closing her eyes and waving her arms around for added effect. "Two starry eyed young lovers starting out on their journey together, just like me and Ernie, or Romeo and Juliet."

"Settle down Shakespeare. I don't even know the guy. He might be an axe murderer for all I know."

"Well, there you go," giggled Joan, "That would solve all our problems!"

Frankie burst out laughing. "Feel like a walk to the lake? I need some fresh air."

"Sure. Let's take some sandwiches with us."

Down at the lake, Frankie fed her sandwiches to the ducks. She felt sick. She was dreading her meeting with Robert and how he was going to react. *Oh, by the way, I want you to help me kill Joan by injecting her with a lethal drug overdose.*

What the fuck was she thinking? Was she totally insane? But then she looked over at the lovely lady sitting there in her wheelchair, talking to the ducks each by name, and imagined her lying in the nursing home, being left to die in misery. She just had to bite the bullet and ask him. It was the right thing.

The end of the day couldn't come quick enough. She just wanted it over with.

Joan looked so contented sitting there next to the water, feeding and talking to the ducks.

"Won't you miss all of this?" asked Frankie.

"Of course, dear, but that's already been decided for me. Pretty soon I won't know Daffy from Daisy or my bum from my elbow. Anyway, what I miss most is my Ernie. I just want to be with him now. That's all I want. I'm ready to go."

They both sat there in silence, the only sound coming from the ducks squabbling over their pieces of bread. Frankie imagined being a duck. Life would be so much easier. Just swim around, eat and shit. Have the occasional root. Lay the occasional egg. Easy.

"Come on, let's keep walking," said Frankie as she grabbed Joan's wheelchair.

They walked the entire circuit of the lake, stopping occasionally to sit and admire the view and the huge array of waterbirds that lived there. It was so peaceful, but Frankie knew it was just the calm before the storm. They got back to Joan's unit just before Frankie's knock off time.

"Okay Joan, I'm off now. Wish me luck." Joan grabbed Frankie by the hand and pulled her close.

"Frances, this means everything to me. You're my ray of hope in this dark time of my life, and I'm eternally grateful for what you're doing."

"I haven't done anything yet, so don't get your hopes up."

"I have every faith in you dear." Frankie actually believed her. Someone finally had faith in her. After all these years.

"I'll try not to let you down." Frankie leaned over and kissed Joan on the cheek. "See you tomorrow."

Frankie stood in the car park, leaning against a post. Seeing Robert walking towards her, she felt a giant knot in her stomach and a lump in her throat. She wished the ground would open up and swallow her.

As he got closer, a strange look came over his face.

"Woah!" he said, his eyes wide and his mouth hanging open. "Frankie! What happened to you?"

"What? What do you mean?" Surely, he couldn't see the terror she was feeling, could he?

"You look amazing!" he continued, circling around her, checking her out from all angles.

"Oh," she remembered. "Joan's handiwork."

She was glad Joan had picked today to make her look this good. Maybe it would help her stay out of jail.

"Wow." Robert was lost for words, still staring at her. Frankie could feel her face turning red, but with the amount of makeup slathered on her, surely he wouldn't notice.

"So where do you want to talk?" asked Frankie, diverting the attention away from herself.

"I thought we could go and have a coffee if you like. Sound okay?"

"Sure," said Frankie, wishing he'd suggested copious amounts of alcohol instead. Her nerves were out of control.

"Jump in," he said as he led her to an old Hilux ute, opening the passenger door for her. "Excuse the mess."

His car was surprisingly tidy compared to its outside appearance. "This is old Bessie. She came with me from the farm, and I can't part with her."

"That's nice," said Frankie with a hint of sarcasm, knowing that she was about to turn his mood from happy to fuck knows what. After what she was about to say, maybe he'd want to run her over with old Bessie.

"So, I've gotta tell you Frankie, I'm a bit disappointed."

"I know, these clothes. I left my evening gown at home. Sorry," joked Frankie.

"Ha. No, your appearance could never disappoint me. It's the chocolates. The Roses. I thought for sure you'd win the comp. No more big nights for you before an important match! It was a great night, by the way. I haven't danced that much in years."

"Yeah, it was a fun night. I haven't danced that much *ever*. If you call being thrown around dancing."

"And sorry if I offended you when I invited you back to my place. I didn't mean…"

"You wanted to sleep with me?"

"Yeah. Well, I don't mean I didn't mean I wanted to sleep with you, I just mean I didn't mean…"

"It's OK, don't stress about it. You mightn't even want to talk to me soon."

"Why wouldn't I want to talk to you? Are you having an affair with Tom as well as Liam now?" he laughed.

I wish it was that simple, thought Frankie. They pulled up at the café. It was an old, restored homestead overlooking the river. Frankie was relieved it was in a quiet spot. Hopefully no-one would hear what she was about to say.

As they walked in, Frankie noticed the waitress staring at her while she was showing them to their table. She quickly disappeared to the bathroom and looked in the mirror, still surprised by how amazing she looked. She took a deep breath before going back out to face her fate.

Robert was beaming at her as she sat down, clearly impressed with her new look. Good. She needed all the help she could get.

They ordered their coffee and Robert leaned forward in his chair.

"So, Frankie, you wanted to talk to me about Joan? Seems like you two are getting on like a house on fire. Pardon the pun."

"Yep, we are. She's an amazing woman. How long has she got?"

"They don't know for sure, but probably a couple of years."

"No, I mean until they make her move out of her home."

"Oh. Well, Maggie wants her out by the end of next month. There's an audit happening then. It happens every three years. It's a total pain in the arse. These dickheads in suits come in and go through everything with a fine-tooth comb. If they found out Joan was having her episodes and still living alone, the home could lose its licence. I know she doesn't want to move, but there's no other option. We'd all be out of a job otherwise."

"What if I told you there *was* another option?"

"Like what? Kidnap her? Kidnap the auditors? Actually, that second one would be a good option. Waste of everyone's time if you ask me."

"No. Not kidnap her. Look, I don't know how to say this, so I'm just going to say it. Joan wants to die. She's had enough and I don't blame her. If I was her, I'd want the exact same thing. I want to help her. I want to help her end her life the way she chooses, not the way everyone else chooses, especially all the doctors. I think she deserves to go out with dignity, and if I don't help her, no-one else will."

Frankie's heart was racing as Robert just sat there staring at her, not saying a word.

"And … I'm going to need your help."

Robert's eyes got wider. "Are you fucking *mad*? You're telling me you want to kill her?" he was raising his voice.

"Ssshhhhh," said Frankie annoyed, looking around. "It's called euthanasia. It happens all the time."

"I know that. I'm not a moron! But what the fuck Frankie, you can't just go around killing people willy-nilly. There are these things called *laws,* you know! Do you realise you'd get done for murder and end up spending the rest of your life in fucking prison? What are you thinking? Are you on drugs?"

Frankie actually wished she was. This was becoming the nightmare she feared it would be.

"So, what are you going to do? Hit her on the head with a hammer? Drown her in the bathtub? Roll her into oncoming traffic?" Now Frankie was getting pissed off.

"Calm the fuck down Robert and stop being such a *dick*!" snapped Frankie.

Robert let out a bellowing laugh. "Oh, *I'm* being a dick? Who's the one saying they want to *kill* someone? Fucking hell! That's rich, Frankie!"

"Fuck you! I should've known you'd be a fuckwit just like all the others!"

Frankie leapt to her feet, knocking over her chair and ran out of the café, swearing to herself and fighting back tears. She could hear Robert calling after her, so she sprinted as fast as she could around the corner and out of sight. She ran into the nearest alleyway and fell on the ground, holding her head in her hands. She couldn't believe she'd been so stupid. What *was* she thinking? She'd just fucked up *everything*. All in a matter of minutes. She'd never be able to show her face at the home again. It was all over. She'd let herself down and she'd let Joan down. She held the bluebird hanging around her neck and cried. She just wanted to go home. Wherever that was.

CHAPTER TEN

Frankie woke to the sound of gentle knocking.

"Frankie? Are you okay?" It was Ruth's voice outside her door.

"Yeah, fine," muttered Frankie.

She glanced at her phone through her bleary eyes. It was midday. Her fix it pills had once again done their job.

"Come down for a coffee and I'll make you something to eat," said Ruth.

Frankie realised she'd been sleeping since six pm the day before, and it wasn't long before the memories of everything she'd avoided for the past eighteen hours came flooding back to haunt her once more. She groaned, dragged herself out of bed and stumbled off for a shower.

Ruth's smiling face greeted her as she wandered into the dining room.

"Frankie. I was getting worried. You didn't come down for dinner or breakfast. Are you okay?"

"Don't ask," said Frankie, shaking her head as Ruth handed her a cup of coffee.

"So, no work today?"

"Nope. I can't go back. I think I've just fucked everything up yet again. I'll be lucky if the cops don't come looking for me. I'll probably have to leave here soon."

"Oh no, Frankie. Why?"

"Because I trusted someone. Serves me fucking right."

Ruth left Frankie to drink her coffee and went into the kitchen. She returned with a plate of food and sat down at the table with her.

"So, Frankie. Tell me what's happened."

Frankie leaned back in her chair and looked up at the ceiling.

"You remember me telling you about Joan, the lady who wants me to help her die?" Ruth nodded. "Well, I made the mistake of telling Robert about it and he totally lost his shit. He thinks I'm some psychopathic killer on the loose. He's probably already told everyone about it. I won't ever be able to show my face there again and once the department finds out, I'm fucked. I'm *so* pissed off at myself. I should've known better. I thought he was a nice guy but obviously my judgment is shit as usual. And Joan… I've let her down."

Tears started to well up in Frankie's eyes. "She was so happy that I was going to help her." Frankie started to sob as Ruth got up and hugged her. "Why is my life always such a fucking mess?"

"It's okay, Frankie. Everything will sort itself out. You haven't done anything wrong. All you did was try to help someone."

"Don't you mean try to *kill* someone?" sniffled Frankie.

"But you haven't! There's no crime in talking about it. And how do you know Robert has told everyone?"

"Of course he would have. He thinks I'm a fucking *psycho*. He'll probably try and get me locked up for all I know. I'm gonna have to leave here Ruth."

"Please don't rush into anything right now Frankie. Things probably aren't as bad as you think."

"They probably *are*, going by Robert's reaction. Sorry Ruth, I'm not hungry."

Frankie pushed away her plate. "I'm just going to bed."

"I'm here if you need to talk, Frankie. For what it's worth, I think you're amazing. To want to do that for someone is the most courageous thing I've ever seen. Joan is lucky to have a friend like you."

"Well not anymore," blubbered Frankie as she rushed out of the room.

Back in her room, Frankie started pacing the floor. What was she going to do? Where would she go? She couldn't go back to Melbourne. Maybe she'd just jump on a train and go. Anywhere. She'd find a job somewhere. Maybe she could go fruit picking. Or do some waitressing. Her allowance would be cut once they found out she'd left the home. Maggie would probably report her to the Department and then all hell would break loose. She'd be in trouble with the law. Again. Another black mark against her name. She needed to get the fuck away from this place.

She took out her suitcase and quickly stuffed everything in. Yet another place she was running from and, the way things were going, she'd be living like this for a long time to come. She took one last look at her room and wandered down the stairs to say goodbye to Ruth.

Ruth wasn't in the dining room. Or the kitchen. She could hear voices coming from the sitting room at the front, so she walked up the hallway and poked her head around the doorway. She could see Ruth sitting there talking to someone. As she got into the room, she saw the person Ruth was talking to. It was Robert.

She dropped her suitcase. Robert looked up at her, a worried look on his face.

"Frankie. I need to talk to you."

"Better make it quick. I've got a train to catch," she snarled.

Ruth stood up. "I'll leave you two to talk." She gave Frankie a smile as she quickly left the room.

"Sit down Frankie," said Robert in a quiet voice, patting the spare seat on the lounge next to him. "Please?"

Frankie reluctantly sat down in a chair on the opposite side of the room, her arms crossed.

"What are you doing here? Did you come to arrest me? How did you even find me?"

Robert let out a nervous laugh.

"Which question will I answer first?" Frankie glared at him with daggers. "Sorry. No, I'm not here to arrest you. I found you because you'd written your address on the report we did last Friday. And... I'm here because... I'm sorry."

"For what?" snapped Frankie sarcastically.

"I'm sorry for what I said to you. You just took me by surprise, you know? I wasn't expecting it."

"Oh, you weren't expecting that I was a psychopathic killer? Well now you fucking know. So, look out, you might be next!"

Frankie was getting angrier by the second. Robert slowly went over and knelt down next to Frankie's chair.

"Frankie. Stop it. I'm sorry. I know where you're coming from. I know what you're trying to do. I understand now. Frankie… I think you're incredible. I don't want you to go."

Robert put his hand on Frankie's arm and looked at her with watery eyes. Frankie sat there not saying a word, stunned by the sudden turnaround. They both sat in silence for several minutes as Robert continued to look at her, stroking her arm.

"It's my dancing isn't it," she said, trying to make light of an intense moment. "It gets everyone."

"Yep, you've nailed it!" laughed Robert as he grabbed her in a big bear hug.

Frankie laughed and put her head on his shoulder, feeling like the weight of the world had just been taken from her and tossed into oblivion.

"Do you really?" whispered Frankie.

"Really what? Think you're a great dancer?"

"Think I'm incredible?"

Robert held her by the shoulders and looked her directly in the eye.

"You have no idea. I've never met anyone like you, Frances Hadfield."

He slowly leaned over and kissed her. This kiss was definitely not a friendship kiss. Frankie felt a dizzying warm rush surge through her entire body. She just wanted him to swallow her up.

Robert rested his forehead on hers. "So, does this mean you're staying?" he whispered.

"Maybe," smiled Frankie. "Better get rid of my suitcase."

"I'll wait here for you," said Robert, grinning at her with a look she'd seen before. It was only now that she realised what it meant.

As Frankie made her way back to her room, she passed Ruth in the dining room, looking at her with a big smile on her face. Frankie paused outside the doorway.

"He's a lovely guy," whispered Ruth, holding both thumbs up. Frankie grinned and ran up the stairs two at a time.

Robert was waiting at the front door for her. "Let's go. My car's out the front. Thank God I caught you in time. Otherwise…"

"You'd never see me again."

"No, otherwise I would've had to chase every train leaving Ballarat till I found you!"

He opened the car door for her and bowed like a chauffeur as she got in.

Frankie was shellshocked. In that one brief instant, everything had changed.

"So, where are we going?"

"Well, I know where I'd like to take you right now, but we'll have to get back to work. I promised Joan."

"So, you've seen her?"

"First place I looked. I thought for sure you'd be there. She was really pissed at me when I told her we'd had a fight. She thinks the world of you, you know. She told me about what she'd asked you, among other things."

"What other things?"

"Well, like how wonderful you are, and what an idiot I'd be if I let you get away."

Frankie laughed. "Oh really, so is that why you came to find me?"

"No. I came because I'd already figured that out."

He reached over, grabbing Frankie's hand and squeezing it. "Promise me you won't try and run away again?"

Frankie thought for a moment. "Not without telling you first."

Robert shook his head. "Frankie, Frankie, Frankie. What am I going to do with you? Hmmmm … let me think …" A cheeky grin came over his face.

"Ha. You wish," laughed Frankie.

The truth was she wished for the same thing. A truth that both excited and terrified her. Frankie was relieved to arrive at Golden Leaves so she could focus on something else.

"We better go and see Joan first and put her out of her misery." Robert paused. "Sorry, poor choice of words."

How ironic, thought Frankie. *That's exactly what Joan had asked for. To be put out of her misery. Her potential misery.*

They went to unit four, Robert standing back while Frankie knocked. "Hello. Eureka?"

"I found it!" came the reply.

The door swung open to an elated Joan.

"Oh Robert, you found her!" She opened her arms so Frankie could give her a hug. "Oh, thank God. I thought you'd gone for good, Frances."

"Almost. I was thinking about it." Frankie looked at Robert.

"I convinced her to stay, Joan. I told her there was another excursion day coming up and I needed a quizmaster. I guess she just couldn't resist."

Joan shook her head. "Come in you two, have a cuppa with me."

"After you," Robert ushered Frankie in. "Can I just ask – what is this Eureka thing you two are talking about?"

"It's a memory test Robert," said Joan, "so Frances knows my mind is sound. She says Eureka and I tell her what it means. You of all people should know what it means by now."

"Yes. I found her." He stood and stared at Frankie, making her uncomfortable.

"Just like the Greek tale of Cupid and Psyche" said Joan wistfully, obviously delighting in the romance filling the room.

"Oh, here she goes again," sighed Frankie shaking her head. "Shakespeare's back. I think you've got your characters mixed up, Joan. It's actually Cupid and Psycho." Robert let out a huge bellowing laugh.

"I studied Greek mythology at school, Frances. I know *exactly* what I'm talking about!"

Frankie went into the kitchen and made the tea and coffee.

"So, now that the cat's out of the bag Robert, what's the plan?" asked Joan, staring at Robert intently.

"Well, as I told you earlier Joan, it's not an easy thing to do. There's lots of things to consider and lots of hurdles to jump over. Not least of them being the fact it's illegal."

"It shouldn't be," piped up Frankie.

"Yes, I understand that Frankie, but you can't use that as an argument in court when you've been accused of murder."

"Surely there's a way around all these things? There has to be! Can't we just run away somewhere and do it?" asked Joan.

"What, and hope no-one wonders where we all are?" answered Robert.

"I could just say I'm leaving to go to another home."

"There'd be mountains of paperwork. They wouldn't just let you wander off to God knows where. They'd need to tick all the boxes, especially with the audit coming. No-one will be able to fart without the auditors knowing."

"What if we said we were taking Joan on a holiday?" asked Frankie. "Aren't they allowed to go on holidays?"

"Yes, they can go on holidays, but it's usually with their family, not the staff."

"I'll just say I'm taking my two favourite staff members on a holiday to say thank you. Is there any rule against that?"

"I don't know. Can't say I've ever seen it happen. I guess we could use the argument that I'm a trained nurse and could take care of you, but I think they'd find it highly unusual, and a bit suss, to be honest."

"We just need to come up with a convincing story," said Frankie. "Maybe something like - Joan wanted to have a last adventure before she moved out of her unit."

Robert sat and scratched his head. "The story's the least of our worries. Do you both realise what's involved in all of this? There's the drugs we'd need…"

"You could steal them!" interrupted Frankie.

"Then there's the problem of what do we do once we've done it?"

"You could throw me in the river or dump me in the forest, I really don't care." said Joan.

"We're not dumping you anywhere!" said Robert, clearly getting frustrated. "I just think this is way too risky, and I don't want to be like some criminal, sneaking around stealing drugs and dumping bodies! Plus, we have to consider what would happen to us once everyone finds out. It'd be the end of us! We'd both end up in prison. Is that what you want for yourself?"

They all sat in silence, mulling over everything Robert had said.

Joan started to get teary. Frankie went over and put her hand on Joan's shoulder.

"Don't worry Joan, I'll find a way through all this. I promise."

Robert looked at Frankie with raised eyebrows. "I *will* find a way Robert!" said Frankie, getting annoyed.

"Okay then, let's see how incredible you really are, Frankie. Go ahead and surprise me. Surprise us both. I have every faith in you."

Frankie gave Robert an angry look.

"I mean it!" laughed Robert. "I *do* have faith in you."

"So do I!" seconded Joan.

"I'm glad someone does," muttered Frankie to herself. "I'll start working on a plan. I've already made some notes."

"Well, I have to go. I've got a meeting with Maggie this arvo." said Robert. He looked at Frankie. "I'm giving her an update on your recent behaviour. Apparently, there's been some complaints."

Frankie glared at him.

"*Joking!*" laughed Robert as he put his arm around her. "*My* only complaint will be if you don't let me make you dinner tonight."

"Ooh, Frances, watch this one. He's up to no good," laughed Joan.

"Can he cook though?" said Frankie to Joan, pretending Robert wasn't in the room.

"Hey, I make a wicked lamb roast. Taught by my own dear mother. Do you like lamb?"

"*Yes,*" they both replied in unison, making Robert laugh.

"Well, how about I pick you up around seven, Frankie?"

"Ok, I'm game. Should I bring some Mylanta? You know you'll have to measure up to Liam."

"Who's Liam?" asked Joan, confused.

Robert laughed, gave them both a kiss on the cheek and left for his meeting.

"I knew it," said Joan. "I just knew it."

"Knew what?"

"I knew you two would be perfect for each other. From the moment I laid eyes on you, I knew it."

"We'll see. He might be a shit cook. That'll ruin everything." laughed Frankie.

"I think this calls for another makeup session, Frances. He'll be like putty in your hands! Let's have a wine!"

Frankie felt like she was a teenager again, drinking with her girlfriends while they got ready to go out. The only difference was this time, her makeup would be awesome.

CHAPTER
ELEVEN

Frankie emptied her suitcase on her bed and hung everything back in the wardrobe, except for her only dress. One which she'd paid a lot of money for but had never mustered the courage to wear. She felt like a million dollars after Joan had once again worked her Broadway glamour magic, so jeans just weren't going to do her justice tonight. As she went downstairs to iron her dress, she could hear voices coming from the games room. She poked her head around the corner to see Pete and Ruth chatting. They both instantly stopped talking and stood staring at her.

"Hey," said Frankie "I won't be here for dinner tonight, Ruth."

"I'm not surprised looking like that! Dinner with Robert?"

"Yep. How'd you know?"

Ruth laughed. "My god, Frankie, the poor guy doesn't stand a chance."

"You look like a movie star, Frankie!" grinned Pete.

"Oh, thanks Pete. Not Godzilla, I hope."

Pete burst out laughing. "No. You're beautiful. Like Audrey Hepburn."

"You just want more Fantales, don't you Pete?"

"Yep!"

Ruth walked over to Frankie and whispered, "So, I guess you won't be coming home tonight?"

"No idea. I haven't tasted his cooking yet."

"Well, if first impressions are anything to go by, I'll bet his cooking won't disappoint." She gave Frankie a nudge and a wink.

Obviously, Robert had made a good impression on Ruth. Frankie was relieved; she trusted Ruth's judgment.

"Come and show me before you leave," said Ruth as she went to prepare dinner.

Frankie looked at herself in the mirror. She could hardly believe it was her. The sexy little black dress still fitted her. It hugged every curve of her body, leaving very little to the imagination. She took a deep breath and smiled at her reflection. She really *did* look like a movie star. Robert was in for a huge surprise, and she couldn't wait to see the look on his face. Socks were about to be knocked off, along with a lot more no doubt. Filled with excitement, she bounced downstairs to see Ruth.

"Woah. You're *definitely* not coming home tonight!" gasped Ruth. "You look so beautiful, Frankie. And sexy! Should I send Pete along as a bodyguard?"

Frankie laughed. "It's ok, I have my caustic personality to keep me safe."

"Oh Frankie, you're one in a million." Ruth hugged her.

"Well, wish me luck."

"I think Robert's the one who's gonna need all the luck tonight. I want to hear *all* the nitty gritty tomorrow, okay?"

"Every sordid detail," smirked Frankie as she spun around with her hand on her hip and strutted out of the room.

As she looked through the sitting room window, she could see Robert pulling up outside. She watched him get out of the car, dressed in jeans and a fitted button up shirt. He looked really good, even better than the night at the pub.

Her heart was racing now. She took a deep breath to calm herself as she opened the front door.

Robert froze on the steps.

"Hi," said Frankie nonchalantly with her hand on her hip.

"Hi. I'm here to pick up Frankie. Can you please tell her I'm here?"

"She's not here. But I'm free, so you'll have to make do with that."

She slowly walked down the stairs and gave Robert a kiss on the cheek. Robert was still standing in the same spot, staring at her.

"What?" she asked.

"I should've brought the limo. I didn't say black tie, did I?"

"What, this old thing?" Frankie did a twirl in front of him, rubbing her hand down her thigh.

Robert grinned at her with that familiar look as he ran over to open the car door for her. He got in the car, still visibly flabbergasted.

"Can I say Frankie, you look… absolutely *stunning!*" He started fanning his face.

"Are you hot?" asked Frankie, milking the most out of the moment.

"Hot? It's an inferno in here!"

Robert shook his head and started driving, constantly looking over at her and shaking his head some more.

Frankie was feeling pretty pleased with herself. Ruth and Joan would be proud.

"So, you never told me where you live. Have you got housemates?"

"Oh God no, I've done the whole housemate thing. I couldn't stand it. Guys are such pigs. Well, not all guys! I was constantly yelling at them to clean up their shit."

Frankie laughed. "You should've seen where I used to live. My aunty and cousin are the biggest pigs you could imagine. They won't even move their fat lazy arses to put something in the bin."

"Really? I can't imagine you living in a place like that."

"Neither can I anymore. Thank God. Fuckwit Christian actually did me a favour."

"Who's Christian? The drug dealer?"

"Yep. I can thank him for getting me out of that shithole and having me deported here."

"Thank you, Christian! The dumbest fuckwit to ever walk the planet. Look at what he's missing out on!" He looked at Frankie, again shaking his head.

The car pulled into a gravel driveway. "Here we are. Home sweet home." The house was nothing like Frankie expected. It was an old colonial style house with a huge wrap around verandah, surrounded by beautiful trees and gardens.

"Wow" said Frankie. "It's gorgeous. How long have you lived here?"

"I bought it a few years ago. It was my grandparents' house. My brothers didn't want it so I was lucky enough to get it. I love it here."

"I can see why." Frankie looked around in amazement.

"Come on, I'll show you round." He grabbed her hand and led her through the front gate down to the house. He pointed to the vines growing all along the verandah. "These are some of my babies. My grapevines. They'll be next year's vintage."

"So, you're already a winemaker?"

"Ha. Well, I try to be. I've actually got a special bottle of red to have with dinner tonight. It's from my first vintage. Do you like wine?"

"Well yep, but I'm no expert. I pretty much drink anything, so it'll probably be wasted on me."

"I seriously doubt that, Frankie. Come on, let's go inside."

He led Frankie through the house. It was like stepping into someone's parents' home, with everything in its place, all clean and tidy. It took her by surprise. She wasn't sure if she liked it, or whether it was freaking her out. What young guy takes so much pride in a house? She suddenly felt uncomfortable and out of her depth.

"This is my family." Robert pointed to a row of framed photos on the living room wall. "Mum and Dad, my brothers and their families."

"God, you look like your dad."

"Yeah, everyone says that. He's not a bad old bloke."

"Where's Amy?"

Robert looked surprised. "In a drawer."

"Can I see her?"

He paused for a moment, opened one of the drawers and handed a photo to Frankie. Robert and Amy were both sitting on horses holding hands. "She really *is* a stunning redhead. Look how happy you are."

"Yep, we were. She was an amazing girl. I've spent the last six years pining for her, but you know what? Lately I've realised it's all pointless. She's gone and she's not coming back. It's time to move on." Frankie was surprised by Robert's sudden change of heart. He took the photo from her and put it back in the drawer. "Anyway, let's have a drink. What would you like? I've got Guinness!"

"The magic word," said Frankie, glad for the change in conversation. "Liam will be jealous."

"Tom too. By the way, Tom thinks you're a total hottie."

"What?"

"Oh, don't worry, he's happily married to a lovely girl. Doesn't stop him from appreciating talent when he sees it though."

"So, is *that* why he brings my beer to the table?

"Actually, he does that for all the girls, sorry. But turn up in that dress and he'll do whatever you want!" Frankie laughed.

Robert handed her a Guinness in a pint glass and clinked his glass against hers.

"Dinner smells amazing. I can't believe you can cook. So, your mum taught you?"

"Sort of. I used to hang out with her in the kitchen a lot and just picked stuff up."

"So do you see your family much?"

"Usually every few months. They still do the whole family birthday get together thing, believe it or not."

"Wow, they sound amazing. You're so lucky."

Robert took Frankie's glass and put them both down on the table. He put his arms around her and held her against him. "I am lucky. Lucky I met you."

He kissed her, this time with a passion that made her weak at the knees. "I mean it, Frankie. Since I met you, I feel like living again. I can't even explain it. You're just so…"

"Angry?"

Robert threw his head back and let out a roar of laughter.

"Yes! Angry. Passionate. Sexy. Vulnerable. *Real!* You're just so *real*, Frankie, and it's a fucking breath of fresh air!" He kissed her again. "I could really get used to this."

"So could I. A man cooking me dinner and pouring me pints of Guinness. Just like Liam and Tom!" she teased.

Frankie sat and watched Robert prepare everything for dinner. She felt like she was on another planet. Who was this guy?

Who was she? The whole situation felt so unexpected and way out of her comfort zone. Thankfully the Guinness was taking the edge off.

"You okay, Frankie? You've gone quiet."

"Yeah, I'm okay. I'm just not used to this."

"Having dinner cooked for you?"

"Just all of this." Frankie shrugged her shoulders and suddenly felt incredibly awkward, like she was some kind of imposter. She felt an overwhelming urge to run.

Robert walked over and grabbed her hands. "It's okay, Frankie. I'm not going to hurt you. I'd never do that."

"How do you know that? That's what everyone says."

"I'm not everyone. I care about you, Frankie. Sorry if I've come on a bit strong and freaked you out, but seeing you in that dress…

Come on, let's have a nice dinner. No pressure. I'll take you straight home afterwards. Okay?"

Frankie nodded with a nervous smile.

The lamb was amazing. So were the baked vegies and home-made gravy. Frankie wondered what the hell was wrong with her. Why was she so terrified of Robert? She couldn't think of a single reason to make her think he was an arsehole or was going to hurt her. So, what was her problem? She was definitely attracted to him. Who wouldn't be? He had everything going for him. Was she really that screwed up that she'd throw away something so good for no reason? Why couldn't she just be normal for once?

After dinner they sat on the lounge talking and drinking Robert's red wine. Frankie rested her head on Robert's shoulder.

"I'm sorry," she said softly.

"Sorry for what?"

"For being such a fuck up."

Robert laughed and put his arm around her. "You're no fuck up, Frankie. You're a gorgeous girl. You just need some time that's all. That's okay, I'm not going anywhere."

"Where the hell did you come from?"

"Mildura mate," joked Robert with an Aussie ocker accent.

Frankie laughed, looked up into his eyes and kissed him.

"I think I've changed my mind, Robert. I don't want to go home."

The intimacy they shared that night was something that Frankie had never experienced before. Robert gently caressed every inch of her body, slowly drinking her in like she was a fine wine. The smell of his body was intoxicating, and she revealed her inner most self to him in all its raw, beautiful glory. Their passion was so intense it left her breathless. They made love the entire night, stopping only long enough to quickly catch their breath. Just as the sun came up, they finally drifted off to sleep, legs and arms wrapped around each other.

The alarm woke them. Frankie opened her eyes as Robert kissed her and squeezed her tight. "Good morning, beautiful."

"Morning," smiled Frankie.

Robert stroked Frankie's hair. "You are one sexy woman, you know that?"

"You're pretty sexy yourself. You can cook me a lamb roast any time!"

Robert kissed her neck. "I reckon we've got about five minutes till we need to get up."

"Better not waste it then."

They made love one more time before dragging themselves out of bed.

In the shower, Robert lathered Frankie's body all over, carefully washing every inch of her skin. He was such a gentle, passionate lover that it made her ache for him. All she wanted to do was spend the day in bed with him. All the guys she'd been with before had been too busy getting their own rocks off to even consider or care about what might pleasure her. Robert was the exact opposite. No wonder Amy was smiling so much in that photo.

"I'll make some breakfast," said Robert as they got dressed. He looked at Frankie as she pulled on her dress. "Oh God, I could just eat you for breakfast instead."

He grabbed her, pretending to gnaw on her neck, giving her tingles. "I have to get away from you or we'll never get to work." He shook his head and walked out of the room.

Frankie followed him out to the kitchen and sat watching him make coffee. What a surprise packet he'd turned out to be. She thought back to when she first met him, and how she'd thought he was a bit of a dick, telling stupid corny jokes and being a clown all the time. But there was so much more to him. A bit like her really. She'd shown more of herself to Robert in one night than she'd ever shown to anyone else in her whole lifetime. She wondered if he knew that.

"You know," began Frankie, twiddling her fingers, "last night, I've never been like that with anyone. *Ever.*"

"Really? How lucky am I then." He stopped what he was doing and went over to put his arms around her. "And *I've* never gone through the whole night with anyone like that before. I just didn't want it to end. You blew my mind." He gently kissed her and went back to finish making breakfast.

As they sat eating toast and drinking coffee, Frankie thought of work and how different everything was going to feel now. What a whirlwind this had been, ever since she arrived. And last night was a night she'd remember for as long as she lived.

Robert drove her back to Learmonth House and waited while she ran in to get changed. She raced past Ruth who was in the dining room.

"Hi Ruth. Sorry, can't talk now, I have to get to work." Ruth had a big smile on her face. "See ya," she yelled as she passed Ruth again before running out the door.

"It's gonna be a long day," yawned Frankie on the drive to work. "How much sleep did we have?"

"Too much," said Robert, putting his hand on Frankie's leg.

They pulled up in the car park. As Frankie started to get out, Robert pulled her back. He gave her a long passionate kiss. "I'll be thinking about you all day today."

"Good." said Frankie. "I was just thinking about how much I enjoyed you tearing my dress off last night." She ran her hand up the inside of Robert's leg and kissed his ear, gently biting his ear lobe.

Robert moaned. "Frankie, don't. Stop. Don't… stop." They both laughed and got out of the car, Robert adjusting himself on the way in.

CHAPTER TWELVE

Frankie knocked on the door at unit four. "Eureka," she called out. No answer. She knocked again. "Joan? Hello?"

Turning the handle, she pushed the door open. Joan was sitting on the lounge with headphones on. She looked up and saw Frankie, "Hi Frances. Come in, dear," then took off her headphones and fiddled with the remote.

"I found these old movies when I was going through my photos. They're from way back. Ernie had them all transferred onto DVDs. Look at this bloke," she said excitedly, pointing at the TV. "See the one standing next to Ernie? Well, he was also a producer. He and Ernie were great friends. We'd known him for years. Anyway, it turns out he was selling cocaine! Apparently, he was one of the biggest dealers in New York. Ties to the mafia, the whole bit! It was a *huge* scandal. Poor Ernie. You could've knocked him over with a feather!"

"So, what happened to him? Did he go to jail?"

"Ha! No, he didn't. He knew people. People with connections. Apparently, he did a deal with the police and got off. Can you believe it?"

"What kind of deal?"

"I'm not sure. Ernie didn't have anything to do with him after that, but there were a lot of other arrests around the same time."

"So, he threw people under the bus to save his own arse."

"It certainly appeared that way. We hardly ever saw him or heard of him after that."

"Probably 'cause he'd been murdered by the mob!"

"Maybe. But he didn't die in jail, that's for certain."

"That's what *we* need Joan. Someone to throw under the bus to keep us out of jail. Someone like…"

"Like who, dear?"

"No idea." said Frankie. But she did have an idea. A big idea.

"Anyway," said Frankie, changing the subject. "Eureka."

"I found it," she laughed, holding up her old DVDs.

"So, tell me, how did your dinner go with Robert? Is he a good cook?"

Frankie sat on the lounge next to Joan and stared out the window.

"He's a fantastic cook Joan. I was very impressed."

"So, good in the bedroom too, I take it?"

"Joan!" gasped Frankie, trying to act surprised.

"Oh Frances, I was a beautiful young thing once too, remember? I know how these things work. Well?"

"It was amazing Joan. I've never felt anything like it. Sorry, too much information."

"Don't be silly," Joan laughed. "I knew it as soon as I saw you today. Your face looks different. It's meant to be I tell you. I knew it from…"

"The day you met me. Yes, I know." Frankie gave Joan's arm a gentle squeeze. "You love all this lovey, dovey romantic stuff don't you Joan!"

"Love makes the world go round Frances. I've always believed that. I think that's why I found my beautiful Ernie, because I was open to love."

"Oh, hang on, I'll just grab my violin," teased Frankie.

"You're exactly the same, Frances, you just don't quite believe it yet. I know. Under that tough exterior lies a gentle loving soul, as soft as summer rain on a rose petal," recited Joan as she batted her eyelids at Frankie.

"Very funny, Shakespeare. You're making me nauseous."

"So, when are you seeing him again?"

"I don't know, probably when I pass him in the corridor, I guess. Anyway, we need to start focussing on our plan. We don't have a lot of time. I was going to start thinking about it last night but—"

"You got tied up." Joan giggled.

"No, I didn't get tied up Joan, stop it." Frankie laughed. "I'll make us a cuppa. We've got some work to do."

Frankie handed Joan her tea and sat with her on the lounge.

"We need to talk about your son. What are you going to tell him?"

"Nothing," said Joan flatly. "I don't think he'd care either way."

"I'm sure that's not true. You can't just leave and not tell him you're going. Plus, he'll need to sort things out after you've gone, won't he?"

"Yes, but that's *his* problem"

"So, you're seriously not going to tell him you're going? For good?"

"No."

"Joan! How do you think he'll feel once he finds out? He'll be out for blood. Mine!"

"He might feel a bit guilty that's all. Maybe he won't even feel that. I just don't see the point in telling him. He'll just pretend that he cares, when obviously he doesn't. It'll be like a sideshow. I don't want that. I just want to drift away quietly without all the fuss."

"What if you wrote him a letter? You could tell him that way. I just think he needs to know."

"No! He doesn't!" Frankie had never seen her so angry before. Joan hauled herself off the lounge into her wheelchair and went into the bedroom. After a few minutes, Frankie followed.

Joan was sitting by the window staring out. Frankie sat on the bed next to her and held her hand. The pair of them sat together in silence for several minutes.

"You know Frances, one of the hardest things I've ever had to learn in my life is that sometimes the people you love the most are the ones who hurt you the most. My son abandoned me years ago. He never forgave me for letting Ernie treat him the way he did. But you know what? If I had gotten my way and let Daniel come home, he wouldn't have got his life together. He'd probably be dead in some gutter by now. Ernie saved Daniel's life! Why can't he see that?"

A torrent of grief came pouring out of Joan as Frankie hugged her tightly, rocking her back and forth. Frankie knew exactly how that felt. Hiding that hideous monster out of sight was a mammoth task, but an ultimately futile one.

"You're still his mum, Joan. Nothing will ever change that. He doesn't know how lucky he is. I'd be proud to have you as *my* mum."

Joan smiled at Frankie with red teary eyes.

"I'm just lucky to have met you, Frances. You're like my little ray of shining light."

"Sorry Joan, but I'm going to have to ask you again. Eureka?"

"I found it?" Joan looked confused.

"Phew. I thought you'd totally lost the plot there for a minute, calling me a shining light!"

Joan let out a cackle. It was good to see her laughing again. Frankie hated to see her in so much pain.

"Sangas and duckies?" Joan nodded.

The fresh air and warm sunshine were a welcome relief. They wandered down and sat by the lake, feeding Joan's feathered friends and swapping stories. Who knew how long they had left to do this. What a shame Joan couldn't share moments like this with her only son. It made Frankie want to scream.

She wished she could grab Daniel around the neck and shake the shit out of him.

"Joan, I've got an idea, and please don't say no just yet. How about recording a video for Daniel?"

Joan sat up straight in her wheelchair, ready to object.

"Uh!" Frankie held her finger up to her lips. "Hear me out. You wouldn't have to send it to him. He'd only get it after you've gone. But I really think he needs to hear everything you told me, and I think it'd make you feel better. I just don't want you leaving with unresolved stuff."

Joan sat and thought, not saying a word. Suddenly her eyes lit up.

"I could record my memoirs!"

"Exactly! Tell the world all about the beautiful Broadway dancer who fell in love with a handsome producer."

The entire walk back, Joan chattered about the stories she was going to tell. This was exactly the idea that Frankie had been looking for. Joan's life would mean something and would never be forgotten. Frankie wondered to herself which one of them was more excited.

Back at the unit, Joan searched for her video camera.

"I just don't know what I've done with it. I'm sure I had one somewhere. Maybe I've lost it. Bloody Alzheimer's!"

Frankie laughed. It wasn't often she heard Joan swear.

"Don't worry, I'll buy you a new one. I'll get a tripod too so we can set it up properly."

They spent the rest of the afternoon writing notes about the stories Joan was going to tell. Frankie had never seen her so animated. She'd heard a lot of the stories before, but the longer Joan reminisced, the more and more intricate and interesting the stories became. This was going to be wonderful.

Joan went into the bedroom, returning with a roll of cash.

"Here Frances, take this."

"Jesus! Did you rob a bank?"

"No dear. I always have cash around. I don't believe in all those cards. The government use them to track you, you know."

"Yep, sure they do." Frankie smiled at her, giving her a kiss on the cheek. "I'm off now. See you tomorrow, movie star!"

Frankie spotted Robert in the car park, leaning against his car waiting for her. He looked so different today. His nurse's uniform wasn't hiding anything anymore. She was imagining him naked.

"Hey beautiful. Where've you been hiding today?" He grabbed her around the waist and gave her a kiss.

"Actually, I've been busy with Joan."

"Wanna get busy with me?" Robert gave her that grin. All the sensual delights of the night before came flooding back to her.

"I'd love to, but I have to buy a video camera. And a tripod."

"Ooh, Frankie, I like the way you're thinking!"

Frankie laughed. "It's actually for Joan. She's recording her memoirs. Can you help me set it up though? I'm hopeless with all that tech shit."

"Sure. Maybe we can give it a test run as well. Better get the waterproof model!"

Frankie laughed as Robert scooped her up and sat her in the car.

"Why sir, you're so strong!" said Frankie in a high pitched southern American accent, batting her eyelids at him.

"Yes Ma'am. That I am. I can bring down wild animals with a single blow."

"I know," said Frankie, running her claws down his shirt.

"So, memoirs hey? That should be interesting. She sure does have some stories. So," Robert paused, "are you still thinking about the whole euthanasia thing?"

Frankie nodded. "And I might have an idea how we can get away with it."

"Okay, let's hear it. You know how sceptical I am about the whole thing."

"Nope. I'm not telling you *anything* until I've got the whole plan worked out."

Robert looked at Frankie and shook his head.

After arriving at the shopping centre and choosing the video equipment, Frankie took out the roll of cash from her bag at the counter to pay for it.

"Drug money?" asked Robert, pretending to whisper.

"Shut. Up." she elbowed him. The shop assistant stood staring as she took the notes from the roll. "It's from my night job." she whispered back, loud enough for the assistant to hear. "This is just one night's takings."

"I don't doubt it." Robert raised his eyebrows at the assistant, making her look away in embarrassment.

Arriving back at Learmonth House, the motion of the car ride had almost sent Frankie to sleep. She yawned and gave Robert a kiss. "I'll see you tomorrow. I really need to get some sleep."

Frankie dragged herself inside. She could hear a ruckus coming from the lounge room. It sounded like a poker game was well underway.

"Frankie!" they yelled to her as she gave them a wave on her way past, not stopping to chat. Ruth was at the end of the corridor, standing there smiling.

"My God, Frankie, looks like *you* had a good night! Gonna fill me in?"

"Oh Ruth, mind if I take a raincheck? I can hardly stand up I'm so tired. But all the sordid details I promised you? They're all true!" she grinned.

"Ha. Good for you, Frankie. I'll see you later then."

Frankie slowly climbed up the stairs, stumbled to her room and sat on the bed. She tore open the box and plugged the camera into the wall before flopping back down on the bed. She was too tired to go for a shower. Or even to get undressed. She closed her eyes and was instantly asleep.

CHAPTER THIRTEEN

Frankie slowly stretched, looking at the time. Six-thirty. It had been a long time since she'd had such a restful sleep without the help of pills or alcohol.

She sprang out of bed and looked out the window. It was a beautiful, sunny day and she was looking forward to her morning walk to work.

Standing under the water, she lathered herself up and closed her eyes, remembering the sensation of Robert's hands on her skin. His gentle, sensual touch was like a drug, and her body was aching for more. Recalling the feeling of him being deep inside her, she slowly brought herself to orgasm as the warm water rushed over her body.

As she dried herself, she thought about the day ahead. She imagined Joan at home, making herself glamorous for her big debut in front of the camera. That was something she loved about Joan. She wasn't afraid to show the world who she was.

Frankie got dressed and skipped down the stairs for breakfast. "Morning, morning everyone!" She gave Ruth a big smile. "Beautiful day out there."

"It's certainly sunny in here!" Ruth put her nose into the air. "I think I can smell love in the air as well."

"I can smell bacon. I'm starving."

Frankie filled her plate and poured herself a cup of coffee, quickly telling Ruth about her amazing night with Robert. She spoke about his lovely home, what a good cook he is, and how it all took her completely by surprise.

"Maybe you were expecting the same old rubbish you've had before."

"Yeah, I think you're right. Which reminds me, can I run some ideas past you later?"

"Sure. What are you up to this time?"

"Payback."

"Ooh," Ruth grinned, rubbing her hands together. "I'll be waiting with bated breath."

Frankie ran upstairs to collect the camera gear before heading out to work.

Lost in thought on her morning walk, the silence was suddenly interrupted by a loud tooting, followed by a wolf whistle. Robert pulled over to give her a lift.

"Jump in!"

Frankie ran over, leapt into the passenger seat and gave Robert a big strong bearhug.

"Wow! I should leave you alone more often. Oh, hang on, what am I saying?"

"Morning," Frankie grinned.

"Good sleep then, beautiful?"

"The best. I had an even better shower. You were there."

"Oh, was I? Goddamn, I missed it! Tell me about it."

"Well, I was all lathered up from head to toe, and you were caressing my slippery wet body with your big strong hands as I kissed your neck, and then you turned me around and pushed me up against the wall and..."

Robert stared at her, his mouth hanging open. "And?"

"Can't remember the rest."

"Oh, are you serious? Come on Frankie, you're *killing* me here!"

Frankie sat there smugly smiling, enjoying every minute of teasing him. "I brought the camera. Do you reckon you can help me set it up?"

"Hmmm. Let me see. That would mean you owe me."

"Okay, what do you want?"

"The end of the story."

"Name the time and place, and I'll be there."

"Twelve thirty. Meet me in the carpark."

"Okay." They both grinned at each other. This was going to be a memorable lunch.

After arriving at Golden Leaves, they knocked at Unit four.

"Film crew!" yelled Robert.

The door opened and, as expected, Joan was looking even more glamorous than usual. She was wearing a stunning red evening dress, the type you'd see at a fancy black-tie ball. Her matching jewellery was encrusted with diamonds and rubies, and she wore a bright red flower in her hair. "Good morning, your highness." Robert bent down and kissed Joan's hand. "We're looking for Joan. Have you seen her?" Joan giggled.

"Joan! You look amazing!" Frankie circled around Joan to admire her. "That dress is … Wow!"

"This dress is actually what I wore to the very last event with Ernie. It was one of his favourites."

"I can see why he loved it. Bet he loved taking it off too," said Robert as Frankie slapped him.

Joan laughed and nodded. "Yes, it used to do the trick, alright."

"Dresses have a habit of doing that." Robert grinned at Frankie.

"Anyway…" Frankie interrupted. "Let's get this show on the road."

Robert helped Frankie set up the equipment as Joan supervised, instructing them on where she wanted to sit, what she wanted in the shot, where the best light was and how close the camera needed to be.

"Anyone'd think you've done this before," said Frankie.

"Oh, sorry dear if I'm barking orders. It's just second nature to me from my showbiz days. *'Stand there. Do this. Look that way. Don't frown. Stand up straight'.*"

"That's good, because I have absolutely no idea what I'm doing!" said Frankie as she looked through the camera lens, fiddling with the zoom button.

"Okay lovely ladies, I'll leave you to it. Give me a shout if you need help. I'll make sure no paparazzi get through the gate." He patted Joan's hand and gave Frankie a kiss. "See you at twelve thirty. *Sharp.*"

"Yes, sir! Twelve thirty sharp!"

As Joan sat on the lounge, Frankie focussed the camera on her.

"So, Joan, are you going to start at the very beginning?"

"Yes, I thought about it last night. I'll start with my childhood. Daniel probably doesn't even know about any of that."

"Okay, well let's do this!" Frankie pressed record. "Action!"

She sat listening as Joan told the tale of her childhood, something Frankie hadn't heard before. Her family had suffered through poverty and tragedy. Her father had been killed in a mining accident when she was little, leaving her mother to bring up three children on her own, surviving mostly on the generosity of kind neighbours and whatever measly money her mother could make by mending clothes for other people.

One of her brothers had also died from whooping cough not long after their father's death. Frankie was horrified but fascinated by Joan's story. To think this woman sitting in front of her came from such a tragic childhood was unbelievable. It was like something you'd see in a movie.

"Cut."

They took a break while Frankie made Joan a cup of tea. "Wow Joan, this is fantastic. But, I had no idea you'd had such a tough life."

"Oh, everyone did it tough in those days. Dad wasn't the only man to die in the mines. It happened all the time. It was still a good life though. Mum loved us and took care of us best she could. I think Michael dying really knocked the wind out of her sails though. She never really smiled much after that."

Frankie could tell Joan was enjoying every last minute of this. Her face lit up when she was telling her story. Joan quickly finished her tea, eager to keep going.

On the story went, into her later childhood years. Joan spoke about her dreams of becoming a dancer and trying to scrounge up enough money for ballet lessons. She spoke about the year her mother gave her a pair of second-hand ballet shoes for her birthday and how she never took them off, dancing around the house constantly. Suddenly Joan stopped mid-sentence.

"What happened then, Joan?"

Joan sat staring at the camera with a faraway look on her face.

"Joan, what happened then? Joan? Joan?" She sat there staring into the distance. "*Joan!*" Frankie knelt down in front of her. "*Joan! Eureka!*" Joan didn't move.

"*Fuck!*" yelled Frankie. "*Fuck, fuck, fuck!*"

Frantically she raced out of Joan's unit and sprinted down to the main building. Rushing through the doors, she slowed down to a quick walk, trying not to draw anyone's attention. She had to find Robert. He wasn't in the dining room. She quickly went to see Clare.

"Oh, hi Frankie! How—"

"Where's Robert? Clare? Where's Robert?"

"I think he's at the clinic with…"

Frankie ran over to the clinic entrance. As she looked through the glass doors, she could see Robert talking to Maggie. She waved her hands frantically trying to get his attention. He wasn't noticing her, so she started tapping on the glass. Finally, Robert looked up, smiled and waved. Maggie also looked over and gave her a wave.

Frankie gestured to Robert to come out.

"Can't you wait till twelve—"

"Quick! It's Joan! There's something wrong with her. Hurry!"

Frankie dragged Robert by the arm out of the building. She was now almost hyperventilating.

"Frankie! Calm down! Tell me what's wrong!"

"I don't know! She's just sitting there staring!"

When they arrived at Joan's unit, she wasn't where Frankie had left her.

"Oh fuck! Where is she?" Frankie yelled.

Robert checked down the hallway.

"She's here."

Frankie rushed into the bedroom. Joan was sitting in her wheelchair staring at the wall. Robert turned her around and bent down to talk to her.

"Joan. Can you hear me? It's me. Robert." He looked at her eyes and checked her pulse. "Come on Frankie, help me get her onto the bed."

"What's wrong with her?" sniffled Frankie, distraught.

"She'll be okay. She's just having an episode. I better let Maggie know."

"*No!* Don't let the doctors near her. They'll want to take her away!"

"Frankie, she needs to be checked properly. We can't leave her alone while she's like this."

"I'll stay with her! Just tell me what I need to do. I'll do it. *Please* don't tell Maggie."

Robert sat and stared at Joan. She was almost asleep. He took a deep breath and looked at Frankie.

"You realise what you're asking me to do?"

"I know, just tell them some bullshit. Just say I couldn't get the camera working, and you just came up to fix it, and everything was fine. *Please. Please* don't tell them!"

"Did you tell anyone else?"

"No. I only saw Clare, but I didn't tell her anything. *Please* Robert." She was squeezing his arm, staring at him in desperation.

"Fucking hell, Frankie. Okay. But you need to listen to me. You need to watch her. Make sure her breathing stays like it is now. Any change at all, you need to get me. If it gets slow, or fast, or irregular, or changes at all, you get me. If she starts changing colour, you get me. If she starts saying weird shit, you get me. If she does anything at all, you get me. Okay? I'm trusting you."

"Yes. I promise."

Frankie started to cry. Robert put his arms around her.

"It's okay. Don't cry Frankie. She'll be okay."

He sat with her as they watched Joan fall asleep.

"You okay?"

"Not really," sniffled Frankie. "But I won't take my eyes off her I promise. Where will you be if I need you?"

"Same place you found me. But if you need to come looking for me again, I doubt we'll be able to keep hiding this." Frankie nodded. "I'll be back to check on her as soon as I can. Don't forget, any changes at all…"

"I'll come and get you."

"Good girl." He kissed Frankie and went back to the clinic.

Frankie sat next to Joan for what felt like an eternity. She watched her sleeping, timing her breathing to make sure it wasn't changing. She kept checking her pulse to make sure it wasn't racing. She kept feeling her forehead to make sure she wasn't getting hot or cold. She held her hand and talked to her. She told her how amazing their first recording session had been and begged her to get better so they could finish her story. She told her about the weather outside. She told her how she felt about Robert and what a good cook he was. She talked and talked and talked to her, about anything she could think of, praying that it might magically snap her back to reality.

Robert returned an hour later to check on her.

"How's she doing?"

"She's just been sleeping. Her breathing's steady though and she hasn't really moved."

Robert checked her pulse and looked at her eyes. "She seems stable. She probably just needs to sleep it off." He smiled at Frankie "You'd make a great nurse, Frankie."

"Fuck no, I couldn't stand it. I'd be a basket case!"

"I've never seen anyone move so fast!" he laughed. "Frankie Gonzales. Fastest nurse in all of Mexico."

"Well, it scared the *shit* out of me!"

"I know. It takes a bit of getting used to."

Joan started to stir. Frankie held her hand as she opened her eyes, staring at the ceiling.

"Joan?" whispered Frankie. Joan smiled.

"I found it," she whispered back. Frankie hugged her, crying happy tears.

"What have you found Joan?" asked Robert.

"Eureka," said Joan.

He smiled at Frankie. "Of course. Your password. Your memory's better than mine Joan."

Frankie stayed by Joan's side for the rest of the day. She rested in bed most of the afternoon, Frankie bringing her drinks and chatting with her. Joan couldn't remember talking about Michael or her ballet shoes, but she remembered talking about her mother and father.

"I think we'll leave the recording for today, Joan. You've been through enough for one day." Frankie paused. "Can I just ask you – what's it like?"

"What's that, dear?"

"When you have these episodes, what's it feel like?"

Joan sat and thought. "I can't really remember anything except… I dreamt that I was falling. Then nothing. I just woke up."

"Well, you scared the shit out of me. Thank God you're okay."

"I'm sorry, Frances. Thank you for staying with me. They're probably going to take me away now aren't they. They said if I had any more turns, they'd have to transfer me."

"No, they won't. They don't know. Robert covered for us."

"He's such a good man, Frances. Don't let that one go whatever you do."

Frankie smiled. "If you say so, Joan."

CHAPTER FOURTEEN

Robert returned to check on Joan as Frankie was getting ready to leave.

"You okay?" He put his arm around her.

"Yeah, I am now. Do you think I should stay with her tonight?"

"She should be okay now. It's been six hours."

He went into the bedroom where Joan was tucked up in bed reading a book. "It's good to have you back, Joan. I think you gave our Frankie a bit of a fright!" He laughed as he checked her pulse.

"Yes, I know. I'm sorry." She grabbed Robert's hand. "And thank you Robert, Frances told me what you did. If it wasn't for you two, I'd be…" Tears started running down her cheeks.

"Shh… it's okay, Joan."

He sat on the bed next to her and held her, patting her gently on the back. "Now, I just want you to rest tonight. No going out nightclubbing, alright? I'll tell the kitchen to bring your dinner here. I'll be back to see you in the morning, okay?"

Joan nodded. Robert gave her a kiss on the forehead.

Frankie said goodbye and they both left the unit.

"So, she's okay?"

"Yeah, she's fine. But just be prepared, Frankie. This is going to keep happening. And more often."

Frankie felt a sense of panic building inside her.

"So, by more often, do you mean…"

"Can't say for sure, but it's only been a few weeks since the last one."

Fuck, thought Frankie. *I have to get this shit sorted. And soon. Like right now.*

Robert opened the car door and Frankie jumped in. He stopped and looked at her. "Sure you're okay?"

"Yes. No. I don't know!" Frankie slapped her hand on her forehead. "I've just got a lot to do."

"You gonna tell me what's going on, Frankie?"

"I will soon."

Robert drove her home. "Hey, seeing we missed out on our hot lunch today, fancy dinner with Liam tonight?"

"Why? Are you busy?"

"Funny girl. How about I pick you up at seven?"

"Sounds good. I need a beer after today."

Frankie gave him a quick kiss and raced inside. She desperately needed to talk to Ruth.

"Hey, Ruth. Got time for a chat?"

"Sure. Just preparing dinner, but I can chop and listen at the same time."

Frankie quickly closed the door to the hallway and sat down at the table. Ruth put down her knife and sat at the table with her. "What's going on, Frankie?"

"Well… I've come up with a plan and I want your honest opinion. I've been racking my brain trying to think of a way to get around the whole jail thing, and I think I've found it."

"Okay, let's hear it."

"The other day at Joan's, I was watching a video of this bloke she knew who was this huge New York drug dealer and he got caught, but, he didn't go to jail."

"Why not?"

"He did a deal with the cops."

Ruth opened her mouth to talk but Frankie continued, "By dobbing in other dealers. He threw all the others under the bus to save his own arse!"

Ruth sat there looking confused. "Sorry, you've lost me Frankie. What's this got to do with you?"

"Don't you see? Who is the one person I know who might be valuable to the cops? Who could I throw under the bus to save my own arse?" Frankie paused. "And who deserves everything they get after what they did to me?"

Ruth sat and thought, then a smile came to her face. "Oh…"

"Exactly!" Frankie was excited. "Christian. I'm going to go see him."

"You're *what*?"

Frankie excitedly rattled off her whole plan, step by step, in every minute detail, while Ruth sat there looking more and more horrified by the minute, the colour draining from her face.

"So? What do you think?"

"I'm terrified, Frankie. Terrified something bad will happen to you."

"You worry too much, Ruth."

"Sometimes being afraid keeps you alive! Are you going to tell Robert?"

"*Shit* no! Well, not until it's over. He's not going to be happy, but it'll solve the problem of jail hopefully. And get me the money I need for the farewell."

"What farewell?"

"Joan's. That's the next plan on the agenda."

Ruth shook her head. "You never cease to amaze me, Frankie."

Frankie gave Ruth a kiss on the cheek.

"Thanks for listening to me ramble on once again, Ruth. You're a great friend. Oh, I won't be here for dinner. Robert's taking me to the pub."

"Have a stiff drink for me while you're there!"

"I thought you didn't drink?"

"I don't!"

Frankie laughed and ran upstairs to get ready. Now that she'd verbalised her plan to Ruth, it all seemed a lot clearer in her mind. Everything was falling into place.

This was going to work. It had to.

She just had to decide exactly *when* she was going to do it.

Robert held Frankie's hand as they walked into the pub and made their way to the bar.

Tom looked at them from behind the bar with a grin on his face. "Well, hello, hello! I see you two survived the other night."

"Yep, but we've had a close call since then," Robert laughed, as Frankie elbowed him and started turning red.

"Sit down guys, I'll bring your drinks over."

"Fancy another survival challenge later?" whispered Robert in Frankie's ear as they sat down.

"You know me. Always up for a challenge. Anyway, I need to finish my story."

Tom arrived with their pints. He quickly pulled up a stool and sat down.

"So, how's it all going? I hope Rob's looking after you, is he Frankie?"

"He's taking very good care of me, Tom. He even cooked me a baked dinner the other night."

"You sly dog. Already pulled out the big guns, hey?"

Robert shrugged his shoulders "Can't help it if I'm an amazing cook."

Tom laughed. "I've actually tasted Rob's cooking and as much as I hate to admit it, he is a decent cook."

"Decent?" Robert objected. "That's the last time I invite *you* over!"

"Well, your chef *here* knows how to cook a parmy. I think I'm going to have one again tonight," said Frankie.

"Good choice," said Tom nodding his head. "Well, enjoy you two. Better get back to it."

"Come on," said Robert grabbing Frankie by the hand and dragging her towards the bistro. "The sooner we eat, the sooner we can have dessert."

"Hungry, are you?"

Robert gave her that look.

"Ravenous."

After sitting back down at their table, Frankie's mood turned serious. "I'm going to start a foundation for Joan."

Robert grabbed her hand. "You're always thinking up ideas, aren't you? I love that about you."

"I'm serious!" Frankie snapped, pulling her hand away.

"Okay, okay, I didn't say you weren't! So, tell me about it then."

"Well. I'm going to contact Daniel and…"

"Who's Daniel?" Robert interrupted. Frankie glared at him. "Sorry."

"Joan's son. Daniel. I'm going to contact him and tell him to start up a charity which will raise money for research into Alzheimer's. Then every year he'll have a fundraiser with all his rich and famous mates and make lots of money and everyone will think he's a hero, when in actual fact he's a gutless scumbag piece of shit who threw his mum into a nursing home and left her to die."

Robert sat there looking stunned, not saying a word.

"I'm also going to get him to send Neil Mason down for Joan's farewell. And pay for it. I just need to work out where…"

"Hang on, hang on" Robert interrupted again, "how exactly are you going to get him to do all of this? I think I missed that bit."

"Well, part of her memoirs will be about Daniel. About his life of drug addiction and crime and God knows what else he got up to. The part he doesn't want anyone to know about. The part that could totally fuck up his career."

"So, what you're telling me is, you're going to blackmail him?"

"I guess. But don't forget, he's going to benefit from it too. Everyone will think, oh, what a wonderful son, he must have loved her so much, how kind he is, blah, blah, blah. He doesn't deserve it, but I don't really care, as long as Joan's remembered and something positive comes out of it. Anyway, the arsehole can afford it. He lives on Sydney Harbour, for fuck's sake."

"Wow." Robert sat there staring at Frankie. "Wow."

"Ooh," said Frankie with excitement as the waitress brought out their meals. "Yum!"

Robert sat there, still staring at Frankie.

"Come on, I thought you were ravenous!"

Robert picked up his cutlery and slowly started to eat. "So, when is this all going to happen?"

"As soon as Joan finishes her memoirs. All I have left to do is organise her farewell."

"Oh *God*, do I even want to know about that?"

"I bloody hope so, because I'll need your help!"

"But we haven't worked anything out yet about the whole…"

"*You* haven't worked anything out yet. But *I* have. I told you I would."

"So, what have you…"

"I'll tell you when it's done."

"Frankie…"

"When it's *done*! You just need to trust me. All I need you to do is to decide which drugs we'll need and work out how to get them."

"Oh, is *that* all." Robert shook his head.

"Surely it can't be that hard. You work in a clinic *full* of drugs every day."

"Yeah, I do, but if I get caught stealing them, that's a whole different ball game."

"I'm sure you'll figure it out. That's your only job. Apart from…"

"Oh yes, that's right, apart from *killing* her."

"Well, show me how to do it and *I'll* do it. I don't care!" Frankie was getting annoyed again. "Why can't you get past the whole *killing* thing? It's not killing her. It's setting her free. It's saving her from soul destroying torture! Why can't you see that?"

Tears were starting to well up in her eyes.

"Hey. It's okay. I understand where you're coming from. I really do."

"But?"

"But nothing. I understand. Okay?"

They both finished their meals without saying much.

"Let's get out of here. Is that still okay?" He grabbed Frankie's hand. She nodded.

They gave Tom a wave as they were leaving.

"Compliments to the chef!" yelled Frankie.

On the drive home, Robert started chuckling to himself.

"What's so funny?"

"You're just so full of surprises, that's all. I never know what you'll come out with next. And what's the story with Neil Mason?"

"He reminds Joan of her husband, so I'm going to plan a romantic dinner for them on her last night as a surprise. I just hope he's a nice guy and will go along with it. He is an actor after all, so it shouldn't be too hard."

"She might change her mind after that and decide Neil Mason is worth living for."

"Can't you just see it. Joan chasing him around in her wheelchair."

They both laughed and made jokes the whole way home about what might happen between the two of them on Joan's final night.

As they pulled into Robert's driveway, there was a car parked outside his gate and a man standing on his veranda.

"Who the hell's that?" he said as they got out of the car and walked towards the house. "Bro!" yelled Robert as he recognised his brother, walking up to give him a hug.

"Robbie. Good to see you man." He patted Robert on the back.

"Frankie, this is my brother, Adam! Adam, this is Frankie."

"Nice to meet you, Frankie," Adam put out his hand and gave her a big firm handshake.

"You too, Adam."

"Come in!"

They all went into the house. "What are you doing here? Where's Mel and the kids?"

"They're at home. I'm on my way up to the farm, so I thought I'd take a detour and come and get you on the way."

"Come and get me? What for?"

"Can we sit down?"

"Oh sorry, sure, do you want a drink? I've got beers or I can make you a cuppa. Frankie?"

"No thanks," both Adam and Frankie said in unison.

"It's Mum," said Adam. The smile on Robert's face instantly vanished. "She's been diagnosed with breast cancer."

"Oh *fuck!* When?"

"A few days ago. She's been feeling off for a while, so Dad made her go to the doctor. They gave her a blood test and that's when they found it. But it's…"

"It's what?" Robert was on the edge of his seat staring at Adam.

"It's stage four."

"*Fuck!*" Robert stood up and started walking in circles, his hands over his mouth. "What the fuck? Why didn't they find it before now?"

"You know what Mum's like. She hates doctors. Dad's apparently been nagging her to go but she's left it too long."

"Oh *fuck*. So, what now? What are the doctors saying?"

"They've told her she might only have months left. If she has treatment, that could give her anywhere up to five years they reckon. But…"

"What?"

"She's refusing to have treatment."

"*What the fuck!* She *can't!* What the *fuck* is she thinking?"

"Well, she can. Ultimately, it's her choice."

"What about Dad? What's he saying about it all?"

"He's not saying much at all. I think he's shell shocked. He just keeps saying '*it's your mother's choice.*'"

"Fucking hell. We need to talk some sense into them!"

"I know Robbie. That's why I came to get you. Michael's heading up tomorrow. I thought the three of us might be able to get through to her. Especially you."

"So how long have you known?"

"I only found out today. Michael rang me. Dad had only just rung him, even though they found out three days ago."

"*Fuck,* they're hopeless! I'm gonna kick Dad fair up the arse when I see him!" Robert paused his pacing to look at Frankie. "I'm sorry Frankie. This is all just so…"

"Don't be sorry. I'm just so sorry to hear about your mum. It's horrendous for you all."

Robert sat next to her and hugged her. She could feel him starting to sob. Adam stood up and went into the bathroom. Frankie held Robert as tight as her arms could squeeze. "I'm so sorry, Robert." She didn't know what else to say. What else *do* you say to someone who is about to lose their mum. At least he was getting some warning, which is more than Frankie got.

"I'm just gonna run Frankie home," said Robert as Adam emerged from the bathroom. "I won't be long."

"Nice to meet you, Frankie," said Adam, "I'm sure I'll be seeing you again some time."

"You too Adam. I hope so."

They pulled up outside Learmonth House. Robert sat staring straight ahead. "Good luck with everything. I hope you can get your mum to change her mind."

Robert looked over at her and smiled.

"Thanks, beautiful. So do I. She's pretty stubborn though. Almost as stubborn as you."

Frankie laughed. It was good to hear him making jokes.

"Not sure how long I'll be gone, but I'll keep you posted. See you when I get back." Robert leant over and kissed her.

"I'll be here. Drive safe."

Frankie felt a pain inside her as she watched Robert drive away. She had absolutely no doubt now. She was falling in love with him.

CHAPTER FIFTEEN

It was unusually comforting to hear Clare's melodic morning greeting as she walked in.

"Good morning, Frankie. How are you?"

"Morning Clare. How are you going?"

"I'm good thanks. Rob rang and he won't be coming in for probably a few days, so Maggie will talk to you before you start today."

"Oh, okay. Is he having a holiday?" she said, joking.

"Um, not sure, but I think it's a family matter. He didn't say exactly, but it didn't sound like he was having fun."

"Okay thanks Clare."

Oh my God, are her eyes painted on? Frankie smiled to herself. She walked through the doors and met Maggie heading towards the clinic.

"Morning, Frankie. As I'm sure you already know, Rob will be away for a few days."

"Yep, Clare told me." Maggie looked at Frankie with a strange grin on her face.

"Okay… Anyway, he said that he'd given you plenty of things to go on with. Helping Joan get all her things in order."

"Yep, she's got a lot of stuff to sort through, so I've got plenty to keep me busy, that's for sure."

Frankie was dreading the thought of Maggie somehow finding out about Joan's episode.

"Okay, great. We'll have to lock in a moving date for her soon too, before the auditors come. So, if you can help her get packed that would be great. If you need anything just come and get me. I won't be far away."

"Okay sure, thanks Maggie. See you later."

Frankie took a deep breath, realising with Robert away now, she'd have to manage the whole situation on her own.

Oh, please God, don't let Joan have any more fucking episodes.

At unit four, Joan opened the door looking happy and vibrant, immaculately dressed as usual, this time in a stunning emerald green dress with matching jewellery.

"Good morning, Frances! Aren't you going to ask?"

"How are you?"

"No. Eureka. And yes, I'm fine. I feel wonderful today."

"You look wonderful too, Joan. That dress is gorgeous. All ready for our film shoot?"

"Oh yes!"

Any opportunity to be in the limelight made Joan come alive. Frankie smiled at the thought of Neil Mason surprising her on her final night. But there were a lot of hurdles to jump before then.

"By the way Frances, I have a gift for you two."

"You two who?"

"You and Robert."

"Oh really? You don't need to do that! But can it wait? Robert had to go home to see his parents for a few days. His mum's been diagnosed with breast cancer."

Frankie told Joan all about what had happened after Adam's arrival the night before, and how Robert's mum was refusing to have treatment.

"That's a terrible state of affairs for his family. I can relate to her though. She might as well enjoy what's left of her life while she can. Once the doctors get hold of her, she'll have to lie in hospital having poison pumped into her and then she'll be too sick to do anything!"

"I don't think it'll be like *that* the whole time!"

But maybe Joan was right.

"Anyway, that's enough sad stuff for one day. But I just want to add, *please* don't have any more days like yesterday, Joan. I don't think my nerves could handle it."

Frankie laughed, but she was deadly serious. If Joan *did* have another episode, the whole plan was fucked.

"I'll try my hardest dear, I promise." Joan crossed her fingers.

"Right, let's get this show on the road!" Frankie set up the camera while Joan fussed about, making sure the light was right, and she was sitting in the right spot.

"We're up to the bit where you get your first pair of ballet shoes. And… action!"

The pair of them spent the whole morning filming. They had several breaks to drink cups of tea and coffee and go over what they'd filmed. Frankie was once again enthralled by the story of Joan's rich and colourful life full of so many contrasts. She'd seen poverty and loss, glamour, wealth and fame, as well as heartbreak and love of epic proportions. It was like watching a Hollywood movie, full of twists and turns.

At lunch time Frankie made some sandwiches which they took down to the lake and shared with Joan's ducky friends. "I wonder what will happen to all my ducks when I'm gone."

"They'll lose all their excess belly fat, for one thing" joked Frankie. It was a sad thought though. No more Joan coming to the lake and sitting here feeding them, talking to them, calling them each by name. No doubt they'd be looking for her long after she was gone. Frankie started to get teary.

"They'll miss you, Joan. That's what will happen. And so will I." Frankie gave Joan a big hug as her tears started.

"Oh Frances, I wish I'd met you a long time ago. You're like a granddaughter to me. We could have had such fun together. Such mischievous fun." Frankie continued to cry and Joan patted her back to comfort her. "At least we've met each other now, that's the main thing."

"I would've loved to have met you when you were young," snuffled Frankie, wiping her nose. "Imagine all the stuff we could've got up to."

"All the hearts we would have broken," added Joan.

They started laughing, making up stories about their imaginary wicked escapades, mostly involving rich, sexy men. They were still laughing when they got back to Joan's unit.

"So where are we up to now, Joan? You've just got your job on Broadway. Is Ernie next?"

"Well, not quite. There were a few others before him."

"Joan! You never told me that!"

Frankie continued filming, relishing the stories of Joan's romantic conquests. As she finally got to the part where she met Ernie, Frankie could tell that their connection was different to all the others. Almost like they were destined for each other. Almost like it was meant to be. Almost like…

"Frances."

"Oh sorry, what?"

"Can we have a tea break?"

"Of course." Frankie went into the kitchen. "Joan, your story is amazing! It's like watching a movie."

Joan giggled. "I'm actually remembering things I'd forgotten about for years. I don't know where it's all been hiding!"

"Well, it won't be hiding anymore." Frankie handed Joan her tea. "Soon the whole world will know about you."

"Are you going to make it into a movie?" Joan laughed.

"No." Frankie sat down next to Joan. "I was going to wait to tell you this, but I think now's a good time. I'm going to organise a charity to be set up. The Joan Middleton Foundation. It'll raise money for Alzheimer's research."

Joan sat there with her mouth open. "The Joan Middleton Foundation?"

"Yes, the Joan Middleton Foundation. Daniel's going to help."

"Daniel?"

"Yes, Daniel. He just doesn't know it yet."

Joan's eyes were wide with excitement. "Oh Frances, I don't know what to say!"

"Well, that's a first!" Frankie rubbed Joan's arm. "It's going to be great Joan. There'll be fundraising events each year, and everyone will know about you. All the money will go towards finding a cure for Alzheimer's." Frankie knelt down in front of Joan and grabbed both her hands. "And it'll all be because of *you*!"

Joan started making squealing noises like a child discovering their presents on Christmas morning. Frankie had never seen her so excited. "I wish I could go to the fundraisers!"

Frankie laughed. "Don't worry, you'll be there. You'll be the star of the show!"

"Frances, how can I ever thank you? This is just so wonderful!"

"Don't thank me just yet," Frankie paused. "We still have to do something which you're probably not going to like."

Joan's smile vanished as she stared at Frankie.

"I want you to tell Daniel's story now. From the start. I need you to tell me everything, including all his dark times."

Frankie explained to Joan this was the most important part and without it, there would be no incentive for Daniel to do anything, including helping with the foundation.

"So, you want all the dirt on him? I can't betray my own son."

Fuck, he's betrayed you and left you here to rot like a piece of garbage, you owe him nothing.

"It's okay Joan, no-one will ever need to see it. Anyway, once Daniel realises how great this foundation is going to be, he'll kick himself that he didn't think of it first." Frankie left it at that. Joan wasn't stupid. She'd know *exactly* why Frankie needed all the dirt on Daniel.

"Okay then, let's just get it over with I guess."

Joan took a deep breath and set herself up in front of the camera again.

It was a traumatic afternoon for Joan, reliving all the heartbreak Daniel had caused to both himself and his parents. It brought Joan undone several times, making her sob uncontrollably from the grief she'd been suppressing for so many years. It was awful for Frankie to watch her in so much pain, but she was also glad that Joan was releasing it. Surely that was a good thing. To let go of all the hurt. To feel it once and for all and then get rid of it. To clean out all the dark closets we drag around with us our entire lives.

After many hugs, tears and cups of tea and coffee, their filming was done for the day. Joan looked exhausted. She sat on the lounge with her head back, closing her eyes.

"You did an amazing job, Joan. I'm so proud of you."

Joan opened her eyes and looked at Frankie. "I never thought I'd be able to do anything like that. That was one of the hardest things I've ever done."

Frankie put her hand on Joan's. "You were very brave."

Joan paused. "You know what? As horrible as it was, I feel better after speaking about all that. It's a bit like all those jobs we keep putting off because we hate doing them, but once they're done, we feel better."

"Like cleaning out the closet."

"Exactly!" Joan let out a huge breath. "I feel like a wine! Would you like to have one with me, Frances?"

"I'd love to, Joan. I think you've earnt one after today!"

The talk of wine steered Frankie's thoughts back to Robert. That was another horrendous thing that was headed their way. Robert losing his mum. Fuck.

"Cheers, big ears!" They clinked their glasses together. "Did you know Robert makes his own wine?"

"Really? No, I didn't know. He's just full of surprises, isn't he?"

"It's not bad either. I tried some the other night. Apparently, he wanted to start a vineyard years ago."

"Ernie and I had friends who owned a vineyard up in the Dandenongs. Not far from our holiday shack. We spent many a wonderful night with them around the fire drinking their wine. They even named one after me once. It was a sparkling wine. They called it Fancy Dancer, because I used to show them some of my dance moves after I'd had a few too many glasses."

Joan had a huge smile on her face. "The good old days." She looked at Frankie. "I've got more to tell you about the Love Shack, but that will have to wait for another day. When Robert's back."

"Ooh, the Love Shack. I can't wait. Just keep it clean, okay?"

"Oh no dear, that's completely out of the question." Joan chuckled.

"Okay, too much information. Speaking of Robert, I need to ring him."

Frankie went outside.

"Hey, you."

"Hi. How's it all going? How was the trip?"

"Long. At least I got to catch up with Adam, which was good. But Mum, she's fucking adamant about it. All of us have been trying to convince her to do something, but she just digs her heels in. She's *so* stubborn!"

"Like me, hey?"

"Oh, she's worse. By far!"

"Oh, that bad."

Robert laughed. "It's really good to hear your voice. I miss you. Plus, I'm pissed off that we missed out on our survival challenge."

"I think your mum's survival challenge is more important for now."

"Yeah, you're right. I just don't know what we're gonna do. Dad's being fucking useless, just going along with everything Mum says."

"Well, maybe he's got a reason for doing that. He has known her the longest."

"Yeah, well maybe he's also losing his shit. I don't understand why he isn't trying to get her to *do* something like the rest of us."

"Have you asked your mum what she wants?"

"We already know. She doesn't want treatment."

"That's what she *doesn't* want. Do you actually know what she *does* want?"

Robert sighed. "Not really. To die, obviously."

"I'm sure she doesn't want to die. Who'd want to leave a family like yours behind?"

Robert started getting upset. "I just don't understand it! Sorry Frankie, but I better go. I'll talk to you soon, okay." He hung up.

Frankie longed to tell him how much she missed him. How much she wanted to hold him. How she was falling in love with him. But that would all have to wait. She went back inside.

"How's his mum?"

"Stubborn."

Joan just sat and nodded as though she understood it perfectly. Frankie understood it too. Then she imagined it being her own mum in that position. Her own mum refusing treatment. Frankie would have reacted exactly the same way, fighting tooth and nail to convince her to prolong her life, even if it wasn't what she wanted. She then realised how selfish human nature is. Trying to keep loved ones alive at all costs. Even if that cost was the loved one's God given right to choose for themselves. It just didn't make sense. It was all wrong.

CHAPTER SIXTEEN

The following day Frankie and Joan spent the morning reviewing all the recordings to make sure everything was just right. The first recording had captured Joan's episode, along with Frankie's panic and the frantic conversation with Robert afterwards.

"Oh, that's awful Frances. I look like a stunned mullet! Can you get rid of that bit?"

"No Joan. I think we should leave it in there. It shows people what it's like for you when this happens. The world needs to see this stuff!"

"I suppose so." Joan went quiet.

"It's okay, Joan. Remember why we're doing this. People *need* to be shocked. They need to see the reality of what this disgusting disease does to people like you."

"Yes Frances. You're right. I guess I'd forgotten about that. I was too busy thinking about my fundraisers."

Frankie didn't know whether to laugh or cry. "Joan, trust me, your fundraisers are going to kick arse!"

"You really think so? It's just a shame I won't be there to see."

"You never know, maybe you'll be watching from somewhere else. You and Ernie together. Just promise me that you'll send me a sign if you're around. Maybe send me a duck." Frankie started laughing.

"Okay, it's a deal. Sounds like a bit of a challenge though. I was thinking more along the lines of turning lights on and off, or pushing photos off shelves. All the typical ghost things."

"Pftt. That stuff's for hacks. I'm expecting much more than that from *you*."

"Okay then. A duck it is!"

They both laughed as they imagined various ways Joan could make a duck appear. As much as she didn't want to, Frankie realised it was time to talk about the hard stuff. Time was running out. She went into the kitchen and came back with a cuppa for Joan.

"I saw Maggie yesterday and she was talking about setting a date for you to move."

Joan's face froze as she sat staring straight ahead. "And?"

"She didn't say when, but she said it would be before the auditors come, which I think is the end of next month."

Joan sat there silent.

"I don't want your last day to be spent here, Joan. I want it to be somewhere nice that you choose. Somewhere that makes you happy. We'll get you out of here somehow. Maybe tell them we're taking you on a holiday." Frankie paused. "This all feels so wrong, planning things for your final day. It must be so much worse for you. Are you okay?"

Joan smiled with a contented look on her face. "I'm more than okay, dear. I'm the luckiest woman in the world to have someone like you. Someone who would do this for me. I'll be forever grateful to you, Frances. As I've said before dear, I'm ready."

Frankie sat down and held Joan's hand. "I'm just not sure *I* am."

"It's okay, Frances. I'll always be with you in here." She put her hand on Frankie's chest. "And I already know where I want to spend my last day."

Frankie looked at her through watery eyes. "Where?"

"Sorrento."

"Wait. Isn't that in Italy?"

Joan giggled. "No, not that one. The Mornington Peninsula. The Bella Donna Hotel it was called. It was beautiful." She gazed into the distance. "Ernie took me there many years ago. It was one of the most romantic nights of my life. And the sunset! My God, I've never seen anything like it. The colours were breathtaking. We drank champagne and danced on the balcony overlooking the water like we didn't have a care in the world. It was the night Ernie gave me my eternity ring. I fell in love with him all over again that night." Joan looked at her ring and then at Frankie. "That's where I'd like to spend my last day."

Frankie smiled. "That sounds perfect."

Joan's face lit up with excitement. "I've still got the dress I wore that night. It was Ernie's favourite. That's what I'll wear."

Joan sounded like she was preparing for a ball rather than her own final departure. She went straight to her bedroom to look for the dress. Frankie could hear Joan muttering to herself as she searched through her wardrobe. She went outside to call Robert.

"Hey Frankie. How are you?"

"Hey. I'm fine. How about you? How's everything going?"

"Not great. Mum hasn't changed her mind about anything. We're all trying, but it's not making one bit of difference. I think she's more worried about feeding us all than she is about her fucking cancer."

"She's probably just loving having all her boys home."

"Yeah, she actually said that. It's weird you know, but I reckon this is the happiest I've seen Mum in a long time. It's freaking me out. She's acting like everything's great. Like there's nothing wrong."

"Maybe she's just trying to make the most of it."

"Yeah. By the way she wants to meet you."

"What? Did you tell her about me?"

"Of course I did! The whole family wants to meet you. Adam's given his tick of approval."

"Oh, has he now? After the whole five minutes of meeting me?"

"Yep. Plus, I told him all about you on the way up here."

"Oh great. Not everything, I hope."

"Everything. Every. Minute. Detail."

"Fuck, Robert!"

Robert burst out laughing. "He can't wait to see you in that dress."

"You bastard!" Frankie yelled. Robert just laughed harder. Frankie started laughing too.

"You're in big trouble now! Just wait till I see you."

"Ooh, I can hardly wait. What are you going to do to me?"

"Torture you. Slowly. Every inch of your body will be burning." She could hear Robert starting to get turned on. Then she heard Joan calling out to her. "Oh shit, sorry I have to go. Joan's calling."

"Oh, you're good Frankie. You really *do* know how to torture a person."

"I know! I've had years of practice being a cruel heartless bitch. Hey, when are you coming back?"

"Not sure yet, probably in a day or two. Why? Are you missing me?"

"Just wondering. I've finished Joan's filming so I'm about to organise her farewell."

"Oh, okay." Robert went quiet.

"Yes. I am missing you." Frankie could feel herself blushing.

"That's the best thing I've heard all day. Apart from the torture, of course."

Frankie laughed. "Better go. Good luck with your mum. Try and have a good time with your family."

"See ya, Frankie. I'll talk to you soon." He blew her a kiss and hung up.

Frankie went back inside.

"Oh, sorry dear, I didn't realise you were on the phone. How is Robert?"

"He's okay"

"You seem a bit sad. You miss him, don't you?"

"Yeah, I do miss him. It's just that…"

"What dear?"

Frankie sat and started nervously twiddling her fingers.

"I think I'm terrified, Joan. I'm starting to really like him. I mean *really* like him."

"Well, that's wonderful!"

"It's just that… sometimes I think I should just run away."

"So that you don't get hurt?"

Frankie nodded.

"That's your fear talking, Frances. You're telling yourself that Robert will do what everyone else has done to you. Like your parents leaving you, your boyfriend betraying you, your own family abusing you. But that's the past. Leave it where it belongs. You need to grab what makes you happy with both hands and don't let go."

Frankie smiled. "You're right, Joan"

"Now, come and I'll show you the dress I'll be wearing."

They went into the bedroom and lying on the bed was a creation you'd expect to see on a screen Goddess in an old movie. It was made of sky-blue satin with flowing lace over the top. It had diamantes along the neckline and around the edges of the matching silk scarf. Frankie just stood there with her mouth open.

"Oh my God Joan! It's beautiful!"

"Isn't it? Ernie had it made for me in New York as a surprise for my birthday. He chose the colour because it matched my eyes." Joan held the dress up under her chin. "He always had an amazing attention to detail. Have a look through my wardrobe Frances. Maybe there's something in there *you'd* like to wear."

"Probably not. I'm more a jeans kind of girl."

"Nonsense. You'd look stunning in a dress. You've got a beautiful figure, and you need to show it off."

"I don't really wear dresses." Then Frankie remembered the dress she wore to Robert's and the effect it had on him. "But I might have a look."

Joan sat and watched as Frankie chose some, holding them up for Joan's opinion.

"That's it!" said Joan as Frankie held the black dress up against herself. It was an elegant off the shoulder design with a low-cut neckline and fitted all the way down to a slightly flowing hemline. "Try it on!"

A few minutes later Frankie came out of the bathroom. Joan looked up and gasped with her hands up to her mouth.

"Oh, Frances look at you!" Frankie stood in front of the mirror in Joan's bedroom, spinning from side to side, hardly believing she was looking at her own reflection. The dress fitted her perfectly. She felt like a celebrity.

"Joan, this is gorgeous!"

"It's yours, Frances. I didn't think I still had it, to be honest. Now I know why I kept it. It was waiting for you."

"Oh Joan, thank you!" Frankie squealed with delight. "It's the most beautiful thing I've ever owned. I absolutely love it!"

"Now we just need some jewels."

Joan went over to her jewellery boxes. "Here, try this." She handed Frankie a choker necklace encrusted with diamonds and emeralds. She put it on and stared at her reflection. "Perfect," said Joan. "The emeralds really bring out your green eyes. I've just got to find the matching bracelet. It's here somewhere."

Frankie felt like she'd been magically transported to an exclusive high end designer house in Paris where women with insanely rich husbands spent their days drinking champagne and looking down their noses at everyone while trying on ludicrously expensive clothes.

"Here you are." Joan handed Frankie the matching bracelet along with a pair of emerald and diamond earrings. "Can you see some boxes up on top of the wardrobe Frances?" Frankie took them down for Joan to look through. "No, not that one. No, no. Oh, here they are." She handed a box to Frankie. Inside was a beautiful pair of black stilettos with a fine high black heel and diamante studded straps. "See if they fit you, dear."

Frankie tried on the shoes which were a perfect fit. She put on the earrings and bracelet and stood in front of Joan.

"Oh, you look divine, Frances! With your hair and makeup done, you could go anywhere with anyone, I don't care who they are."

Frankie looked in the mirror, holding her hair up. She did indeed look divine. She'd never looked so incredibly beautiful in all her life. She felt like she could conquer the world.

"My god Joan, I can't believe how different I look. I feel like a movie star."

"Robert will lose his marbles when he sees you in this."

Frankie laughed. He really would lose his marbles. His reaction to the last dress she wore would be nothing compared to this. She couldn't wait to wear it.

"Well, that's us sorted dear!"

"Sorrento won't know what hit it when we turn up. They'll think the Royals are in town!" Frankie laughed as she spun round and round in her beautiful black dress. She thought back to her mum's favourite saying, *who do you think you are? The Queen of England?* and she wished her mum could see her now. She would be so proud of her, standing here looking like a beautiful princess.

Frankie got changed and handed the jewellery back to Joan.

"No dear, that's for you to keep. It belongs with the dress."

"No Joan, I can't take that!"

Joan looked at Frankie with a serious look on her face.

"What do you think I'm going to do with it? I don't need it now. Please Frances, take it! Think of it as a gift. My gift to you. Then when you wear it, you can think of me."

Frankie hugged Joan.

"Thank you, Joan. It's way too much but I promise I'll take good care of it. You know, I reckon if you were my real grandmother, I would have spent my entire childhood playing dress ups with you. Who knows, you might have even convinced me to wear dresses instead of jeans."

"I would have insisted on it!" laughed Joan.

Frankie packed away all the dresses and shoes and went out to pack up the video camera.

"I'd really like to record some footage of you at Sorrento. Would that be okay with you?"

"I think that's a wonderful idea. Not that I'll get to see it, I guess."

"Don't worry I'll show you. I wouldn't share it with anyone without showing you first."

"So, who *are* you going to share the videos with?"

"Well, obviously Daniel. And don't worry, I'll make sure he doesn't get the one about him, just all the good ones that he can use for your fundraisers. I'll be talking to him soon about the foundation." Frankie paused. "You realise he's going to want *me* dead as well when he finds out you're gone?"

"Well, maybe I'll tell him if he ever does anything to hurt you, I'll come back and haunt him for the rest of his life!"

"I don't think a duck's going to scare him."

"Depends where I peck him!" They both burst out laughing.

"Imagine it. Every time he looks out at the harbour from his lounge room, there you are. Just floating there. Watching. Waiting." Joan laughed until tears ran down her face.

Frankie picked up the camera equipment.

"I'm heading off now Joan. There's something I have to do tomorrow, so I won't be coming in. I'll just ring Maggie in the morning and tell her I'm sick. But I'll be back on Friday, okay?"

"Oh. Is everything okay, dear?"

"Yeah, it's fine. I just need to sort something out that's all." *Sort someone out, more like.*

"Okay then. Take care, Frances. I'll see you soon."

"You take care too. No more episodes, okay! Promise?"

"Okay. I promise."

Frankie kissed Joan on the cheek and gave her a quack as she waved goodbye.

CHAPTER
SEVENTEEN

Pete was muttering in the lounge room as Frankie walked down the hallway in Learmonth House. She stood in the doorway to see him busily setting up chairs around the table.

"Oh, hey Frankie. There's a poker match tonight. Do you wanna play?"

"That depends. Are there Roses on offer?"

Pete shook his head. "The Roses are only for the Saturday comps. You haven't put your name down yet for Saturday. Are you playing? It's bocce."

"Not sure yet, but I will if I'm here. Is that okay?"

Pete thought for a moment. "I'll put you on the board as a maybe. So do you wanna play poker?"

"Sure," Frankie smiled at him. "Sounds great."

Pete pulled up another chair around the table. "See you at seven, Frankie."

Frankie made her way upstairs and flopped on her bed. Crunch time had come. Time to make the call. She laid there going over and over her story until it was crystal clear in her mind. She scrolled through her phone contact list, found 'Christian Bakker' and unblocked the number. Holding the phone against her chest, Frankie took a few deep breaths to calm herself before pressing the green button.

"Hello?"

"Christian?"

"Frankie?" He sounded shocked.

"Yep, it's me. How are you?"

"Um, yeah, I'm okay. I didn't expect to hear from *you*."

I bet you fucking didn't, she thought.

"I know. I just wanted to call and say hi. I didn't want things to be bad or awkward between us. You don't mind, do you?"

"Well, no I guess, but I thought you'd probably hate me."

"Hate you? How could I hate you?" *I despise you; you piece of shit!* "We had so many good times together, Christian. And I just wanted to say sorry about how I carried on. You know what I'm like, getting angry at the drop of a hat. I lost my temper, and I took it out on you. And… I'm sorry." Frankie added some tears for effect.

"Frankie don't cry. I'm sorry too."

The tears got louder. "Are you? Really?"

"Of course I am! I felt bad about you having to leave Melbourne."

So you fucking should! "Oh Christian, I'm so glad to hear you say that. It ripped my heart out having to leave with us being on bad terms. I haven't been able to sleep. I know I shouldn't be ringing you, but I just couldn't stand it any longer!" The tears were really flowing now. "I just really miss you."

"I miss you too, Frankie."

"Do you? I was so scared that you might have forgotten all about me. I just wish I was back there with you right now. I miss you so much." More tears. *Fuck, I deserve an Oscar for this.*

"So where *are* you, Frankie?"

"I'm in Albury. I'm working on a farm there. It's boring as batshit but it's also been good to have some space to think about everything."

Christian laughed "Wow. Never thought I'd see *you* on a farm. So are there cows or what?"

You dumb shit. You have no idea who I am or what I'm like.

"I know, I thought the same thing! Imagine it! Yeah, they've got cattle, and they grow wheat and other stuff. It's pretty hard work, actually. But on the upside, it's good for my figure. I've lost a bit of weight, and I've really toned up."

"Really? You already looked good."

"Oh, you're just saying that."

"No I'm not! You always look good."

"Not as good as you I bet. I've really missed being with you."

"Oh yeah?" Frankie could imagine him puffing up his chest, admiring himself in the mirror.

"You have no idea. It's driving me crazy. Every night I wish you were here so I could feel your body next to me. I don't think I've ever masturbated so much in my life!" She giggled, pretending to be embarrassed. "I really need to come and see you Christian. That is, only if you want me to."

"Of course I want to see you, Frankie. Anything I can do to relieve the tension."

She giggled some more "Well, I can get a lift down tomorrow with one of the other farmhands. They're going home so they can drop me off in town on their way through."

"Okay, tomorrow sounds great!" *I bet it does. You arrogant wanker.*

"Please don't tell anyone though. I'm not actually supposed to be anywhere near you remember. But I'm sure a few hours won't hurt. No-one has to know."

"Don't worry, I won't tell a soul. Just don't bring a baseball bat this time," he laughed.

"Oh God, I'm so sorry. How embarrassing. I promise no baseball bats. But I do promise to leave you weak at the knees."

"Yeah, baby. Bring it on. What time you coming?"

"Probably around ten or eleven, I'd say. I'll message you when I'm almost there. I can't wait to see you, Christian."

"Me too, Frankie. I'll be waiting."

"See you then, sexy." Frankie blew him a big kiss and hung up.

She threw herself back onto the bed, laughing hysterically. She couldn't believe how easily he'd fallen for her story. Now that she'd had time away from Christian, she couldn't understand how she'd ever been attracted to him in the first place. Maybe she'd always been so stoned she just didn't know any better. She felt like a totally different person now. The thought of having sex with him now repulsed her. After what she'd experienced with Robert, Christian was nothing but a dud. In every way.

Ruth was in the kitchen as Frankie burst in. "It's done!"

Ruth looked confused. "Which one?"

"I just rang fuckwit and he's fallen for it." Frankie laughed out loud and pumped her fists in the air. "I'm meeting up with him tomorrow."

"Now you've just got the hard, dangerous part to go." Ruth was clearly not sharing Frankie's excitement.

"Don't worry Ruth." said Frankie. "Nothing's going to happen to me."

Ruth put her hands on her hips. "Do you want me to come with you?"

"No, it'll be fine. Seriously."

"I could hide around the corner or something?"

Frankie laughed, but Ruth just stood there looking worried. "I'll be fine. I promise. Okay?"

Ruth nodded as Frankie went back upstairs.

Opening her wardrobe, she took her drug stash out of her coat pocket and tipped it onto the bed. All the remnants of her drug-fuelled life with Christian, not that it was any kind of life at all. As she picked up the two vials of Rohypnol, a shudder ran down her spine as she remembered all the scumbag arseholes who used to buy these from Christian, to do God knows what with. Or to do God knows *who* with.

Everything about her time with Christian in his seedy little world now made her feel sick to her stomach.

After getting everything ready for the next day, Frankie sat on the bed going back through the plan over and over in her head, from the moment she'd get off the train in Melbourne to the moment she'd get back on it. She was ready. *Yeah baby, bring it on.* Frankie laughed. *You'll be sorry you said that.*

The poker night was a rowdy affair as usual. The packet of Fantales that Frankie had donated as a prize obviously added to the competitive atmosphere. She'd never seen a bag of lollies being fought over so ferociously. They all spent hours yelling and laughing, trying to cheat without anyone noticing. Pete was trying his best to keep everyone under control without much success. It was hilarious to watch. Frankie hadn't laughed that much in a very long time. Around ten o'clock everyone called it a night. Ruth and Frankie helped Pete pack up the room.

"I can't believe you won, Pete. Were you cheating?" Frankie teased.

"No!" objected Pete, hiding his Fantales behind his back. "I'm just too smart for everyone else."

He grinned and left, looking very pleased with himself.

"So," asked Ruth, "what time are you leaving tomorrow?"

"I'll catch the nine am train."

"And what time will you be coming back?"

"Well not sure, but I'm guessing…. Let's see, ten thirty there, drinks, drugs, sleep, money, train, I reckon, I should be back by five at the latest." Frankie grinned.

Ruth stood there looking horrified. "Can you leave his address with me? If you're not back by five, I'm calling the police."

Frankie laughed, then realised Ruth wasn't joking. "I'll see you in the morning before I go and I'll give it to you then, if it'll make you feel better. Honestly, I'll be back before you know it."

She kissed Ruth on the cheek. "Don't worry. Goodnight."

Making her way up the stairs, Frankie felt a small seed of doubt creeping into her mind. What if something *did* go wrong? What if Christian found out what she was up to? What if the drugs *didn't* work? What if someone turned up and caught her? What if someone kidnapped her and stole all the money? Suddenly all the what ifs were attacking her from every angle.

As she sat looking at herself in the mirror, she took some deep breaths trying to calm herself. *You can do this. The plan's sound. It will work. Just relax. Relax. If you don't do this, then everything else is fucked. You're doing this for Joan. Just remember that. This has to work. You can do it.*

She stared into her own eyes until it felt like she was looking at someone else. She noticed every little speckle in her eyes. There were so many different colours, but Joan was right about the emeralds. They really did bring out the green in her eyes. She thought about Joan and the beautiful dress and jewellery she'd given her. And then she thought about Robert. She really missed him. As much as she hated him being away, the timing had turned out perfectly. At least she didn't have to make up stories and lie to him. She set her alarm for six am and plugged in her phone to charge. Turning off the light she closed her eyes, hoping that she'd see Robert in her dreams.

Ruth was making the morning coffee as Frankie arrived in her little black dress.

"Wow, dressed to kill today!"

"Hopefully not. Just stun."

Frankie chuckled as Ruth poured her a coffee.

"Here." She handed Ruth a note. "This is Christian's address. But I'll message you when I'm on my way back, okay? Just so you don't send the cops out looking for me."

"Make sure you do, Frankie. Cause if I haven't heard from you by five..."

"It'll be way before then."

She took a few gulps of her coffee and smiled at Ruth with as much confidence as she could muster.

"So, have you got everything? You don't want some breakfast first?"

"No way could I eat right now. And yes, I think I've got everything. Phone check, notebook check. Magic potion check." Her witch voice made Ruth laugh.

"Just be bloody careful!" Ruth slapped her arm.

"Ruth! Language! You'll hurt my sensitive ears. See you when I get back."

Walking through the front door, Frankie realised she'd passed the point of no return. *Oh fuck. Please God, let everything go to plan today. Please, please, please.* She took lots of deep breaths as she walked briskly to the station. A passing motorist whistled at her. *Sexy dress, check. Now it's showtime!*

As she sat at the station, she went over and over what she needed to do. The story was so well rehearsed in her mind, it almost felt real. She just needed to keep her nerve and stay focused.

The train ride to Melbourne felt like an eternity, partly because she didn't have the usual distraction of listening to music. Her phone's battery power was the lifeblood of her operation, so it had to be conserved.

The announcement for Deer Park Station came over the loudspeaker. *Shit is getting real now.* She sent a message to Christian.

'Hi sexy. Can't wait to see you. I'll be there within the hour', ending the message with heart and fire emojis. His reply came a minute later; no words, just thumbs up and dribbling emojis. *Fuck I hate you,* she thought.

She felt sick at the thought of having to pretend she missed him. He disgusted her. How quickly everything had changed, and she knew why. She'd finally met some good people. People who actually cared about her. People who weren't soul sucking parasites in search of their next meal. But mainly it was because of Robert. He'd opened up a whole new universe for her. She wished he was here with her right now.

"Next stop, Southern Cross Station" abruptly interrupted her thoughts. Again, she checked everything in her bag. It was all in the same place it was last time she checked, and the time before that.

Leaving the station, she headed for the nearest bottle shop, where she bought a bottle of JD and two shot glasses. They were also an important part of the plan; something she couldn't risk leaving to chance.

As Frankie reached the corner near Christian's apartment, her heart was racing. For the ten thousandth time, she went over everything again in her mind.

"Get your fucking shit together!" she muttered to herself, desperately trying to stop herself from panicking. She thought about Joan, about her videos and her dresses. She thought about her love stories of Ernie. She pictured Joan's face in front of her, crying and begging for her help. It reminded her of the real reason she was here and suddenly, everything became clear again.

CHAPTER EIGHTEEN

Right, let's get this done, she thought.

Taking a deep breath, she stood up tall, her head held high, and strode down to the apartment building, ringing the buzzer.

"*Yeees?* Who is it?" Christian's pathetic attempt at humour disgusted Frankie even more.

"Oh, hello sir, I seem to be lost. I'm looking for a handsome, well-built man who apparently lives in this building. Goes by the name of Christian?"

"Well, looks like you've found him! Come on up."

Maybe I could stab him in the heart after I drug him. She suddenly imagined a tiny Joan sitting on her shoulder. "*Don't do it dear. He's not worth it.*" Frankie chuckled to herself as she entered the familiar lift, punching button three. Pressing the record button on her phone, she zipped it into the side pocket of her bag.

She strutted towards Christian's door to find him standing there waiting, dressed only in a pair of baggy jeans, leaning on the doorway with a big smile on his face. She put her arms out towards him, holding up the bottle of JD in celebration.

"Christian! Oh my God, I've missed you!" She threw her arms around his neck as he picked her up and swung her around.

"Frankie! Woah, you look *great*! And yeah, *alright*!" he said, pointing at the bottle.

Frankie gave him a big kiss, trying her hardest to ignore his darting tongue.

"I thought it's about time for a fucking party! And a party wouldn't be complete without JD, now would it?"

"No way. Come here you!" Christian wrapped his arms around her, grabbing her arse with both hands and carrying her into his apartment, kicking the door closed. She again imagined Joan on her shoulder, waving her finger. *"Don't do it dear."*

Christian threw Frankie down on the lounge and fell on top of her, kissing her roughly with his prickly face, running his grubby hands quickly up her legs and underneath her dress. She laid there pinned down, pretending to reciprocate, desperately fighting off the urge to belt him with a heavy object and escape.

"Wait! Christian." He kept going, oblivious to her words.

"Christian! Hang on a sec! I need to tell you something!"

Christian eventually stopped his drooling, groping onslaught and paused, panting heavily in her face. *"What?* Have you got your periods?"

Tiny Joan was there again, warning her not to stab him. "No, there's just something I need to tell you about."

Christian sat up with a groan and leant back on the lounge, crossing one of his legs. He was obviously pissed off. *"What?* What's wrong?"

Frankie sat up and pulled her dress back down, putting her hand on his leg.

"Nothing's wrong. Actually, I've got something really exciting to tell you. A business proposition."

Right, this is it she thought. *Don't fuck this up!*

"Well," she said with as much enthusiasm as she could muster, "I've met this couple out in Albury who've got this amazing business. It's a bootleg business. They make all their own alcohol; I've actually tried it and it's *really* good! They make everything – rum, vodka, bourbon, scotch, you name it, they make it. Anyway, at the moment they're only selling it in New South Wales, but they want to expand, and they're looking for a distributor south of the border. And I thought of *you!* It'd be perfect! You've already got all the contacts, and the profit margin is *huge*. It could make you rich!"

Christian had a smug look on his face.

"*Alcohol?* Why would I want to sell alcohol, when you can just walk into the nearest bottle shop and get it?"

"Not for ten bucks a bottle you can't! Imagine the amount of profit venues could make buying their spirits for that price. You sell it for fifteen, there's sixty bucks a case profit straight up! Even at twenty bucks it's still cheap and you'd make a hundred and twenty a case! Apparently, it's going gangbusters in New South Wales so they're starting up another factory in Victoria."

"So how much are we talking about?"

"I think at the moment they're selling about a thousand bottles a week, but the new setup's going to be a lot bigger." Frankie looked at Christian with wide eyes. "Imagine how much money you could make!"

"Worth thinking about, I guess. So, who *are* these people?"

"I only know them as Tony and Jane. I don't even know if that's their real names. They obviously don't go round advertising what they do. They only told me because I got to know them pretty well and I told them I used to do a bit of courier work."

"Really? What else did you tell them?"

Frankie kissed Christian on the cheek. "Don't worry, they don't know anything about you or what you do or where you live. I'm not that stupid. All I said was that I might know someone who'd be interested. Do you reckon you'd have the people to do it? You'd need trucks obviously."

"Yeah, probably. Blacky's family owns a freight company. He already helps me out with the big jobs."

"Blacky?"

"Blacky. Jeff Blackwood. Don't you remember him?"

"Is he the guy that brings in the shipments?"

Christian laughed. "Fuck no, that's Ferrucci. You remember Blacky. Him and his missus invited us over that night, and we were jumping off the balcony into the pool. Remember?"

Frankie laughed. "Oh yeah, I remember. That was funny. We were all so fucked up that night."

Frankie took the shot glasses out of her bag and poured the JD. "Here's to those nights and more to come." She handed a glass to Christian "Cheers." They sculled their shots. Frankie leaned over and started kissing Christian. "Have you still got that bottle of baby oil in your bedroom?"

"Mm," murmured Christian as his hands went back to where they left off.

"Go and get it. I want to give you a rubdown. Show you what you've been missing."

Christian jumped up and went into the bedroom. With her heart racing, Frankie quickly took one of the vials from her bag. Her hands were shaking so much it took all her concentration to snap off the lid without spilling it. Quickly she poured it into his glass, topping both up with JD.

As she struggled to compose herself, Christian returned with the baby oil.

"Cheers!" said Frankie handing him the glass. They both sculled their shots, and she quickly refilled them again, before he had a chance to notice the taste of her treachery.

"Are you trying to get me pissed?" he said, downing his third shot.

"Yes, I am. So I can take advantage of you. Now take your clothes off."

"I like the sound of that." He unzipped his jeans and stood in front of Frankie as she slid them off, his semi erection right in her face. Not so long ago it would have been a welcome sight, but now all she wanted to do was get as far away from him as possible. But she had to keep up the act, just long enough for the drugs to do their work.

"Lie down. I'll do your back first." She could tell that Christian just wanted to get straight to the sex, so she needed to distract him. "Come on, I'm gonna make you wait until you can't stand it. Over you go!"

He sighed and reluctantly laid down on the floor on his stomach. Kneeling beside him, she poured baby oil all over his back and down his legs. She massaged his back, digging her thumbs in hard, making him squirm and groan.

"Feel good?"

"Uh huh. I know what would feel even better. My cock inside you."

"Yes, it would, but you'll just have to wait." She slowly ran her hands down his legs, taking as much time as she could, hoping the drugs would hurry up and kick in. "So, what do you think about the business idea? Maybe you could even get the big guys involved."

"What big guys?"

"You know, like the importer guy?"

"Ferrucci? I doubt it. He's strictly Colombia."

"What, cocaine?"

"Cocaine, heroin, *fuck* Frankie, why all the questions?"

Frankie quickly bent down and started kissing the back of Christian's neck, running her hands in between his legs to distract him. He pushed himself up and rolled onto his back. She continued to kiss him as he grabbed her, pulling her onto him. She slowly ran her tongue down his neck and chest, doing anything she could think of to avoid having sex with him.

Christian suddenly stopped groping her and rolled over, trying to sit up. Frankie stopped and looked at him. "What's wrong?"

"Fuck, Frankie!" He slurred, still trying to get up. "What've you…"

"Christian! What's the matter?" Frankie pretended to be concerned, but she realised the game was up and the time for pretending was over.

Christian slumped on the floor, making strange moaning sounds as his eyes rolled back in his head, dribble running from the corners of his mouth. After cautiously pushing him with her foot, Frankie rolled him onto his side, propping him up with cushions on either side. She felt his pulse. It was racing, but at least he was alive. His breathing was fast and shallow. Frankie was panicking, but it was done now and there was no going back. *What if I've used too much? What if I've fucking killed him?* A million thoughts were hurtling through her mind. She paced around in circles, struggling to catch her breath. Again, she checked Christian's vital signs. His heart was still racing but his breathing was slowing. Surely that was a good sign. She sat on the lounge trying to get herself together. *Right come on, stick to the plan. Stick to the plan.*

She collected Christian's phone, the bottle of JD and the shot glasses, throwing them all into her bag. Next, she went into the bedroom and pulled back the bedside table, revealing his secret trap door. Holding her breath, she pulled on the latch and lifted it, letting out a cry of relief. "*Yes!*" There it was in all its glory; his entire stash. She lifted out the grey duffle bag and unzipped it, revealing wads and wads of cash wrapped in rubber bands, several plastic wrapped drug bricks and two handguns. Her heart felt like a jackhammer trying to smash its way through her chest; she'd never been so terrified in all her life.

Trying to calm herself, she pictured Joan back on her shoulder. "*It's okay dear, don't panic. Just do what you need to do and leave. It's over now.*" Flipping the trapdoor closed, she pushed the bedside table back in place.

As she crept back into the lounge room, she imagined Christian standing there, waiting to kill her. To her relief he was still on the floor exactly where she'd left him. Fumbling through her handbag, she took out her notepad and scribbled a message, her hands still trembling.

Now it's YOUR turn to start again. I've got everything on tape. If you ever come looking for me, I'll send it all to the police and you'll be a <u>DEAD MAN!</u>"

She tore off the note, leaving it in the middle of the table.

Carefully and methodically, she went back over everything once more in her head, making sure she'd taken care of every minute detail. She took out her phone, pressed stop and replayed the start of the recording. The sound was much clearer than she'd expected it to be. She bent down to check Christian one last time. Finally, his breathing and pulse had normalised. As she picked up her bags, she scanned the room again before walking out, quietly closing the door behind her.

Outside in the fresh air, an overwhelming torrent of emotion hit Frankie like a freight train. She ran over to the gutter and vomited several times, the JD burning like fire on its way back up. Apart from the phone call delivering the news of her parents' death, this had been the most intense, gut-wrenching moment of her life.

All the way back to the station, she fought the overwhelming urge to run, trying her hardest to appear normal. Not like someone who had just double-crossed, drugged and robbed their drug dealer ex-boyfriend. Or like someone who was carrying a bag full of money, drugs and guns. She was breathing so heavily that she started to feel lightheaded. *Just get on the train and get back. That's all you have to do.*

Finally arriving at the station, she chose a seat at the far end of the platform, away from everyone else. She now wished she wasn't wearing her sexy dress. The last thing she needed was to draw attention to herself.

Eventually her train pulled in and she quickly got on the front carriage nearest to the guard, hoping that would lessen her chances of running into any trouble. She sat in the single seat at the front of the carriage, hiding the duffle bag on the ground under her feet.

Taking out Christian's phone, she switched it off and removed the sim card. That's when she remembered she'd promised to message Ruth.

"On my way back now. Everything's ok"

Less than thirty seconds later Ruth replied.

"Thank God, see you soon."

Frankie leant back and closed her eyes, only to see Christian's angry face staring back at her.

The day replayed over and over in her mind until she wanted to scream. No doubt it would haunt her for a long time to come, but then she remembered the reason she'd chosen to do it all in the first place. It was her get out of jail card, and somehow, she'd managed to get exactly what she came for. Christian had spilt the beans on his mate Blacky and the big guy Ferrucci. *Surely if Ferrucci ever finds out what Christian told me, he will be a dead man. So, mission accomplished!* She smiled to herself. She'd really pulled it off. Without a hitch. She could hardly believe it had gone so well.

At the back of her mind though, she could sense a big black hole. What she'd done to Christian felt very wrong. It wasn't because she thought he didn't deserve it, but she felt tainted in some way, like she'd sold part of her soul. All she wanted to do was get home and have a long hot shower to wash the repulsive smell of Christian off herself.

Her phone pinged. It was another message from Ruth.

"Robert's looking for you. I told him you're on your way back from Melbourne. That's all I said. Sorry."

"Fuck!"

Frankie's mind raced. What was she going to tell him? She wasn't planning on keeping it a secret from him, but she would have liked more time to think about it. Now, she had about five minutes. The train was almost at Ballarat. *I'll just tell him everything. I was going to anyway. I don't have anything to feel guilty about. Do I? I made out with Christian a bit, but so what. I only did that so he'd trust me. Big deal. I didn't have sex with him. Plus, I told him I'd come up with a plan, so it wasn't like he didn't know.*

She swallowed the big lump in her throat and tried to compose herself.

Robert was waiting at the far entrance to the platform as Frankie got off the train. Her heart started racing as soon as she saw him. She wasn't sure if it was from happiness or fear. As she got closer, the look on his face decided for her. It was fear.

Oh fuck, here we go.

"Hi, you're back!" Frankie smiled nervously, putting her arm around Robert and giving him a kiss, hoping he didn't notice the sweaty stench of another man.

"So are you. Good trip?" he asked with a sarcastic look on his face.

"Um, yeah, I guess so. How about yours? How's your mum?"

"Dying." Frankie knew right then she was in for a fight, no matter what she said from that point on.

"So, you couldn't get her to change her mind?"

"Nope. Thought I'd come back and surprise you. Looks like I've managed to do that."

"So did you go to work?"

"Yep. Went to work. Joan told me you had something to take care of. Maggie told me you were sick. So, I went to see if you were alright, and then Ruth tells me that you've gone to Melbourne. What the fuck's going on Frankie?"

"Look, I just needed to do something. I told you that! I told you I'd come up with a plan and that I'd tell you about it once I did it. Don't you remember?"

"Well, it seems like every other bastard seems to know about it *except* for me!" Robert was starting to raise his voice.

"I couldn't tell you!"

"Why the fuck not?"

"Because you would have freaked out!"

Robert grabbed Frankie tightly by the arms. "Why would I have freaked out Frankie? Why?"

"Let go of me!" she yanked her arms away and started storming out of the station and into the carpark. "I didn't tell you because you would have overreacted. Just like you're fucking doing now!" People nearby were stopping to stare at them.

"*What!*" yelled Frankie at one couple of onlookers. "Mind your own fucking *business!*" They quickly turned away, whispering and shaking their heads.

Robert followed close behind her.

"*Tell* me Frankie. Tell me *why*. What have you been doing? It's *him* isn't it. You've been to see *him*! Haven't you! Tell me!"

Frankie was getting angrier by the second. "*Yes!* I've fucking been to see him! But it's not what you think!"

"Well, what the fuck *is* it then? You sneak off to Melbourne without a word to me, to do fuck knows what! And in that fucking *dress*! What am I *supposed* to think? What would *you* think?"

Frankie stopped and swung around to look Robert in the face. "I don't know Robert and I don't fucking *care!*" she screamed. "Just take me home, alright?"

"Fine!" Robert yelled.

Frankie hurled the duffle bag into the back seat of Robert's car and flounced into the passenger seat. Robert got in and slammed the door.

"Well?" he said.

"Well, what!" she snapped.

"Are you going to tell me what the fuck's going on?"

"Not here in the middle of the bloody car park!"

"Well, shut your fucking door and we can go back to my place and talk there!"

Frankie slammed her door and stared out the window as Robert screeched out of the car park for the silent drive back to his place.

CHAPTER NINETEEN

By the time they arrived at Robert's place, Frankie's anger had turned to guilt and shame. Every wicked thing she'd done today had fucked things up between her and Robert, and she hated herself for it. She looked over at him, tears streaming down her face.

"Come on, let's go inside."

He grabbed the duffle bag and his suitcase from the back and led Frankie inside.

"Is it okay if I have a shower?" Frankie asked as soon as she was in the door.

Robert paused, staring at her.

"I know what you're thinking, but I didn't sleep with him! I fucking *detest* him!" Frankie hung her head and started to cry.

Robert went over and gently lifted her head. "Just go and have your shower, then we can talk." He went into the bedroom and got her a t-shirt.

Frankie slowly wandered into the bathroom. She stood crying under the hot water and scrubbed her body as hard as she could stand, trying to remove every last trace of Christian from herself. She wished she could scrub her insides as well.

She finally emerged from the bathroom to find Robert sitting on the lounge. He patted the seat next to him.

"Feel better?"

Frankie nodded, slowly sitting down on the lounge.

"I want to tell you everything, but you're probably going to hate me when I tell you." She started to cry again.

"Well, why don't you let *me* be the judge of that."

Frankie took a deep breath.

"Okay, so the other day, Joan showed me a video of this guy they knew in New York. He was a big drug dealer and he got caught. But… he didn't go to jail, because he gave the cops what they wanted."

"Drugs?"

"No. He gave up all the other drug dealers to save his own arse."

Robert sat there frowning, looking confused.

"Okay, so in a nutshell, I went to Christian's and recorded information about his drug contacts, then I stole all his stash and his phone. I've got everything."

"You what?"

"I recorded information about—"

"No, I heard that bit. So, you stole his *stash*?"

Frankie slowly walked over and picked up the duffle bag before sitting back on the lounge and unzipping it on her lap.

"Holy *fuck*! *Frankie*, what the *fuck*! Jesus *Christ!*"

Frankie tipped the entire contents of the bag out onto the lounge.

"What the *fuck*, Frankie! Are you *mental*? Are you trying to get yourself *killed*?" Robert stood up and started pacing the room.

"I thought it all through. He doesn't know where I am, and anyway, he wouldn't dare to try and find me. I've got too much intel on him now."

"Intel? Are you some kind of vigilante now? Fucking hell, Frankie! There's *guns*! Not to mention a fucking truckload of cocaine or heroin or whatever the fuck *that* shit is! Do you seriously think he's not gonna come after you? Oh *fuck*!"

Frankie sat quietly as Robert continued to pace, speculating loudly about the various treacherous outcomes which were inevitably headed her way. After several minutes of ranting, he finally flopped back down on the lounge next to her.

"Do you see why now?"

"Why *what*?"

"Why I didn't tell you."

Robert shook his head, not saying a word.

"Don't you see Robert? I have *everything*. His phone will have all his contacts, messages, everything. I have a recording of him naming the guy who imports cocaine and heroin from Colombia! I have a recording of him naming the guy who distributes for him! I have his drugs and his guns! And his money, some of which belongs to me by the way."

"So, tell me again, *why* exactly this guy won't come after you and murder you?"

"I left him a note saying I'd recorded everything, and if he tries to find me, I'll go to the cops, and he'll be a dead man."

"Hang on, hang on, back up a sec. You forgot a bit. How the fuck did you manage to walk away with his guns *and* his drugs *and* his money right from under his nose?"

"I drugged him."

"*What*? You fucking *drugged* him? Oh my God, this is getting better and better!"

"I bought a bottle of JD before I went there and I spiked his drink."

"Oh fuck, *fuck!* And so, I guess before that, he just all of a sudden decided to spill his guts about all his drug contacts, did he?"

"No, I told him that I'd met some people who were looking for a distributor for their bootleg business."

"What?" Robert was getting more and more agitated.

"I asked him whether he'd have the people to do it. I just made shit up to try and get him to talk."

"And all this is on tape, is it?"

"Yep!"

"Let me hear it."

Frankie paused, realising the last thing she wanted was for Robert to hear every sordid detail of her encounter with Christian.

"I don't think you..."

"Let me *hear* it!" Robert demanded.

Reluctantly Frankie took out her phone. "Robert, just remember, all this was planned before I—"

"Play it." He sat there stony faced, staring straight ahead.

Taking a deep breath, she pressed the dreaded play button, wishing she could make herself disappear; partly so she didn't have to relive the horror, but mostly so she didn't have to witness the disgust on Robert's face once he discovered the level of depravity she was capable of.

They both sat there in silence as the whole revolting scene played out. Frankie felt like she was going to vomit, comforted only by the fact there was nothing left in her stomach.

As she sat there reliving each horrible moment, she despised herself more and more. She felt like a filthy dirty prostitute, lying and cheating to get what she wanted, no matter what the cost. And going by the look on Robert's face, the cost was going to be enormous. That was one thing she *hadn't* factored into her plan. The aftermath of her actions. The effect on her. The effect on Robert. The effect on their relationship.

As the disturbing sounds of Christian's struggle to stay conscious rang out, Frankie trudged into the bathroom and changed back into her dress. She came back out and sat quietly on the lounge opposite Robert, anxiously preparing herself for his final rejection.

Still not saying a word, he finally stopped the recording and looked at her. Then he looked at her dress. "Going somewhere?"

"I guess so, after all that. Don't you want me to fuck off now?"

"You know what, Frankie?" Robert began in a low, serious voice, "In all my life, I've never met anyone—"

"As disgusting as me, yeah, I know. I'm fucked. The recording proves it. I'm just a lowlife scumbag who goes around destroying people's lives. But I never meant to hurt *you,* Robert!" Frankie was crying again.

Robert just sat there, still not moving, watching Frankie as she cried.

"As I was saying, in all my life, I've never met *anyone* who would risk so much to help another person. You did all this for Joan, didn't you? You put your life on the line for her today."

Frankie continued crying, but now they were happy tears.

"As hard as that was to listen to, I know what you must've been going through. I can tell by your voice. I know the sounds you make when you're enjoying yourself, and that ain't them. I can also see why you hate the guy. What a fucking *tosser*!"

The serious look on Robert's face suddenly vanished, like a hypnotist had just snapped him out of a trance.

"So, you don't hate me?" whimpered Frankie.

Robert went over and sat next to her, wrapping his arms around her. Putting his forehead on hers, he looked her straight in the eyes. "I *love* you, Frankie."

"What?" Frankie reeled back in surprise.

"I *love* you!"

"Oh my God! I love you too!" squealed Frankie as she threw her arms around his neck.

"Just please tell me he didn't take your dress off."

Frankie shook her head, grinning. "You're the only one who's ever done that."

"Good, cause I'm about to do it again."

He started kissing her, carrying her into the bedroom, undressing her as they went.

Frankie tore Robert's clothes off like he was on fire. Before they could even make it to the bed, Frankie was wrapped around him as they crashed against the wall, almost devouring each other.

In a raging frenzy of passion they fell onto the bed, desperately trying to satisfy their hunger for each other, finally climaxing together in a glorious, euphoric crescendo.

Falling back in each other's arms, too breathless to even speak, they laid exhausted in the silent blissful afterglow.

Robert stroked Frankie's hair. "Were you scared today?"

"I was terrified," she said softly, tears welling in her eyes. I've never been so scared in all my life."

"I'll never let anyone hurt you, Frankie."

She put her head on Robert's chest. She didn't want to think about Christian for one more second. "So how was it being back with your family?"

"Sad. But also good" Robert paused. "You know, everything felt different this time. I even rode Casper."

"Oh great, you've got another woman. *Now* you tell me!"

Robert laughed. "Seriously though, I haven't even been able to *look* at the horses until now. Mum picked up on it straight away. The first night I was there, she pulled me into the kitchen and said, *'who is she?'* That's when I told her all about you. And that's *also* when I realised it was all over for me."

"All over? That sounds a bit tragic."

"It is. A tragic love story just like Cupid and—"

"Yes, Psycho. It's funny, cause that's about the same time *I* realised. When you left for the farm, I had this really horrible feeling in the pit of my stomach. I've never felt that before and I don't really want to feel it again. So please don't ever leave me again, okay?"

"Never again. My beautiful. Amazing. Brave. Frankie. I promise," said Robert, kissing her face with each word. "But now *you* have to promise *me* that you won't come up with any more dangerous plans without telling me."

"Okay, I promise. Anyway, my next plan involves you, so there's no way I can get around it."

"We'll talk about that over dinner young Frances, but first, I think dessert's calling!"

Their connection had deepened since their time apart and they were insatiable for each other. This was a whole new surreal, sensual world to Frankie, and Robert was like a magnificent thunderbolt from the blue. He took her breath away. She'd never been so blissfully happy, and she'd obviously never been in love before. Not like this.

At dinner they sat drinking Robert's wine, talking and laughing like they'd known each other forever. Robert poured his heart out to Frankie about how terrified he was of losing his mum and she hugged him as he cried.

"You must've been through hell and back losing your parents," he said, wiping his face. "I can't even imagine how hard that must've been."

"It's been shit. But I'm still here. And now you are too. Hopefully one day, some kid somewhere will be crying about losing one of us!"

"Kid? Don't you mean kids?" A look of excitement came over his face. "I can't wait for you to meet Mum. Well, all the family, but Mum especially."

"I can't wait to meet her either."

"I reckon you'll really get along. She was a bit of a bugger when she was young. A bit like you."

"Oh really? Maybe she'll be worried I'll lead her precious son astray."

"If I know Mum, she'll be *hoping* you will!"

CHAPTER TWENTY

Frankie raced into Learmonth House to get changed for work as Robert waited outside. Ruth called out to her from the dining room as she ran past. "Frankie! Are you okay? Is everything okay?"

"Everything's fine, Ruth. Sorry, I've got to get changed. Robert's waiting for me."

"Frankie, wait." Ruth hung her head. "I just wanted to say sorry. Robert kept asking me until I told him. He could tell I was frantic. I'm so sorry."

Frankie hugged her. "I'm sorry too, Ruth. It's all my fault. I shouldn't have got you involved."

"No, I'm glad you did! Someone needed to know where you were going. So, how did it all go? Sorry, I know you're in a rush, but what happened with…"

Frankie held Ruth's hands, looking in her in the eyes, grinning.

"Everything went like clockwork, Ruth! I'll tell you all about it after work, okay? And don't feel bad about telling Robert. I'm glad you did now."

After running upstairs to get changed she hurried back outside and jumped in Robert's car.

"Poor Ruth. I think I put her through hell yesterday."

"I probably didn't help, giving her the third degree. So did she know everything?"

"Yep, Ruth was my sounding board. I had to tell someone; in case I'd missed something. If I'd known how much she was going to worry though, I probably wouldn't have."

"What about Joan? Did she know?"

"Oh God no! She's got enough shit going on."

"Well, I can see now why you didn't tell *me*. There's no fucking *way* I would've let you do it."

"I know. That's why I thought it was the perfect time, while you were away."

"Didn't count on me coming back and catching you red handed, did you!"

"I'm just glad it's over. The only thing left now is to contact Daniel." Frankie smiled "You should've seen the look on Joan's face when I told her about the foundation. She was so excited. Oh, and she wants to spend her last day in Sorrento."

"Sorrento? In Italy?"

Frankie laughed. "No, the one here. There's a hotel there where she went with Ernie. I just have to make sure it's still there."

Robert sat there driving with a serious look on his face, not saying a word.

"You okay?"

"I was just thinking, this'll be Mum next. Her last day won't be far off either." He looked over at Frankie with watery eyes.

"Don't worry, we'll be with her soon."

As they arrived at Golden Leaves, Maggie was in reception talking to Clare.

"Good morning" sang Clare in unison with Maggie. "How are you feeling today, Frankie?" asked Maggie.

"Much better thanks." It wasn't a lie. She *was* feeling better today after a yesterday from hell.

"Oh, by the way, we've got a moving date for Joan. It'll be the twenty second, which gives us almost two weeks. That'll be enough time to get her all packed, won't it?" Frankie felt a wave of panic rush through her. She glanced at Robert. "Uh, oh yeah, I guess so..."

"Oh Maggie, that just reminded me" interrupted Robert. "Joan asked about getting away on a bit of a holiday before the move. She wants me and Frankie to go with her. I'm fine with that. Obviously, I'll make sure she's well looked after. She's become really fond of Frankie since they've been spending a lot of time together. I think Frankie would be fine with it. Frankie?"

She just stood there nodding, gobsmacked. "Her son's obviously too busy to take her. That'd be okay, wouldn't it?"

Frankie couldn't believe what she was hearing. Robert had just made up this big spiel on the spur of the moment, with such conviction that Maggie could hardly say no. She just wanted to scream with excitement and jump all over him.

"Um, I suppose so. It's usually the family that takes them, though."

"I know, but considering her son's situation, that's pretty much out of the question. It'll only be for a couple of days, and I think it'll be really good for Joan's mental health. As you know, she is pretty stressed about the move."

Oh Robert, you are a master! thought Frankie.

"So where does she want to go?" Maggie asked with a puzzled look on her face.

"Sorrento," Frankie quickly chimed in.

"Sorrento?" quizzed Maggie. "In Italy?"

Frankie smirked at Robert.

"No, the one here. On the Mornington Peninsula. There's a hotel there she's been telling me about. She went there with her husband, and she really wants to go back."

"So, we wouldn't be too far away," continued Robert. "We could have her back in a few hours if we needed to."

Maggie scratched her head. "Well, I guess so Rob. You'll just have to make sure your clinic shifts are covered, and you'll need to fill out the release form. Make sure Frankie's on the paperwork as well. I'll have to ring her son and let him know."

"I can ring him if you like," blurted Frankie, "I mean, if it'll save you time, I'm happy to call him."

"Okay… You can if you like. Just tell him if he has any questions, he can contact me. We'll also need him to sign the release form."

"I'll organise that," said Robert.

"Okay, well let me know when it's all done so I can sign off on it. The auditors will be crawling all over this place soon, so make sure you've got *everything* covered."

"Will do, Capitaine!" Robert saluted at Maggie, finally making her smile.

Maggie rushed off with her clipboard under her arm.

As they got outside, Frankie couldn't contain her excitement any longer.

"My God Robert, you were incredible! That was amazing!"

"I'm full of it, aren't I!" he said smugly.

"You should be an actor."

"Like you can talk!" They both laughed all the way to Unit four.

"Knock, knock. Eureka!"

"I found it!" came the muffled cheery response, before the door swung open. "Oh, hello you two! So, you found her then Robert?"

"Yes, Eureka." he laughed. "We have some good news for you Joan. Frankie can tell you."

"Well," began Frankie, "Robert just gave the performance of his life and convinced Maggie to let us take you on a holiday!"

"Oh, that's wonderful! A one-way trip! For me, anyway." Joan laughed happily, but Frankie felt a sharp pang of sorrow stab her in the chest. "Thank you, Robert. I knew you could do it. You could sell ice to the Eskimos."

Frankie laughed as Robert pretended to be offended. "He really could, couldn't he! You should have heard him, Joan. He was incredible."

"I don't doubt it, Frances, not one bit. Now, sit down you two. I have something for you." She pointed to the lounge and disappeared into her bedroom.

"What's this about?" whispered Robert. Frankie shrugged her shoulders.

Joan returned with an old green tin box on her lap. She handed it to them. "This is for you both."

Frankie sat the box on her lap and gently opened the lid. Inside were some old papers, stained yellow with age.

"What *is* this, Joan?" asked Frankie.

Joan just sat there with a huge smile on her face.

As Frankie took the papers out of the tin she found a set of keys, tied together with an old piece of frayed red ribbon. Among the papers was an old black and white photo of a couple standing on a verandah. She held it up to look at it.

"Who's this?" asked Robert.

"That's me and Ernie."

"Is that the shack?" asked Frankie.

Joan nodded. "That was taken the day we picked up the keys."

Robert opened one of the papers and sat there reading it. "Joan, this is a deed."

"What?" shrieked Frankie.

"Yes, it is a deed. The deed to the Love Shack. And now it's all yours. I've made all the arrangements."

"Oh no, Joan, you can't be serious! This is too much!" Frankie just sat there shaking her head.

"Nonsense! I want you two to have it. I want you to have as many happy times there as Ernie and I did. It's probably going to need some work, and you might have to chase the possums out, but you're young and full of energy so I'm sure you'll manage. And Robert, there's plenty of room for your vineyard too. Twenty-two and a half acres to be exact."

Robert was sitting there with his mouth open.

"Joan! I don't know what to say. I just…"

Frankie started to cry and hugged Joan. "Oh Joan, I can't believe this! Thank you so much!"

Frankie then hugged Robert, crying and laughing with excitement at the same time.

"It'll be perfect for you two lovebirds. I'm just happy for you to have it. If Daniel got his hands on it, it would go straight to the highest bidder."

"So, he doesn't know about it?" asked Frankie.

"No dear. There's lots of things Daniel doesn't know. But what he doesn't know won't hurt him. He'll get plenty when I'm gone, don't you worry."

Robert found a map amongst the papers and opened it. "It's in the Dandenongs? You've got to be kidding me!"

"Yes. Lot Twenty-one Currawong Avenue. It's a beautiful, peaceful spot. Surrounded by nature. Mind you, it's probably a bit overgrown by now, but it's the perfect place to hide away and it's still so close to everything."

Robert hugged Joan so hard it almost squeezed the breath out of her. She started to giggle, patting him on the back.

Joan sat there beaming at them. "It couldn't go to two more beautiful people."

They both sat on the lounge, shaking their heads in disbelief.

"Well," said Joan, "I think this calls for a toast."

Robert jumped up. "I'll get it!"

He returned with a bottle of water and three glasses.

"Cheers!" they all said together, clinking their glasses.

"Here's to you, Joan" said Robert, holding up his glass. "You've just completely changed our lives. We'll never forget this."

"Never," agreed Frankie. "To you Joan. The beautiful grandmother I wish I had."

"To you two." Joan raised her glass. "May you love each other for the rest of your lives, just like Ernie and I."

"Or Cupid and Psycho!" added Frankie

They all laughed. "Cheers!"

The three of them spent the morning talking, laughing and listening to Joan's stories about the Love Shack. And as she'd promised Frankie earlier, she didn't spare any of the details. They heard all about the layout of the shack, along with saucy stories about the christening of many of the rooms, causing huge roars of laughter.

Joan was clearly in her element, her face alive with excitement as she relived all her fondly treasured memories.

"We'll take good care of the Love Shack, Joan. I promise." Frankie put her hand on Joan's. "Maybe we could even get some ducks!"

Joan laughed. "Maybe you'll get a stray one wandering in one day."

"If we do, we'll name it Joan." Robert looked at Frankie, confused. "Joan's going to come back as a duck to show me she's still around."

"You two are quackers!" joked Robert, making them laugh. "Anyway, I better get to the clinic. I'll get that paperwork organised. Frankie, are you going to ring Daniel?"

Joan looked at Frankie. "Why do you need to ring Daniel?"

"He has to sign your release form," said Robert intervening, "to give his approval for us to take you on your trip."

"Oh, what a joke. Like he gives a damn."

"Anyway, I need to talk to him about your foundation as well."

"Oh yes!" Joan's face switched from annoyed to excited in an instant. "And the fundraisers!"

"Anyway, my lovelies, I'll see you both later." He kissed them both on the cheek before leaving for the clinic.

Joan looked up Daniel's number in her little book and handed it to Frankie. "You might have better luck getting him to answer his phone. All I ever get is his damn message bank!"

Frankie suddenly felt an overwhelming sadness for Joan. Her life was about to come to an end, and her only child wouldn't be there to hold her hand, to tell her he loves her, to tell her how much she means to him. *He won't even answer her calls for fuck's sake.* Frankie's sadness quickly turned to anger.

CHAPTER TWENTY-ONE

Frankie went outside and rang Daniel's number. As expected, it rang a few times before going to voicemail.

"You've reached Dan. Please leave your name and a brief message and I'll return your call."

"Hello Daniel. My name's Frances and I'm calling from Golden Leaves. I need to speak to you regarding your mother. Can you please call me back urgently? Thanks."

That should get his attention, she thought. *He'll probably think she's finally kicked the bucket. Wanker.*

Her assumption was right. Within five minutes, her phone rang.

"Hello, this is Frances."

"Hi, this is Dan Middleton. I had a missed call from you. Something about my mother?"

"Oh Daniel, thanks so much for ringing me back," she said in a sarcastically cheery, professional tone. "The reason I'm ringing is because your mother would like to go on a short break before she moves from her Assisted Living unit into the Nursing Home part of the facility. You *are* aware she's moving soon, aren't you?"

"Ah, yeah, they told me they were going to move her, but I wasn't sure when."

"Oh good. I'm glad you know what's happening."

Dan tried to speak, but Frankie continued over top of him.

"Anyway, she's requested that two of the staff, one of them being myself, take her on a mini break to Sorrento."

"Sorrento? In It—"

"No! The one here. On the Mornington Peninsula. Apparently, she spent some time there with your father. I'm sure you know all about it?"

"Um, not really, but go on."

"Well, a couple of things. Firstly, we'll need you to sign a release form, giving your permission for the trip. But don't worry, she'll be taken good care of. She'll have a medically trained staff member with her at all times."

"Okay, and?"

Frankie, sensing his distracted indifference, was struggling to keep her composure.

"And, I need you to organise a visit from Neil Mason, your mother's favourite celebrity, as a surprise for her in Sorrento."

Daniel let out a roar of laughter. "You're joking right?"

"Oh no, Daniel, I'm definitely not joking! I'm sure you either know Neil personally, or have contacts who do. Surely it won't be too difficult for you to organise."

Daniel started laughing again. "Is this some kind of joke? Did Mum put you up to this?"

"No, it's not a joke and no, your mother did not put me up to it. She knows nothing about it, which is why it's called a surprise." Frankie could feel her temper starting to rise. "The trip will be in a week's time, the week ending the twentieth."

"So, you expect me to get Neil Mason, the famous actor, to go to Sorrento to surprise my mother, in a week's time?"

"Yes."

"Sorry, who *are* you again?"

She now had Daniel's full attention, and he was starting to get agitated. "My name's Frances. I've had the very great pleasure of spending a lot of time with your mother recently. She really is a wonderful woman. But I'm sure you already know that. You are her *son* after all. And if anyone would love to do something special for her, I'm sure it would be *you*."

"Look lady, I don't know what you're playing at, but I'd like to speak to your manager. *Now!*" Daniel's anger towards her only made Frankie more determined to crush him.

"Oh, I don't think you *would* like to do that Daniel. Not unless you want me to publish the story I've put together on you and Marcus Jenson. I *also* have friends in the business."

The line went quiet.

"It really is a fascinating story," she continued nonchalantly. "You two sure were close, weren't you? He's married with kids now, isn't he? Funny how people's tastes can change. *Anyway*, by the sound of it you two got up to some pretty naughty, not to mention *illegal*, things. I'm just surprised you got away with it. I guess your mate Roger Pratt had a bit to do with that didn't he. And maybe your other mate, oh, what was her name? Oh yes, now I remember, Betty Ford."

"What the *fuck* do you want?"

"Well Daniel, like I said, I want you to get Neil Mason to Sorrento to surprise your mum. This will be her last taste of freedom before her purgatory in nursing home hell, not that you give the slightest damn. Then…"

"How the fuck would *you* know what—"

"Shut the fuck up Daniel and *listen!*" Frankie yelled. "*Then*, I want you to start a foundation in her name, which will raise money for research into Alzheimer's. Each year you will organise a charity fundraising event with all your famous buddies where you will tell your mother's story and raise thousands of dollars for her foundation."

"You're fucking *insane!*"

"Yes, I am Daniel. Insane enough to tell the world all about you and your dirty little secrets. Unlike *you*, I have nothing to lose. I

182

know everything about you Daniel. I have it all on video. In fact, I have your mum's entire memoirs on video. I'll be sending you a copy so you can use them at your fundraising events to show the world what an amazing woman she is. So, unless you want your *very* colourful past plastered all over the media and your career to get flushed down the toilet, you'll do these things for her. Don't think I'm joking either. I couldn't be more serious."

"You're a fucking *bitch*!"

Frankie laughed. "Yeah, I probably am Daniel. But you know what? I'm not the one who threw my mum in a home without a second thought. You don't ring her, you don't visit her, you don't give a shit *full stop*! All she ever wanted was for you to be part of her life. You broke her heart!"

"Yeah, well she broke mine too!"

"Why do you think you've got where you are today? Because they made the hard choice *for* you! Are you seriously that dumb that you don't see that? Your mum wanted you home. It was your dad who stopped it. So that broke her heart too!"

Frankie took some deep breaths, desperately trying not to cry. She could tell from Daniel's breathing that he was also holding back tears.

"Look Daniel, what I'm asking for is *easy* for you. You've got the contacts and resources to do it all. Please. Just do it. For your mum. And you know what? After all this is done, you're going to look like the big hero. It'll be the best PR for you *ever*! And as much as you don't deserve it, all I care about is getting it done for *her, your mum*."

"Yeah, well it looks like you're not giving me much choice here."

"That's because if I did, you wouldn't do it. *Would* you?"

Daniel sighed. "I'll have to make some calls."

"So, it's the week ending the twentieth. Any night that week. In Sorrento. You'll need to arrange Neil's transport there and back.

It'll be black tie. I also want you to set up the Joan Middleton Foundation and send me a copy of the registration certificate so I can give it to her on the same night. And don't worry, I'll make sure she knows it was *you* who set it up."

"Is that all?" he said sarcastically.

"Let me know the date by tomorrow so I can confirm the hotel. I'll be emailing through the release form for you to sign as well. Nice talking to you Daniel."

Daniel grunted and hung up. Frankie pressed stop on the recording and breathed a deep sigh of relief. *Fuck* she thought. *I can't handle much more of this shit.*

"Well?" enquired Joan with a look of anticipation as Frankie went back inside.

"Yep, I spoke to him."

"Oh really? What did he say?"

"He said he's happy to sign the release form for you to go to Sorrento." Frankie grinned at Joan. "I also told him about the foundation, and he's really excited about it! He thinks it's a great idea and he knows lots of people who can help him organise the fundraisers!"

"Oh, Frances that's wonderful!" Joan's excitement slowly turned to a look of confusion.

"What's the matter Joan?"

"It just doesn't sound like Daniel, that's all."

"Don't worry. Once I filled him in on all the details, he's definitely convinced it's a great idea. Maybe Robert's rubbing off on me. You did say he could sell ice to the Eskimos."

Frankie went to find Robert at the clinic. She waved at him through the doors to get his attention and led him outside.

"I just spoke to Daniel."

"What happened?"

"Here, it'll be quicker to hear for yourself." She handed him the phone, pressing play.

He listened, staring at Frankie with a serious look on his face.

"Bloody hell Frankie, how did you find out about all these people?"

"Joan mentioned them when she was recording her session about Daniel. She didn't really say exactly what'd gone on, but I could tell it was pretty bad, so I just improvised a bit!" Frankie grinned at him.

"Well, you obviously guessed right, going by his reaction. So, is he *gay*?"

"Don't know. From what Joan said, it sounded more like a drug fuelled, anything goes type thing. Anyway, whatever it was, he doesn't want the world knowing about it now. Not the great Daniel Middleton, the upstanding talented choreographer!"

"Just remind me to never get on your bad side, Frankie. You're like a bloody tornado of destruction!" he grinned at her.

Frankie smiled, but she'd had enough. Enough of the lies and deceit and threats. The past two days had taken a huge toll on her. She was exhausted both mentally and physically and now she just craved some peace and quiet.

Robert put his arms around her and pulled her against him.

"Let's get away after all this is over. What do you reckon?"

She could feel Robert's comforting words awakening her emotional monster from its slumber. She desperately choked it back down.

"That sounds amazing."

"Maybe we could go to… our Love Shack! Woo hoo!" He picked Frankie up and swung her round and round in the air. "Let's celebrate tonight!"

"Deal!"

Frankie watched Robert as he walked back to the clinic. She wished they could both disappear right now, away from everyone and everything. All she wanted to do was lay in his arms and stay there forever.

Not far to go now. Just keep going, she told herself over and over as she made her way back to Unit four.

"So, let's start thinking about what you're going to take on your trip. And while we're at it, we better start putting some stuff in these boxes before Maggie finds out we've done nothing!"

They sat together as Frankie started writing a list of things to pack for the trip. The heartbreaking reality that this would be Joan's final farewell was stuffed firmly away out of mind. The time for facing that demon would come soon enough and Frankie was determined to make these final days as joyous as possible for Joan.

"What's your favourite food, Joan? I want to make sure the hotel has it on their menu."

"Ooh, let me think. You know, the night Ernie and I were there we had the most amazing seafood. Lobster, oysters, prawns, the whole bit. I remember we were so stuffed we couldn't fit another thing in!"

"I bet you managed dessert." Frankie gave Joan a wink.

"Oh yes, I think we had dessert twice that day!" They both started laughing.

"Well, I can't help you out with dessert, but the seafood I can probably manage."

"I'll save dessert for when I get back to Ernie."

Joan smiled and grabbed Frankie's hand.

"You know Frances, I'll never forget what you're doing for me."

"You realise I'm going to miss you like crazy, don't you?" Frankie hugged her, tears welling in her eyes. "And the Love Shack Joan, you've thanked us *more* than enough!"

"Maybe you can name some of Robert's wine after me."

"How about Ducky's Dessert Wine?" They both laughed, agreeing it was a perfect name.

CHAPTER TWENTY-TWO

Robert was waiting for Frankie at the car with a huge grin on his face. They chattered with excitement about their new Love Shack the whole way back to Learmonth House.

"So, pick you up about six-thirty?"

"Sounds perfect!" Frankie gave him a long passionate kiss before running up the stairs into Learmonth House.

Frankie looked for Ruth, finally finding her outside gardening.

"Frankie. Hi. How are you after your hectic day yesterday?"

"Oh Ruth, I've got so much to tell you!"

"Think we need a cuppa then!"

They went into the kitchen, closed the door and made coffee.

"So, I want to hear every detail. From the start." Ruth leaned forward in anticipation.

"It couldn't have gone better, Ruth. Everything went according to plan. I got it all on tape like I was telling you." Frankie described watching Christian suddenly slump on the ground, unable to move or speak.

"He *is* still alive, isn't he?" Ruth looked worried.

"Well, he was when I left. I'm sure he'll be fine. He's pumped that many drugs into himself, I'm sure a bit more won't hurt him."

Ruth sat there looking mortified as Frankie told her about everything she'd found in Christian's duffle bag.

"Don't worry Ruth, it's not here. I'd never put you in that position."

"But what if he finds out where you are and comes looking for you?"

"He wouldn't be game. He actually told me the name of the guy who imports all the cocaine and heroin from Colombia! There's no *way* he'd want to mess with him! He is stupid, but he's not *that* stupid!"

Ruth stood up and started to pace the floor.

"Well, I hope you're right Frankie. Should you have taken the guns though? Guns *kill* people!"

"Ruth! The amount of drugs in that bag could kill a *city* full of people!" Frankie paused, remembering her moments of terror in Christian's apartment. "To be honest I think I was on autopilot. I just grabbed it all and got out as fast as I could. I guess it's all evidence though, right?"

Ruth finally sat back down at the table.

"I have something else to tell you too Ruth!"

"Oh Frankie, I don't know if my heart can stand any more excitement in one day."

"No, you're gonna love this." Frankie squirmed in her seat with excitement. "Today Joan gave me and Robert her property up in the Dandenongs! Twenty something acres with a holiday house on it! The Love Shack!"

Ruth looked at Frankie with her mouth open. "You're kidding!"

"No! I'm not!"

"Oh, Frankie!" Ruth stood up and hugged her. "That's the best news I've heard in ages! I'm so happy for you! If alcohol was allowed here, I'd crack a bottle of champagne right now."

They both clinked their coffee mugs together. "Cheers!"

They sat talking and laughing in the kitchen for almost an hour. Ruth sat listening as Frankie recalled every sleazy detail of her terrifying encounter with Christian. She also told her about her massive fight with Robert at the train station and its fairy tale ending.

"Anyway, I'm off to celebrate with Robert tonight." Frankie paused, putting her hand over her mouth. "Oh *shit*! I haven't told you about Robert's mum yet, have I? There's just been so much going on, I forgot!" She filled Ruth in on all the terrible details.

"Oh, the poor woman. Poor Robert. When he came here, I had no idea! Please tell him how sorry I am, Frankie." Ruth wiped the tears from her face.

"I will, Ruth. I'm sure you'll see him before we leave anyway."

"So, when *are* you leaving?"

"Next week sometime."

Frankie felt a wave of sadness wash over her. The thought of leaving Ruth, of losing Joan, and then Robert's mum was going to be overwhelming.

"They've set Joan's moving date for the twenty second, so it'll have to be before that."

Frankie told Ruth about her recording sessions with Joan and her phone call with Daniel. She also told her everything she was planning for Joan's farewell in Sorrento.

"Sorrento?"

"Not Italy," laughed Frankie, "the one here."

"Frankie! How do you fit all this stuff in your head?"

"I don't know, but it's about ready to explode. I can't do this shit for much longer! Anyway, I'd better let you go. Sorry Ruth, I've chewed your ears off again. You'll need a holiday after I'm gone!"

Ruth looked sad. "Life will never be the same without you here, Frankie. You've been like a breath of fresh air around the place."

"More like a tornado of destruction, according to Robert."

She hugged Ruth and ran upstairs to get ready.

Frankie stood under the shower, the soothing rush of water helping to wash away thoughts of Christian and Daniel as she focussed only on the upcoming celebrations with Robert.

Frankie jumped down the stairs and into Robert's car, a big grin on her face.

"Let the celebrations begin!"

As soon as they got inside Robert's house, Frankie grabbed Robert's hand, dragging him over to his computer.

"Let's see if we can find it on Maps!"

He sat down at the keyboard as Frankie leant over his shoulder, wrapping her arms around him.

"Okay, let's see. Currawong Avenue. Palm Beach, Wangaratta, Gembrook. Jesus, there's a lot of them. Oh, here we go. Olinda." Robert dragged the little orange man up and down the street as they tried to find Lot Twenty-One.

"I think that's it!" said Frankie pointing. "Can you zoom in on the letterbox?" They could just make out a blurry number '21'.

"There it is!"

The image showed a big metal gate in the distance surrounded by trees, but there was no sign of the house. The whole street looked like it was in the middle of a forest, with only the occasional glimpse of houses through the trees.

"Look at all the bushland! It's amazing!" yelled Frankie with excitement.

They both sat chattering about what they imagined would be hidden behind all the trees, and how exciting it would be to finally see it. Robert talked about having their very own vineyard and what an amazing life they could have together there.

As Robert got up to go and make dinner, Frankie sat back down at the computer. Suddenly she yelled, "It's still there!"

"What is?"

"The Bella Donna Hotel. It's where Joan's chosen for her farewell. It's beautiful. Look!" Frankie scrolled through the photo gallery while Robert looked over her shoulder.

The hotel was a showcase of ornate European architecture with marble floors and high ceilings with carved archways, leading onto the outdoor dining area which was surrounded by huge stone pillars and classical Italian statues.

"Wow, that looks amazing. I can just see Joan sitting there with Neil Mason in all her finery. So… what if he can't make it?"

"Oh God, I don't know. Maybe I should send Daniel a message tonight to keep onto him. What do you reckon?"

"Yep. I've got the release form too, so you can send that to him to sign as well. His email address is on it."

Frankie scanned the document and wrote the email.

Dear Daniel, As discussed today, please find attached the Release Form for your mother's upcoming trip. Please sign it and return it asap. Please also confirm Neil Mason's available dates urgently, so I can confirm the venue. Following our conversation, I told your mother the wonderful news about the big surprise you have planned for her, and she is beside herself with excitement and anticipation. I'm sure your selfless, kind-hearted gesture of creating a charity foundation in her honour will be remembered forever by not only your mother, but many others as well, Neil Mason included. What a magnificent thing you are doing for her and the millions of other sufferers and their families who are affected by this tragic, heartbreaking disease. You are a true philanthropist. I look forward to speaking with you soon, Frances.

"What do you think?"

Robert read it and smiled, shaking his head. "That's great. Talk about reverse psychology!"

"I just hope he does it without a fight. I've had enough fights to last me a lifetime."

Frankie looked up at Robert. "Thanks for cooking dinner again. You'll make someone a great husband one day."

He stared at her with a smirk on his face. "Yes. I do, I mean I will." They both laughed.

"Okay, *send*. Now we wait." Frankie went over and sat watching Robert busily making dinner in the kitchen.

He opened the fridge and took out a bottle of Moet.

"Woah, Moet! You're spoiling me, Robert."

"You deserve it." He popped the cork and filled their glasses. "Here's to us and our new Love Shack. Here's to Joan and here's to a farewell like the world has never seen. And it'll be all thanks to you, my beautiful Frankie."

"To us. Cheers!"

They drank their champagne as Frankie told him all about her plans for Joan's final night. They also talked about Robert's mum, brainstorming ideas about surprises they could organise for her.

As they sat eating dinner, Frankie had a sudden realisation.

"Hey, why don't we also start a foundation for your mum – for cancer research." She pointed to the duffle bag poking out from under the lounge. "All that money could finally go to something worthwhile."

Robert stopped eating and stared at her. "I think that's a fantastic idea! The Barbara Turner Foundation. I love it!"

"So do I. Let's do it! I don't even know how much is in there."

Frankie went over and opened the bag, took out all the cash and counted it.

"A bit over sixty-five thousand dollars. Fifty-five after I take out what he owes me."

"Holy shit!" said Robert. "How much do you reckon all the drugs are worth?"

"Don't know, but it'd be a shitload."

She picked up one of the several bricks wrapped in tape.

"I don't even know what it is. Cocaine I'm guessing. That's what he usually sold. I reckon we should just bury it all somewhere."

"Yep. And the guns" added Robert. "What about at the shack? No-one'll ever find it there."

Suddenly Robert's laptop dinged. It was an email. From Daniel.

CHAPTER TWENTY-THREE

Frankie held her breath as she clicked on the email. Suddenly a huge smile beamed across her face as she jumped up from the computer.

"He's done it! All of it! Neil's coming! The foundation!"

Frankie started to sob, hugging Robert. "I can't believe it!"

She collapsed on the lounge and cradled her head in her hands. It felt like the weight of the entire world had been lifted from her.

Robert sat down next to her, putting his arms around her, "I'm so proud of you. Imagine how happy Joan's going to be."

Frankie wiped her eyes. It was over. Finally, the fight was over. And she'd won. A feeling of lightheaded euphoria consumed her, as though she'd suddenly been hurled into the middle of a dream.

"I'll read it to you," she said suddenly, springing to her feet and sitting back at the computer.

Frances,

Following a huge amount of inconvenience for all parties concerned, I have managed to secure a small window of availability for Neil Mason to visit Sorrento on Thursday the 18th. His plane will arrive in Melbourne at 2.45pm where a driver will meet him. His expected time of arrival at Sorrento will be around 5pm.

I will need the address of the hotel for the driver. At the conclusion of the evening Neil will be returning to Melbourne.

Most importantly, this visit is to be treated with the upmost confidentiality, which I realise may be a challenge for you. I require you to sign the attached confidentiality agreement and return it to me asap. I suggest you read it carefully.

With regards to the foundation, I have instructed my office to make the necessary arrangements to have this processed urgently, ensuring it is finalised by the 18th. I will forward a copy to you once I have received it.

I trust this concludes our dealings.

Dan.

They looked at each other and burst out laughing.

"Oh, I'm sure confidentiality will be a challenge for you!" mocked Frankie in a snobbish voice, roaring with laughter.

"My God, I can't wait to see the look on Joan's face when she sees Neil Mason standing there."

Robert pulled Frankie against him, looking into her eyes. "You are amazing, you know that?"

He kissed her long and slowly, making his way down her neck and shoulders. Carrying her to the dining table, they tore the clothing from each other and made steamy, passionate love right there on the table, sending everything crashing to the ground.

Afterwards they laid there together, naked and panting.

"I hope your table manners improve before Joan's farewell!" giggled Frankie.

Robert stood up and looked at the floor, shaking his head.

"Better clean all this shit up. See what you do to me? It's all your fault!"

Frankie smiled to herself, imagining how much she was going to relish their night in Sorrento in her sexy dress, watching Robert burn with desire for her, unable to satisfy it.

As she began to get lost in her own erotic fantasy, she looked over, watching Robert sweeping up the broken glass. "You're so fucking sexy."

Robert stopped and looked up to see Frankie standing there naked, staring at him.

"Fuck the mess!"

He threw the dustpan across the floor and picked her up, carting her off into the bedroom for another long, sensual night of lovemaking.

As the morning light entered the room, Frankie woke to Robert gently stroking her hair.

"Morning, beautiful."

Frankie's face beamed.

"It's Saturday. Yes!"

She kissed him and rolled over, resting her head on his chest. A couple of hours passed as they lay there together, talking, laughing and making love.

"You hungry?" she asked. "I can make something to eat if you like."

He looked at her. "Hmm, you're not gonna drug me, are you?"

"No need for that. I've already got what I wanted. Mind if I raid your kitchen?"

"Well, the tornado of destruction has already wrecked my bedroom and my dining room, so I guess the kitchen's next."

She laughed as she jumped out of bed, throwing on his t shirt and heading to the kitchen.

"What are you making? Need any help?"

"No. Sit down. I'm making you an omelette."

"Oh yum! I haven't had an omelette for ages."

"It's not just any old omelette either. It's got a secret ingredient."

Robert pulled the duffle bag out from under the lounge, pretending to count the drug bricks. "Is there one missing?"

"Very funny."

"So, what's the secret ingredient? I didn't even know I *had* any secret ingredients."

"I can't tell you, or I'll have to kill you."

"I don't doubt it," he grinned.

As they sat eating their omelettes, Frankie realised how dramatically her life had changed in such a short space of time. She could never have imagined in her wildest dreams the amazing things that awaited her as she boarded that first train to Ballarat, fearing only the worst. She now felt a renewed faith in life, in herself and in other people.

"This is delicious. How did you get it so fluffy?"

"It's a secret, remember?" Frankie raised her eyebrows, pointing her fork at him.

"Oh, yes sorry. Don't worry, I'll get it out of you later."

"I'll never talk! Just like Ruth. Oh, by the way, Ruth wanted me to tell you how sorry she is to hear about your mum."

"Oh thanks. She's pretty cool, old Ruthy."

"Yeah, she's the best. I'd just love to see her get out and enjoy herself for once. All she does is look after all those misfits. Not that *I* can talk. Maybe we could invite her to the shack some time?"

"Why not? The more workers the better. Bring all the other misfits as well!"

Frankie laughed to herself, imagining Pete with his whistle, ordering everyone about.

Her train of thought suddenly changed up a gear. There was a lot to do before next week. She had the whole farewell organised and she hadn't even booked the hotel yet.

"Fucking hell," she muttered.

"What is it?"

"I've just got so much I have to get organised before next week."

"Well, I can help. What do you want *me* to do?"

"I just need you to get the drugs. We couldn't use any of that could we?" She pointed to the duffle bag.

"Shit no, I know what we need. Actually, today might be a good day to do it, there shouldn't be anyone in the clinic. I'll just have to make sure all the paperwork looks legit. That's the *first* thing the auditors will look at."

"I can also see Joan and tell her when we're going." Suddenly the horrific reality of the situation flooded back. "Are you okay with all of this?"

Robert nodded.

"I wasn't before, but I am now. You realise we won't be able to go *back* there though, don't you?"

"I don't think I could go back there anyway. Not without Joan." Frankie started getting teary. "Anyway, got a notepad?"

They sat there together, Robert diligently scrawling notes as Frankie verbally emptied her head of everything she needed to do. The list was long.

Robert methodically prioritised the tasks, writing numbers next to each one.

"I'm *impressed*!" Frankie grinned at him, looking at the list. "You really are a man of many talents, aren't you?"

She kissed him on the back of his neck.

"Don't distract me, Frankie. If you start that shit, it's all over!"

Frankie giggled, kissing him long enough to start distracting him, but not long enough for him to throw the notepad across the floor.

"So, sorry sexretary, where were we up to?"

Robert groaned in frustration, leaning back in his chair. "Ring the hotel!"

"Okay, I'm going, I'm going! No need to snap!"

She looked over her shoulder, pretending to adjust her imaginary glasses as she strutted around in front of him, until they both burst out laughing.

They spent the next hour huddled around the computer. Frankie typed and made phone calls as Robert instructed her, taking notes as they went. Finally, the last task was crossed off the list except for one.

"We've *done* it! What a team!" She gave Robert a high five as he threw the pen down and carried her off to the bedroom.

"So, are you ready?" Frankie asked as they got out of the shower.

"Yeah. I'm ready. Item twenty-three. *Tick!*"

Frankie grabbed Robert's towel, lassoing him in to kiss him. "Maybe we could rob banks after this. Like Bonnie and Clyde."

"Who?"

"Bonnie and Clyde! Haven't you heard of them?" Robert shook his head. "They were outlaws. My dad used to tell me stories about them."

"Well, that explains a lot!" He grinned at Frankie. "I bet they never stole drugs and guns and blackmailed rich arsehole choreographers."

Frankie laughed. "I'm sure they would have. They were bad arse, well, according to my dad anyway."

"Your dad has a lot to answer for."

"He sure does!" Frankie paused. "Like fucking *leaving* me."

Robert kissed her hand. "Come on beautiful, let's go and get this done."

They got dressed and headed out for Golden Leaves.

CHAPTER TWENTY-FOUR

Reception was eerily quiet without Clare's melodic greeting welcoming them; replaced instead by a sign on her desk requesting visitors to ring the bell on arrival.

"I'll meet you up at Joan's unit, okay?"

"Good luck," Frankie whispered as Robert headed through the glass doors to the clinic.

There was something sexy about seeing him here without his nurse's uniform. Maybe she was just high on endorphins from their loved-up morning. Or maybe it was the high of doing something risky. Either way, she felt a surge of excitement rush through her as she made her way to Unit four.

"Eureka?" Everything was quiet. She knocked. "Eureka?" She heard Joan's muffled voice getting louder as the door swung open.

"Oh, Frances! I wasn't expecting you today!"

"Hey Joan. I know, but we decided to drop in."

She kissed Joan on the cheek.

"Robert's getting some things organised for our trip, so I thought I'd come and see you."

"That's lovely dear! Come in."

Frankie sat on the lounge.

"Good news! We've finally got the date organised. It's next Thursday the eighteenth. I've booked the hotel, and we've

organised all the paperwork, so all you have to do now is pack!"
And prepare yourself for your impending death.

Pretending to be excited, all Frankie wanted to do was scream with grief and run away as fast as her legs could carry her.

"Oh, that's wonderful news! Thank you, Frances. You've no idea how happy this makes me. I can't wait to go there. I'm sure once you see it, you'll know what I mean. It's just so beautiful."

"Yeah, I had a look on the internet. It really is amazing isn't it!"

"I just hope we're lucky enough to have another beautiful sunset."

"I'm sure we'll have a lovely night either way."

Frankie was almost bursting, having to keep Neil's visit a secret. She felt like she'd swallowed a hot air balloon.

"Oh, I have no doubt we will. What more could I ask for, spending my last night with my two favourite people?"

Frankie hugged her, trying not to cry. *No more fucking crying. Not till it's over.*

"So, how about I help you pack everything on Monday?"

"I've already started putting a few things in my suitcase. I guess I won't be needing too much. Oh, that reminds me Frances. I've been thinking, when I'm gone, you're welcome to have anything of mine that you'd like. Take it all if you want!"

"No, I don't *want* anything Joan! You've already given me so much. Given *us* so much. I don't *want* anything else."

"Well, it'll probably all just get hocked anyway!"

"Hang on, there is *one* thing. I'd love a photo of you. One of your showbiz photos."

Before she could finish her sentence, Joan was making her way into her bedroom, returning with an album on her lap.

"Here you go!" Joan held out the album.

"No Joan, I can't take the whole album! What about Daniel?"

"Oh, *bugger* Daniel! He wouldn't want it. I'd much rather you have it."

Frankie took the album and flicked through its pages again.

"Thank you. I'll take good care of it. I think a few of these'll end up on the fridge at the shack."

"Don't forget the one in the tin!"

"Oh, I've already thought about that. I'm getting that one blown up and framed. It's going on the wall."

Joan's face lit up.

Frankie knelt down in front of her. "You know we're never going to forget you, Joan. Not *ever*! And neither will anyone else. I'm going to make *sure* of it. I *promise*."

Frankie looked up to see Robert standing in the doorway.

"Oh Robert, come in dear." Joan wiped her eyes.

"How are *you,* Joan? All excited for your trip to *Italia Bella Donna*?" he said in an Italian accent, holding out her arm to kiss her hand.

Joan giggled. "Yes, I can't wait! So what time are we leaving?"

"Well, I thought we might as well go early, then we can make the most of the day."

Frankie sat on the lounge listening to Robert and Joan speak about all the things they could do in Sorrento, but all she could think about was what that day would ultimately bring. Suddenly she felt like she'd been sucked into a vortex. Her vision started going blurry and colourless, rushing at her with the sounds of a loud whirring motor vibrating in her head. The next thing she knew, Robert was sitting next to her squeezing her hand.

"Frankie. Hey. You okay? Here, have a drink." He was holding a glass of water.

She took a sip. "I'm fine."

"You sure?" Robert was staring at her.

She nodded. "So, what were you saying about Sorrento? What time are we leaving?"

Robert grinned at Joan, throwing his hands in the air. "See what I have to put up with, Joan? She never listens to a word I *say*!"

Joan was also staring at her. *What the fuck just happened? What did I miss?*

"*What!*" Frankie was starting to get annoyed by everyone staring at her.

Robert put his arm around her. "We were just talking about leaving a day early and going via the Love Shack on our way to Sorrento."

Frankie's face lit up. "The Love Shack? That's an *awesome* idea!"

She stood up, looking at Joan, then Robert, then Joan again.

"Of *course,* it's an awesome idea!" said Robert, handing her the glass of water again. "Anyway Joan, sorry to rush off, but we've got lots of things to organise. We'll see you on Monday, okay?"

"I'll see you both then. Don't forget your album, Frances."

Robert grabbed Frankie by the hand and led her out of the unit.

"Take care of her, Robert." Joan shouted.

As they slowly walked back to get in the car, he put his hand on the side of her face. "What happened beautiful?"

"I don't know. I just felt like I was in some weird *tunnel* thing."

"You looked like you'd seen a ghost. I thought you were going to pass out. Do you get migraines?"

"No. Maybe I *did* see a ghost. I just remember thinking about Sorrento, and that Joan was going to die there, and then I don't really remember anything except the tunnel."

"Come on, let's get you home."

The drive back to Robert's house was quieter than usual. Frankie sat staring out the window the entire time, not saying a word. As they walked inside, Frankie suddenly stopped and grabbed Robert's hand. "Oh, how did you go? Did you get them?"

Robert smiled, holding up the plastic bag he'd brought in from the car.

Frankie smiled, half closing her eyes. "You're a legend. I love you."

"I love you too. Come on, you're going to bed." He led her into the bedroom and pulled back the doona. "Come on, in you get." He tucked her in and kissed her forehead.

"Aren't you getting in too?"

"Not this time. Now go to sleep." He sat on the bed as Frankie closed her eyes, gently stroking her hair.

A few hours later, Frankie stumbled out into the lounge room, rubbing her eyes.

"Good morning, beautiful! How you feeling?"

She walked over to Robert and put her arms around him. "I'm good. How long have I been asleep?"

"A few hours. Are you feeling better?"

"Yeah, I feel fine. Like I've been asleep for days. What happened?"

"Not sure, but my guess would be some kind of grief response."

"What?"

"I'm just guessing. But from what you told me, it makes sense. Anyway, I'm just glad you feel better. I was getting worried."

"What, that I had a brain tumour or something?"

"No. That it might've been the omelette!"

Frankie laughed, pretending to slap him. "That's the last omelette I make *you*!"

Robert grinned "Promise?" He put his arms up to fend off more slaps. "*Sorry*! *Sorry*! I'm *joking*! Hey, do you feel like going out to dinner? We haven't really celebrated yet. Where would you like to go?"

"How about Italian? To get us in the Sorrento mood. Do you like Italian?"

"I love Italiano! It is, er, how you say, er, bellissimo!"

Robert kissed his fingers like an Italian chef, his accent making Frankie laugh.

"Would Signora prefer to ride in the Ferrari or the Lamborghini this evening?"

"Well, you know what they say about Ferraris."

"No. What's that?"

"What's the difference between a nurse and a Ferrari?"

"Not much? They're both hot and sexy?"

"No. Not everyone's had a Ferrari." Frankie laughed.

Robert gasped "Ooh, I've never been so offended!"

"So, I guess it's the Lamborghini then. Been there, done that, with the whole Ferrari thing!"

As they got ready to leave. Frankie went to the duffle bag, pulling out some cash. "It's my shout tonight, too."

They pulled in at Learmonth House.

"Why don't you come in while I get changed? You can talk to Ruth."

"Okay, I'll come in and see Ruthy!"

They walked down the hallway to find Ruth preparing food in the kitchen.

"Hi Ruth. I've brought a visitor. I'm just gonna run upstairs and get changed."

Looking through her wardrobe, Frankie wished she owned more than one dress. She pulled on her best jeans and the sexiest top she could find, tying up her hair the way Joan had taught her. She realised at that moment how much her dress sense had changed. She now *wanted* the world to see her, she *wanted* to feel feminine and sexy, and she *wanted* to be noticed. Especially by Robert.

As Frankie got back to the kitchen, she stood in the doorway watching. Sitting at the table were Robert, Ruth and Pete, all belly laughing as Robert waved his arms around, no doubt telling one of his funny stories. Pete was grinning from ear to ear with excitement. Ruth looked up and noticed her.

"Here she is! Robert was just telling us about your trip to the lolly factory."

"Oh yeah, that was funny." She looked at Pete. "That's where I got your Fantales, Pete."

Robert quickly stood up. "*What*? You gave Fantales to *Pete*? Is there something you need to tell me?"

Then he looked at Pete. "*Pete*?"

Pete grinned "*Yep*! She gave me Fantales. *Two* packets!"

"*Two* packets? Frankie! What's going on?"

Everyone was belly laughing again.

Frankie walked over and put her arm around Pete. "Sorry Robert, but I do have a bit of a soft spot for Pete." Pete let out a huge laugh.

"*Right*! Well, I'll be keeping an eye on *you* from now on! And you too Pete!" he pointed at Pete as Pete laughed, pointing back.

"Sorry for missing the comp today too, Pete." said Frankie. "Who won the Roses?"

Ruth sat back and crossed her arms with a smug look on her face as Pete pointed at her.

"You're kidding! Two weeks in a row? No way!" said Frankie.

"She cheated!" yelled Pete with his huge grin.

"Oh Pete, I did *not* cheat!" said Ruth, leaning over to slap Pete's hand. "You watched me like a hawk the whole time!"

"You've gotta watch these girls, don't you Pete?" said Robert, winking at him. "Anyway, I'm going to steal Frankie from you now. I'm taking her out to dinner."

"You look sexy," said Robert as they got into the car. "As always."

Frankie's thoughts again drifted to the dress she'd be wearing in Sorrento, and how much Robert was going to love it. *If you think I look sexy now, you just wait!*

"Good evening, sir! Do you have a booking?" asked the waiter.

"Um, no we don't." He looked at Frankie "Whoops," he whispered.

"Let me see," said the waiter as he looked around. "I should have a table available in around twenty minutes. Would that be okay?"

"Sure. We'll come back. Thanks."

They walked down the street towards the nearest pub to have a pre-dinner drink.

As they made their way along the footpath, Frankie suddenly stopped outside a shop window, staring. "Look at that!" The mannequin in the window was dressed in a sexy short red dress.

"Oh yeah, I can definitely see you in that!"

"I love it! I'll be coming back to try that on tomorrow."

They got to the pub and headed to the bar. "Got Guinness on tap mate?" asked Robert, looking around.

"No, sorry mate. We've got Toohey's Old on tap or Guinness in cans."

"I'll just have a JD and coke, please." said Frankie

"Yeah, make it two, thanks mate."

They took their drinks and found a table, quietly joking to themselves about what a shit pub it was; not to have Guinness on tap.

"Cheers," they clinked their glasses together.

CHAPTER TWENTY-FIVE

The waiter smiled at them as they walked back into the restaurant. "Please, follow me." He showed them to their candlelit table, pulling out their chairs and opening their napkins onto their lap.

"Can I get you something to drink first?"

"Feel like some wine, Frankie?"

"Sounds good."

"Got any local reds?" asked Robert "Maybe something from the Dandenongs?"

The waiter looked at the wine list and pointed one out to Robert.

"We have a lovely Yarra Valley Twelve Acres Pinot Noir, which I highly recommend."

Robert looked at Frankie as they both grinned at each other.

"Sounds perfect. We'll try that one. Thank you."

As the waiter left, Robert whispered to Frankie "Twelve Acres! Pffttt! Try twenty-two and a half!" Frankie giggled with excitement.

As they looked at their menus, the waiter returned with their bottle of wine, pouring it into Robert's glass for his approval, before topping up both their glasses.

"Do you really know what you're doing with all this wine stuff?" asked Frankie, sipping her wine.

Robert laughed. "No idea! Actually, I'm kidding. I *do* know a bit about it. I studied viticulture for a few years."

"That's right, I remember now. Before the accident."

"Yep."

"So, how do you feel about everything now?"

"What do you mean?"

"Well, about Amy."

"I'll always care about Amy. She was an amazing, beautiful girl. I really thought I'd never be happy again after I lost her." He grabbed Frankie's hand. "But then I met you."

"So, you're not comparing me to her then, like you said you were doing with other girls?"

Robert laughed. "I can't compare you to *anyone,* Frankie. You're one in a million."

"I hope that's a *good* thing."

He kissed her hand. "It's a *great* thing, Frankie. A *fantastic* thing. Look, as much as I loved Amy, I really believe that I was meant to find you."

Frankie smiled at him. "I believe that too."

They spent a wonderful night at the restaurant, laughing and chattering about their upcoming trip to the shack and Sorrento, and enjoying amazing food and good wine.

They also talked about Robert's dream of starting up his very own vineyard and how he would teach Frankie everything he knew about winemaking.

Frankie couldn't be more excited about the future than she was at that moment. It was like a dream come true.

The waiter returned. "Would you like to see the dessert menu?"

"Frankie?" asked Robert.

"I can wait till we get home," said Frankie with a straight face, looking at Robert as she rubbed his leg under the table.

Robert laughed. "Okay, we're fine thank you. If we can just get the bill." The waiter nodded and walked away.

"Keen for dessert then?"

"Ravenous," she said, as the bill arrived.

She took the wad of cash from her bag, leaving enough to cover the bill plus a very generous tip.

Robert grabbed her hand and led her out of the restaurant, thanking the waiter as they waved goodbye.

Arriving back at Robert's house, he walked over to the stereo. "What kind of music do you like, Frankie?"

Frankie walked over to look. "You've got records!"

"Yeah, I know, I'm a bit of a freak. I just love the sound of the old vinyls."

"Oh, play this one!" She held up *ACDC Back in Black*. "I grew up listening to this! My dad was a *huge* Acca Dacca fan."

"The man has good taste! That's one of my favourites."

He put it on, turning the volume up loud. They danced around the lounge room singing, making sexy gestures at each other to match the lyrics in each song. Their dancing session abruptly ended with *Let Me Put My Love Into You*, Robert no longer able to resist Frankie's seductive dance moves, carrying her off into the bedroom instead.

Afterwards, they laid there talking for hours, finally falling asleep in each other's arms.

"Guess what today is?" asked Robert as Frankie woke up the next morning, rubbing her eyes.

"I don't know, Sunday?"

"No. It's shopping day."

"Oh yes. The dress!" She looked at him. "Are you going to come with me? Most guys *hate* shopping. You realise you're not allowed in the change rooms, right?"

"Says who? That sounds like a stupid rule."

They drove into town and walked into the shop with the sexy red dress in the window.

Frankie found one in her size and disappeared into the dressing room to try it on, leaving Robert to make small talk with the shop assistant.

A few minutes later, Robert put his head around the dressing room curtain, holding a handful of other dresses. "Try these on as well. Come and show me."

Frankie paraded each dress for Robert, the assistant fussing over her.

Robert sat in a chair, just smiling at her and nodding, not saying a word. Frankie finally emerged from the dressing room with all the dresses over her arm.

"We'll take them," said Robert, pulling out his wallet.

"No," said Frankie. "Which one's your favourite?"

"All of them." He turned back to the assistant. "We'll take them thanks."

The assistant quickly started gathering them up before Frankie could change Robert's mind.

"They all look great on you, honey," said the shop assistant. "You need to show off a figure like that! Plus, they're all on sale, so it's a perfect time to buy them!"

"See?" said Robert. Frankie fought her natural impulse to argue with him and decided to let herself be spoilt for once.

The shop assistant gave them a cheery wave as they left.

"Thank you, Robert, they're beautiful!" She threw her arms around his neck, kissing him.

"*You're* beautiful!" Frankie felt like a little girl who'd just been given her first party dress.

"Lingerie next?"

She grinned. "Okay, but *you're* not paying for it."

"Don't argue with me or I'll put you over my knee!" Frankie kept smiling. This was the most fun she'd had shopping *ever*.

As she tried on some sexy lingerie, Frankie chuckled to herself, listening to Robert chatting to the shop assistant. He showed absolutely no sign of embarrassment being in a shop where most men would fear to tread, occasionally poking his head into the change room to give his enthusiastic approval. Once again, after emerging from the change room with her selection, Robert insisted on paying for it.

"I think it's about time we buy *you* a present!" She said as they meandered through the shopping centre.

He held up the shopping bags. "*This* is my present!" He said grinning.

They stopped at one of the cafés for lunch. Frankie leaned over to kiss him. "Thank you for spoiling me today. I feel like a princess."

"Well, now you'll look like one as well."

As Frankie spotted the nearby sports store, she thought about Pete, and Robert's banter with him and Ruth in the kitchen.

"I want to buy Ruth and Pete a present before we go."

"We're not buying Ruth lingerie. Or Pete."

Frankie laughed. "Let's look in the sports store. I'm sure we'll find Pete something in there."

As they browsed through the store, Frankie spotted the whistles. "This is what he needs!" She chose the biggest, shiniest whistle she could find before heading to the counter to pay for it. She also bought a five-hundred-dollar store gift voucher.

"You really *do* have a soft spot for Pete, don't you?"

She laughed. "They need new stuff at Learmonth House. All their sports equipment is old and crappy. I can just see it now; Pete loose in the sports store with a five-hundred-dollar voucher. He won't come out for days!"

"Maybe we should go back in and warn the guy. Imagine the questions!" They both laughed.

"At least *I* won't be here to get an earbashing about it. Poor Ruth. Speaking of Ruth, I know what I want for her."

They stopped at several jewellers to find the perfect gift for Ruth. As she was about to give up for the day, Frankie spotted it.

"Look!" she said to Robert, dragging him over to the window. There on display was a beautiful gold pair of angel wings with a diamond set in the middle. "That's it!" She jumped up and down with excitement, before dragging Robert inside.

She chose a long, delicate chain to go with the angel wings, holding it up against herself for Robert's opinion. Walking out of the shop, Frankie felt elated.

"Just one more stop at the engraver." Frankie had Pete's name engraved on the whistle in large capital letters.

As they made their way back towards the car, Frankie stopped. "Hang on, I just need to run in for a sec," and off she raced, into the supermarket, returning a short time later with a bag.

After getting back to Robert's house, they spent the afternoon relaxing together, talking, listening to music and drinking wine. Frankie emptied all her shopping bags, excitedly admiring all her new clothes and the presents she'd bought.

"I forgot to give you this." She handed the supermarket bag to Robert.

He laughed as he looked inside, finding it filled with bags of Fantales. "I'm going straight over to tell Pete about this!"

They laid on the lounge watching movies that night, eating Fantales and quizzing each other on Movie Star Trivia from the wrappers.

Frankie suddenly sat up. "Hey! Who am I? Born in Scotland in 1947, I moved to Australia with my family at age 7. My acting roles include the characters Stuart McAlister in 'Pianoland', Dr Grant Alanson in 'Dinosaur World', and Major Campbell Cheswick in 'The Birmingham Boys'. I currently own and run a winery in Australia called Double Trouble. My birth name is Glen, but I am known by another name. Who am I?"

Frankie looked at him, hardly able to contain her excitement.

Robert frowned. "I've seen some of them. Who was the character in the Birmingham Boys again?"

"Major Campbell Cheswick. He was the policeman in charge who was out to get them. Remember?" She kept staring at him.

"Hang on, wasn't that…"

"Yes! Neil Mason!" she squealed.

"You're kidding me!" Robert's face lit up. "And he owns a winery! I'll be able to pick his brain about it!"

Frankie laughed. "I can just see it now. You and Joan'll be fighting over him. I'll just have to find something to distract you."

Frankie disappeared into the bedroom and put on her new black lingerie and sexy red dress.

"How about this?" she said as she strutted back out, dragging a chair over in front of Robert and straddling it, before launching into a raunchy striptease.

Frankie realised that she would never have *dreamt* of doing anything like that until now. She would have been far too awkward and self-conscious. But she had no inhibitions with Robert. She felt safe. She wanted to show him everything. And she wanted to *give* him everything.

CHAPTER TWENTY-SIX

"Sure you don't want me to wait for you?"

"No, I really feel like a walk, plus I want to chat to Ruth for a bit. I'll see you over there."

Frankie ran inside to find Ruth.

"Hey Ruth, got time for a cuppa?"

"Hi Frankie. Sure, how was your night?"

Frankie poured them both a coffee and sat at the kitchen table. She told Ruth all about their night and about all the beautiful new clothes Robert had bought for her. She even told her how she'd given Robert a private viewing of her new dress and lingerie.

"My God, all that seems like such a distant memory to me."

"Well, maybe we need to find you a man Ruth!"

"Oh no, that's the *last* thing I need. I've got enough people to worry about here without having a *man* to take care of as well!"

"No, I was thinking more of a man who could take care of *you*."

"And where will I find one of those?"

"I don't know. They just seem to pop up when you least expect it."

"Yes, well the only thing popping up in *my* life is my toaster!" They both laughed.

Frankie sat in silence for a while, preparing herself for what she was about to tell Ruth next.

"We've got the date sorted for Joan's farewell. It's going to be this Thursday, the eighteenth, but we'll be leaving on Wednesday. We're gonna go via the shack on our way, and…" Frankie paused, playing with her coffee cup. "I probably won't be back, Ruth."

"Oh," Ruth's smile vanished. "What, *ever*?"

"Oh, I'm sure I'll come back to visit you, but I won't be back to stay. We're going to see Robert's mum after Sorrento. He wants to spend as much time as he can with her."

"Of *course* he does!" she tried to smile.

Frankie put her hand on Ruth's. "I'll really *miss* you, Ruth. I'll miss everyone, but *you* most of all."

Ruth quickly wiped her eyes. "I'm so happy for you Frankie, I really am. Everything's worked out so well for you, and you deserve every little bit of it. You're a wonderful friend and…" Ruth started to cry. "I'm going to miss you so much!"

Frankie hugged her as they both cried. "I want you to come and visit us at the shack, Ruth. Promise me you'll come?"

"Of course, I'll come!" Ruth laughed through her tears.

"Okay, well, I guess I better get to work."

She kissed Ruth on the cheek before going upstairs to get changed.

As she walked to Golden Leaves, Frankie felt a huge sadness building inside her. She was dreading having to say goodbye to Ruth, Pete and all the others. And saying goodbye to Joan was going to be horrendous on a whole other level. She'd grown to love her like a grandmother.

But she'd also found Robert, who had brought her so much love, happiness, fulfilment, confidence and hope for the future; everything she'd been missing in her life. It was like a double-edged sword. But even with all the sorrow she was about to encounter, she was certain, down to her very soul that the path she was on was the right one. She'd never been so sure about anything in her whole life.

Robert had breathed life back into her. She finally felt alive, as if she'd been woken from a long sleep, like a bear coming out of hibernation, finally seeing the sun after months of darkness. And in Joan's words, she was going to grab it with both hands and never let go. No matter what.

As she walked into reception, once again greeted by Clare's tenacious positivity, she saw her in a whole new light. She'd judged Clare harshly from the moment she met her, but now she realised the world needed Clares; the more the merrier. What a sad thing it would be to be greeted each morning by a moaning, miserable, whinging grouch, instead of a bright, smiling, breath of fresh air such as Clare.

"Hi Clare. Nice to see you. How was your weekend?"

And for the first time, Frankie took the time to really listen to what Clare had to say, finally feeling a kinship with her and a shared belief that the world really is an exciting, wonderful place to be.

"Have a great day, Clare."

Frankie waved as she left reception, feeling a bond with her for the first time. She could tell Clare sensed it too, as she became even more animated and chirpy than usual, obviously enjoying their conversation.

What a fucking amazing feeling this is thought Frankie as she went to find Robert. He was sitting in the dining room, talking with Maggie. As he looked up at her and gave her a quick smile, she could tell they were in the middle of an important conversation, so she blew him a kiss before making her way to Unit four.

"Eureka!"

The door quickly opened. "I found it!!" Joan's face was beaming. "Come in, Frances!"

"Morning Joan. You look happy!"

"I am dear. I'm so excited for our trip. I've got everything packed. I can't wait!"

Joan paused and held Frankie's hand. "Anyway, how are *you* today, Frances? You didn't look well on Saturday."

Frankie smiled "Oh, I'm fine. I just had a migraine coming on, that's all, but I'm okay now."

"Oh no, they're nasty damn things. Ernie used to suffer with them. Not often, but when he did, he'd be in bed for three days."

"Are you sure that wasn't because of you?"

Joan giggled. "Oh, I wish, but I couldn't go near him. He couldn't stand light or noise or movement, he just had to lay there in the dark with a bucket beside him. Poor thing. It was horrible."

"Sounds horrendous." Frankie changed the subject. "So, show me this packing you've done."

Joan led her into the bedroom. Her suitcase was open on the chair, full to the brim.

"Wow, you *have* been busy! How long are you going for again?" Frankie instantly wished she could take her comment back.

Joan laughed, obviously not bothered by it. "I've packed some things that you can take with you afterwards as well."

"Joan, I told you, I—"

"Nonsense, Frances! Don't worry, it's not everything. It's just a few things that I'd like you to have. I was going to leave them here for you, but then I realised you probably won't be back here, will you." Joan looked at her.

Frankie could feel a lump building in her throat, which she quickly swallowed back down.

"No, we won't."

"Sit down, dear." Joan patted the bed. "I've been thinking a lot over the weekend about you and Robert and I realise I've put you both in a terrible position. Everyone here obviously thinks I'll be coming back, so once they find out I've gone, no doubt they'll want to haul you both over the coals and give you the third degree, so I've written some letters which will hopefully explain everything."

Frankie opened the letter Joan handed her.

Dear Maggie

By the time you read this, I will be gone. I will finally be reunited with my one true love, free from the burden of living with this hideous disease.

Please do not look to punish anyone for my passing, as you would be punishing an act of kindness far greater than most of us will ever be lucky enough to witness during our whole lifetime.

As you know, I have been begging the doctors to help me end this suffering without success. I choose to leave this life on my own terms, not on terms dictated by someone else. Surely that is my right as a human being.

I am truly blessed that I have finally found someone brave enough and loving enough to help me, whilst risking their own lives in the process. They deserve only praise and admiration, not punishment or retribution.

I have finally found peace, and I wish you the same.

Joan Middleton

Frankie gently folded the letter back up, tears running down her face as Joan rubbed her arm.

"That's beautiful, Joan."

"And this one's for Daniel." She unfolded the second letter, handing it to Frankie.

Dear Daniel

I'm about to leave for my trip to Sorrento. I won't be coming back. For a long time now, I've been asking the doctors to help me end my life, to save me from the humiliation and torture of spending my final days locked in a nursing home, waiting to die from this hideous disease. I don't want my life to end that way. I want it to end on my terms, while I can still think for myself and make my own decisions.

Frances and Robert have given me the greatest gift I could ever ask for. They have put their lives on the line for me, when everyone else has let me down.

Please do not tarnish my memory by trying to harm or punish them in any way. They have been my only ray of hope in this whole wretched situation, and I will be forever in their debt.

I'm so sorry that we've been distant from each other for many years. It's not the way I wanted it to be, but I've also realised it was the price I needed to pay for you to make a good life for yourself, which you've done, on your own. I'm very proud of you for having the strength to turn your life around.

I also want you to know that I have never stopped loving you, from the moment you were born, and I held you in my arms. You will always be my precious son. Please always choose love and kindness in all that you do.

Until I see you again, I love you, Daniel.

Mum

Frankie wiped the tears from her face.

"It's okay dear. Please don't be sad. I want you to be happy like me. And I *am* happy. Thanks to you."

"I just can't bear the thought of losing you, Joan."

"Come on, let's get some bread and go to the lake," said Joan.

Frankie wiped away her tears and decided that she was going to try and make Joan's remaining few days as much fun as possible.

As they sat by the lake feeding Joan's hungry friends, she noticed one of them chasing the others around, pulling on their tailfeathers.

"Look at that one!" laughed Frankie "That'll be *you* for sure."

"That's Sigourney. Always bossing the others around. I'll be like Daisy over there. Always preening her feathers."

They both laughed as Joan pointed out all her favourites.

Joan kept saying how excited she was to be going back to the Love Shack and show them both around the area. Frankie looked up to see Robert walking down the path towards them.

"Hi beautiful ladies. Feeding time? Sorry to interrupt, but I've just been talking to Maggie."

He told them that he'd asked for some time off to be with his mum, and he wanted Frankie to go with him.

"What I *didn't* tell her, obviously, was that once we leave on Wednesday, we won't be back at all."

"*None* of us," said Joan. "And as I said to Frances, I realise what a terrible position I've put you both in, and I'm so sorry."

Robert patted Joan's hand. "It's all good Joan. I'm sure we'll work it out."

"Who's hungry? It must be lunch time by now." said Joan

"Me!" yelled Robert, throwing up his hand like a kid in a classroom. He grabbed hold of Joan's wheelchair, zooming her back up the path, swerving from side to side, making her squeal and roar with laughter. Frankie watched as they sped off, feeling like her heart would burst with happiness. She loved Robert more than anyone or anything in the whole world, followed closely by Joan. She just wished she could stop time and soak in this moment forever.

Back at the unit Joan was still giggling from her thrill ride.

"I'll make lunch if you like, Joan? You can show Robert the letters you wrote."

"Okay, thank you dear." She went into the bedroom, returning with the letters and handing them to Robert.

Frankie watched from the kitchen as Robert sat on the lounge reading, not saying a word. As he handed them back, Frankie could see tears in his eyes.

"They're beautiful words Joan. Thanks for writing them. It really means a lot."

Frankie came out with sandwiches and tried to lighten the mood. "You should see how much stuff Joan's packed!"

"You girls are all the same. Did Frankie tell you about the mountain of clothes she bought yesterday? I tried to talk her out of getting them all, but she insisted!"

"Oh! Bullshit! You!" Robert burst out laughing.

"And *then*," he continued, "she insisted on trying them on again when we got home, and I had to sit there pretending to look interested while she paraded around in them!" He was rolling around on the lounge in laughter as Frankie attacked him.

Joan sat there giggling as she watched them wrestle on the lounge. "Oh, I'm going to miss this." She laughed. "You two have so much happiness ahead of you."

"Are you sure about that?" said Frankie, giving Robert a final slap.

As they sat eating their lunch, talking, joking and laughing together, Frankie made a mental note to remember this day forever.

CHAPTER TWENTY-SEVEN

"So do you reckon Joan's letter to Maggie will do any good, or just help get us thrown in jail?" asked Frankie as they drove out of Golden Leaves.

"Not sure, but I've been thinking. We probably won't even *need* the letters."

"Why's that?"

"Well, because the only reason they'd do an autopsy to find the cause of death would be if they thought it was suspicious, or unexpected. And because of Joan's age, and her Alzheimer's, I seriously doubt that they're going to think it's suspicious. Especially considering there's scans which show her brain lesions are growing so quickly. I reckon I could give them enough medical background information to keep them happy."

Frankie stared at him wide-eyed. "So, *you're* telling *me* that we could've gotten away with it *all along?*"

He looked over at her. "I don't know, Frankie. I guess I just never thought past the whole killing her thing!"

Frankie started yelling. "You're fucking *kidding* me, Robert! So, you've known this shit all along, but you didn't think to fucking *tell* me? Before I went and stole everything from a fucking *drug dealer? Fuck me!*"

"I didn't *know* you were gonna do that!"

"I *told* you I had a plan to keep us out of jail. But you obviously already knew about one all *along*! *Fuck*! I can't *believe* this! *Stop the car!*"

"Frankie, calm down."

"*Stop* the fucking *car,* Robert!"

He slowly pulled over as Frankie got out and slammed the door, storming off into the distance, throwing her arms around and yelling to herself.

Arriving back at Learmonth House, she marched through the door and upstairs to her room, slamming the door and throwing herself down on the bed. *What the fuck is wrong with him? What has he been thinking all this time? Is he living in fucking Fairyland?* She punched her pillow over and over until eventually her anger subsided. She laid there exhausted. She couldn't believe that everything she'd put herself through with Christian had all been unnecessary.

She heard a gentle knock on her door.

"Frankie? Can I come in?"

She got up and opened the door. "Hi Ruth. Sure, come in. Sit down."

"Is everything okay?"

"Sorry about slamming the door. It's just… fucking *men*!"

Ruth giggled, then quickly stopped, looking serious again. "What's he done?"

"Oh, *nothing*, just that he's known all along that we'd probably be able to get away with Joan's death," she said sarcastically. "without me having to risk my fucking *life* with Christian!"

"Oh," said Ruth

"I just can't *believe* it, Ruth! I mean, he's a fucking *nurse*! He knows all *about* this stuff. *I* don't!"

"To be fair, he didn't know about the whole Christian thing."

"Yeah, yeah, that's what *he* said. But still, *fuck*! He could've at least *thought* about it. I did tell him I was *planning* something!"

"I'm sure he didn't think it was going to be anything dangerous like it was. Surely Frankie. Otherwise, he wouldn't have let you do it."

Frankie sighed. "Yeah, I know. He wouldn't have. He's already told me that. I just wonder what's been going on in his head all this time! It's like it's only all just dawned on him today!"

"Maybe it has. He is a *man* after all. They're not the *brightest* of creatures." Ruth laughed.

"I can see why *you* don't want one now."

Ruth patted her hand. "I'm sure you don't mean that, Frankie. Robert's a lovely guy. He's probably just not thinking straight, especially with everything that's going on with his mum."

Frankie stopped, holding her hand over her mouth. "Oh fuck Ruth, you're right. You're absolutely *right*. I'm such a bitch, aren't I? Of *course* his mum would be all he can think about."

She quickly jumped up. "I need to go and see him."

Frankie hugged her. "Thanks Ruth. I have no idea what I'm gonna do without you!"

And with that, she raced out of the room.

On the way to Robert's house, Frankie realised that she'd been so caught up with worrying about Joan that she hadn't fully understood how utterly distressed Robert must be, knowing that he's about to lose his precious mum. And she could tell by the way he spoke about her that he was the closest to her out of all his brothers. She flashed back to how painful it was to lose her own mum and tears started running down her face. She walked faster and faster. She needed to tell him how sorry she was.

As she finally got to his street, she sprinted the last hundred metres to his house and knocked on the door, trying to catch her breath. Robert opened the door, his eyes red and puffy.

"I'm sorry, Robert." she gasped, throwing her arms around him. "I'm so sorry."

"What are *you* sorry for? I'm the one who should be sorry."

"I've just been so caught up with my own shit, I haven't even thought about how you must be feeling. I'm such a bitch."

"No, you're not. I'm just fucking stupid sometimes."

They hugged and kissed each other before going inside.

"I'm so sorry I yelled at you. I'm such a fucking hothead and I need to stop it."

"Cranky Frankie," he laughed. "Don't change Frankie. I love you just the way you are."

"Yeah, well let's see if you still think that a few years from now."

"Okay, how about sixty?"

"It's a deal." She wrapped her arms around him.

"Feel like a Guinness? I've already had two."

She laughed. "I'd love one please."

Robert poured them a pint each as Frankie watched.

"I thought I might've blown it with you today." His eyes welled up. "I can understand it though, after everything you've put yourself through."

"But that's just it. Everything *I've* put myself through. You would've never let me do it. It's not *your* fault. It's *mine*!"

"Well, all I know is that I never want to lose you Frankie."

"You *won't*. You're the best thing that's ever happened to me, Robert. *Ever*."

As they sat on the lounge cuddling each other, Robert's phone rang, interrupting them.

"They can wait," he said, before glancing at his phone, noticing the number.

"It's Maggie. What the fuck does *she* want? Sorry, better get it."

He picked it up and answered.

"Hey, Maggie." Frankie watched on as Robert sat listening to Maggie. "Yep, she is actually." Robert winked at her. "I'll put her on."

"Hi Maggie…"

"Hi Frankie. Sorry to disturb you, but I've just had a call from your lawyer in Melbourne, Jackie Hooper, and she wants you to ring her. She said it's urgent. She left her number; do you need to write it down?"

It took Frankie a moment to realise who Maggie was talking about.

"Oh, okay, hang on." Frankie grabbed her wallet and searched through her cards, eventually finding the one given to her by the lawyer on banishment day. "Okay, ready."

As Maggie read out the number, Frankie checked it against the number on the card. "Okay, thanks Maggie, I'll give her a call."

"What was that all about?" asked Robert

"Dunno." Frankie took out her phone, switched it back on and rang the number.

"Jackie Hooper."

"Oh, hi Jackie. It's Frankie. Frankie Hadfield."

"Oh, hi Frankie. Sorry to ring your workplace, but I couldn't find your mobile number anywhere. Look, I just wanted to let you know that Christian Bakker's lawyer has been asking questions about where you are. He rang me this afternoon trying to get information, but wouldn't tell me why. Of course, I told him that it's confidential and to basically bugger off, but I just thought I'd better let you know. After what they've already put you through, I just wanted to give you the heads up."

"So, he can't *find* me, can he?"

Jackie laughed. "Officially, no. Realistically, probably. His lawyer's as crooked as they come, like Christian no doubt, so I just wanted you to be aware. And if they *do* try to contact you or harass you in any way, let me know straight away and I can start legal proceedings against them. You just need to say the word."

"Okay. Well, thanks for letting me know."

"No worries, Frankie. Take care. Give me a call if you need anything."

Frankie hung up the phone, the colour draining from her face.

"What's going on?" asked Robert.

Frankie sat staring.

"What *is* it? What's *wrong*? *Frankie*!"

She eventually looked at him. "Christian's looking for me. His lawyer's trying to find out where I am."

Robert jumped up and started pacing the floor, rubbing his face. Finally, he sat back down next to Frankie.

"Tell me where he lives."

"*No,* Robert! I'll just go to the police, like I planned."

"Tell me where he lives!" His voice was getting louder.

"*No!*" Frankie jumped up and started pacing.

Robert grabbed her by the arms, shaking her, his eyes wide with anger. "*Tell me where he lives!*"

He sat Frankie forcefully down on the lounge and grabbed a notepad and pen, dropping it in her lap. "*Write down his address. And his full name. Now*!"

Robert was scaring her. She'd never seen him so angry. His eyes were dilated and full of rage. As she started scribbling, Robert stormed out to the verandah and called someone.

"Hey mate, sorry for the short notice, but I really need to call in a favour. It's urgent."

"Now."

"Okay, see you in ten."

Robert strode back inside, ripped out the duffle bag from under the lounge and took out the two guns. He snatched the notebook from Frankie, crouching down in front of her.

"Stay *here,* okay? You need to *promise* me you'll stay here until I get back. *Okay*?"

"Okay! No need to yell!" snapped Frankie, pretending to be unafraid of Robert's temper.

"*Promise!*"

"I promise!"

Frankie was trembling as Robert rushed out the door and drove off, screeching his wheels in a shower of gravel.

For several minutes she sat there shellshocked, hoping she was about to wake up from some crazy nightmare. She paced around the house in a blur. Round and round and round, just like the thoughts in her head. *What the fuck just happened? What was he going to do? Was he going to kill Christian? Who the fuck was he talking to?* Melbourne was an hour and a half away, so he'd be gone for at least three hours. *What if he doesn't come back? Should I ring the police? Or maybe the lawyer? What the fuck should I do?*

Frankie was frantic. Robert had just morphed into some kind of angry monster in front of her very eyes, just like Jekyll and Hyde, and it scared the shit out of her. She had no idea what to expect next, or what she should do next. Everything was out of control. She needed to talk to someone to try and make some kind of sense of this. There was only one choice.

"Frankie! This is a nice surprise. How did it go with Robert?"

"Ruth, I have no idea what the fuck is going on! Robert's gone to Melbourne with the guns!" She started to sob.

"Frankie! Calm down. Take some deep breaths. Breathe. Breathe. It's okay, Frankie. Just tell me slowly. From the start. What happened?"

"Well," Frankie snuffled between gasps, "I had a call from my lawyer in Melbourne and she said that Christian's lawyer is trying to find out where I am."

"Okay, but they can't, can they?"

"The lawyer reckons they probably can! Anyway, Robert just went into this fucking mad rage and grabbed the guns and made me give him Christian's address, and I'm so scared, I don't know what to do!" Frankie started to sob again.

"Okay Frankie, do you want me to come and get you?"

"No. He made me promise to stay here. Oh, fuck Ruth, what if they find out I'm staying there? What have I done?"

"Just breathe, Frankie. It's okay. Everything will be alright."

Ruth spent several minutes talking gently to Frankie, trying to calm her down.

Frankie snuffled. "Robert was talking to someone before he left. I don't even know who it was, but they've got the guns, so who knows what's gonna happen."

"I think the most important thing at the moment is to try and settle yourself, Frankie. Remember, Robert's not an idiot."

"I hope you're right, Ruth."

"Look Frankie, there's nothing you can do at the moment, so worrying isn't going to help anything. I'm sure he'll be okay. It's a long drive to Melbourne so I'm sure by the time he gets there he would've settled down and had time to think about it. And it's probably a *good* thing that he's got someone with him."

Frankie paused, taking a deep breath. "How did you get so wise, Ruth?" she said, blowing her nose.

"By getting old!" laughed Ruth. "Now why don't you go and try to distract yourself for a while; run yourself a hot bath, put on some music and try to relax a bit. I'm sure he'll be fine Frankie."

"Yep. I think I will. Thanks Ruth. I'm sorry. You always end up being my sounding board. I've put you through so much."

"No, you haven't, Frankie. Look, I'm sure everything will be okay. Now go and enjoy your bath. I'll message you later. Let me know if you hear anything and ring me if you need to talk."

"Thanks Ruth. You're such an awesome friend."

"I'll talk to you soon."

Frankie rang Robert's phone, which went straight to voicemail, so she sent him a message.

"Please be careful and don't do anything stupid. If anything happens to you, I'll NEVER forgive you. Come home safe. I love you xxx"

She then took Ruth's advice, running herself a hot bath. All she wanted to do was run out the front door and keep running as far and as fast as her legs would carry her, but she'd promised Robert she'd wait there for him. She poured herself a large glass of wine, sculled it and poured another, before getting into the bath, sitting her phone beside her.

She laid back in the bath, dunking her head under the water.

CHAPTER TWENTY-EIGHT

Frankie's heart skipped a beat as her phone pinged. It then sank again as she saw the message was from Ruth.

"How was the bath? Are you going ok?"

"Onto my second bottle of wine which is helping. Been trying to ring him but it's switched off."

"I'm sure he'll be back soon. Ring me if you need to talk XX"

Frankie paced the entire house, lap after lap after lap. She looked at all the photos of Robert's family for the tenth time and looked through his entire record collection, doing anything she could think of to try and distract herself.

She looked at the time again. *Where the fuck is he? Why hasn't he answered any of my messages? It's almost fucking eleven!* She swigged down her wine before refilling her glass with the remains of the second bottle. Again, she calculated the amount of time he'd been away, which was five minutes more than the last time she checked. He'd been gone for three hours and thirty-seven minutes. *Come on, Robert. Where the fuck are you? Get your arse home!*

She sent him another message.

"Are you ok? ANSWER ME!"

Frankie threw herself down on the lounge, held a cushion over her face and screamed, punching and kicking the lounge over and over, until she felt exhausted.

After laying there for what seemed like an eternity, her phone pinged.

"On my way back."

Frankie screamed again. *Finally! Thank fucking God! He's alive!* She hugged the cushion and rocked back and forth, sobbing tears of joy.

She quickly sent a message to Ruth.

"He's on his way back"

"That's great news!"

Feeling like she was going to burst with excitement, Frankie jumped around the lounge room, fist pumping the air. She put on *Back in Black*, turned it up loud and headbanged her way through the entire first side.

Finally, she heard Robert's car pull up outside and raced to open the front door. She ran down the steps and jumped into his arms, nearly knocking him over.

"Thank God you're back!" she yelled, hugging him and kissing him over and over. "You scared me to death, you bastard! I was out of my *mind*!"

"Well, I'm back, so you can stop worrying." They made their way inside. "You can also stop worrying about that fucking Christian. He won't be bothering you again."

Frankie stopped, letting go of Robert and looking at him.

"What did you do to him?"

"Let's just say we convinced him not to come looking for you."

She frowned. "You didn't *kill* him, did you?"

Robert shook his head. "No, but if he ever comes near you, I fucking *will*!"

"Who's *we*?" she stared at him.

"It doesn't matter, Frankie. I'm going for a shower."

"Can I join you?" Frankie followed Robert into the bathroom.

"So, living it up in the jacuzzi while I've been away?" he said, pointing at the bubbles left around the bath.

"Yep. And I've also been into your wine, sorry. Not sorry."

"I *thought* I could smell my Twenty-Two on you."

He pulled her against him and kissed her. "Mm, nice vintage that one."

She pulled up Robert's shirt to take it off, noticing several grazes on his chest. "*Fuck* Robert, what *happened* to you?"

"What," he said, looking down. "I dunno. You tell me. You *were* pretty wild the other night!"

"*Stop* it! Tell me what *happened*! I need to *know*!"

Robert grabbed her by the shoulders and looked her in the eye.

"No, you *don't* Frankie. Please, just *leave* it, okay? Trust me. All you need to know is that you're safe. That's all that matters."

Frankie started to sulk as they got under the shower, Robert wincing as the hot water hit his chest.

She shook her head, grumbling at him in frustration. She slowly and gently washed every inch of Robert's body, carefully scanning for injuries as she went.

As they laid quietly in bed that night, Frankie asked, "So are you *ever* gonna tell me what happened?"

Robert put his finger up to her lips. "Shhh, Frankie. Go to sleep."

She rested her head on his shoulder. There was no way she could sleep. A million things were running through her mind. A million questions with no answers. She laid there listening to the sound of Robert's breathing. He was already asleep. *What the fuck happened to him tonight?* Scenario after scenario played out in her mind for hours until she finally drifted off to sleep, mentally exhausted.

As the sun streamed into the bedroom Frankie opened her eyes. Robert wasn't lying next to her, so she threw on a t-shirt and wandered out into the kitchen to find him making breakfast.

"Sleeping Beauty's awake. Are you hungry?"

"Not really," she said, rubbing her head. "I think I had too much wine last night. How long have you been up?"

He looked at the time. "One hour and seventeen minutes precisely! I didn't want to wake you. You were thrashing around last night. Talking in your sleep, the whole bit."

"Really? What was I saying?"

"I couldn't make it out, but you were yelling at *someone. Me* probably!"

"Yeah, probably. I was probably yelling '*where the fuck are you!*'. I must've said that to myself about a thousand times last night."

He handed her a cup of coffee and gave her a kiss. "I'm sorry I put you through that last night. I probably freaked you out."

"Yeah, actually you did. I've never seen you like that before."

"I know. Not many people have, thank God. I'm not proud of it, but if anyone threatens someone I love, then lookout. I can't help it, Frankie. I just see fucking *red.*"

"Yeah, I noticed that. And I thought *I* was a hothead!"

"Oh, you are," he grinned, "I just save all mine up for one big explosion."

"Oh God, I hope no-one pisses us both off at the same time!"

Robert laughed. "They'll be *dead* if they do!"

He put his arm around Frankie. "So, you ready for our big adventure tomorrow?"

Frankie nodded. After the trauma she'd gone through the night before, all she wanted to do was get the hell away from Ballarat. God knows what was going on in Robert's head, and whether he would ever tell her what went on with Christian or who his mystery accomplice was.

"I'm not looking forward to saying goodbye to Ruth and the others though. You know, if I didn't have Ruth to talk to, I would have gone insane last night."

Robert stopped and stared at her. "So, what did you *tell* her?"

"Everything. Well, as much as I knew. Which obviously *isn't* everything!"

"Well, she probably thinks I'm a fucking psychopath now."

"Well, *are* you?" Frankie raised her eyebrows at him. "She already *knows* I'm one, so what's the difference? Anyway, you don't need to worry about Ruth. She's cool."

Their drive to Golden Leaves was much quieter than normal, Frankie still shell-shocked from the night before. "This feels so weird," she said softly as they pulled into the car park.

Robert grabbed her hands. "Look Frankie, I *will* tell you everything, but after all this is over, okay? I just want you to focus on your time with Joan for now. Just trust me, okay? Everything's going to be fine." He leant over and kissed her. "I love you, Frankie. Remember that."

Frankie sighed. "I love you too."

She jumped out of the car and walked into reception, greeting Clare with a smile and a wave before heading straight to Unit four.

Approaching Joan's open door, Frankie could hear music coming from inside. She knocked and went in to find Joan singing to the music and packing things into boxes.

"Eureka!" shouted Frankie.

"I found it!" beamed Joan.

Frankie gave her a big hug. "You've been busy!"

"I haven't stopped Frances. I'm just so excited, I had to do something before I went mad!"

"Yes, I know what you mean," said Frankie, recalling her previous night of terror. "So, we'll pick you up about eight in the morning, okay? Then we can be up in the Dandenongs before lunch."

"Oh, there's a wonderful place up there to have lunch. Ernie and I used to go there all the time."

"We can do whatever you like Joan! This whole trip is all about *you*!"

Joan giggled with excitement. "I can't wait to see the place again. Oh, I found a couple more photos last night. Here."

She took an old yellow photo envelope from the bench, handing it to Frankie.

Frankie slowly looked at them. "Is this at the shack?"

"Yes dear. Isn't it beautiful?"

Frankie sat there gobsmacked. It truly *was* beautiful. It looked like a rainforest. Joan was standing next to a creek, surrounded by huge gum trees and big bushy tree ferns. The other photo showed Ernie dressed only in shorts, standing in front of the shack holding a shovel.

"Ernie had just planted our tree in that one. See?" Joan pointed to the small plant next to him. "It's a crepe myrtle. The symbol of love, peace and good fortune. It was the sacred tree of Aphrodite, the Greek Goddess of Love."

"Trust *you* to choose that!" Frankie laughed. "My God, Ernie really *was* a good sort wasn't he. Look at that body!"

"Yes, he was. I can't wait to see him again." Joan smiled wistfully "I wonder if our tree is still there."

"Well, we're about find out! These are amazing, Joan, I can't wait to show them to Robert."

They spent the morning drinking cups of tea and coffee, excitedly going over all their plans for their trip, making sure Joan had everything packed that she'd need.

"I hope I'm as organised as you, Joan. I haven't even *started* packing yet!"

"Well, I've got your outfit for dinner packed, so that's one less thing for you to worry about."

Ah yes, the dinner. Frankie's thoughts started to swirl. *The dresses. The music. The dancing. The beautiful hotel. Neil Mason. Joan being beside herself with excitement.*

"How about we visit your duckies?" suggested Frankie.

"Yes, that sounds lovely Frances."

They meandered their way slowly down to the lake for the afternoon, chattering constantly about anything and everything.

They stopped to sit and watch the ducks, feeding them and laughing at their antics. Frankie was surprised how peaceful she felt, considering what was looming on the horizon. Joan also seemed totally at peace to be leaving her life behind. She truly believed that she was about to be reunited with Ernie, so Frankie understood why she had absolutely no desire to stay. If Frankie was in her position and shared her beliefs, she would want the exact same thing. To simply be reunited with Robert. That would be all that mattered.

As Frankie said goodbye to Joan at her unit that afternoon, she realised this would be the very last time. The end of an era was approaching, and Frankie was determined to make it the most beautiful ending imaginable.

CHAPTER TWENTY-NINE

"How did everything go with Maggie?" Frankie asked as they drove out.

"Amazingly well, actually. Turns out my replacement worked with Maggie years ago and they were good mates. After I finished my handover, she even gave me this."

He handed Frankie a piece of paper. It was a letter signed by Maggie giving Frankie four weeks' compassionate leave to attend to family matters.

Frankie was gobsmacked. "Oh my God, that's *awesome*! And it's not even *my* family!"

Robert grinned at her, putting his hand on her leg. "Not *yet*. But you realise once they meet you, there'll be no escaping!"

Frankie smiled. She longed to be part of a happy family again. To be surrounded by people she loved and who loved her back. Not like the worthless parasites she was unlucky enough to be related to back in Melbourne.

"I can't wait to meet them all." Tears started to well in her eyes.

Robert looked over at her "Hey! What's the matter?"

"It's just going to be so great to have a family again." Tears were running down her face.

Robert pulled over on the side of the road and held her close while she cried.

"I can't even *imagine* how much you must miss them."

He lifted her face to look at him, wiping away her tears. "But I promise you, I'll always be here for you. *Always*." Robert held her until all her tears were shed.

On their drive home, Robert said "Hey, I know what'll cheer you up."

Parking outside Liam's he grabbed her hand. "You okay?"

"Yeah, I'm fine." She pulled down the visor to check her eyes in the mirror.

"You look beautiful. Come on."

They walked in to find Tom behind the bar.

"Hi guys! How's it going? The usual?" asked Tom, holding up two fingers.

"Thanks mate," said Robert.

"So, you're off early tomorrow?" asked Tom as he slowly poured the Guinness.

"Yeah, around eight I reckon. Thanks again for checking on the house for me."

"No worries at all Rob. I hope everything goes okay with your mum, well as good as it can anyway. Give her my love. And the rest of the family."

"Yeah, I will for sure. You'll have to come and visit us at our new place too."

Tom glanced at Robert, then at Frankie. "Sounds great, can't wait to see it!" He handed them their beers.

"Thanks Tom. I'm gonna miss this place," said Frankie.

"I'm sure you'll be back. Well, I *hope* you will anyway!"

"Of course, we will." Robert pointed at Frankie "Try keeping *this* one away from a good Guinness! Not to mention my wine collection!"

They went and sat at their regular table. Frankie looked around. "I really *will* miss this place." Frankie paused, staring at Robert. "It was Tom, wasn't it?"

"What?"

"It was *Tom,* wasn't it?"

"What was Tom?"

"Last night. It was you and Tom."

"What makes you think it was Tom?"

"I don't think it was; I *know* it was."

"Oh really. I think you and old Ruthy have been making up stories again."

"Whatever." Frankie smirked at him.

They finished their beers and got up to leave, taking their glasses back to the bar on the way out.

"See you later guys. Good luck with everything." Tom shook Robert's hand.

"Thanks Tom, I'll keep in touch and let you know how everything's going."

Frankie leant over and kissed Tom's cheek. "Thanks for all your help, Tom. With everything."

Tom grinned as they waved and left.

Frankie smirked at Robert as they got into the car. He laughed, shaking his head as they drove off.

"I'm scared," Robert joked as they pulled up outside Learmonth House.

"What about?"

"Ruth! She'll probably have it in for me now!"

Frankie nodded and burst out laughing as Robert stared at her.

They walked in and found Ruth in the kitchen preparing dinner.

"Hi Ruth," said Frankie, giving her a hug.

"Oh, hi Frankie. Hi Robert. Glad to see you both survived last night."

Robert smiled and put his head down.

"Thanks for talking to me last night, Ruth. You saved my life."

"Any time, Frankie. Hopefully you won't have to go through *that* again any time soon!"

She glared at Robert. "Honestly Robert, I nearly had a heart attack when Frankie went off to Melbourne, and now you've nearly given me *another* one!"

"I know. Sorry, Ruth. It was all a bit hectic last night."

"*Hectic*? More like *terrifying*! Anyway, I'm just glad that you're both alright." Ruth paused, "I know you were just protecting her. Hopefully *one* day I'll find a man willing to risk his life like that for *me*!"

Frankie grabbed Ruth by the hands. "You *will* Ruth, I just know it."

She reached into her bag and pulled out the little gift-wrapped box.

"Here, have a seat, Ruth." They all sat at the table as Frankie handed her the box.

"What's this?"

"Just a little something so you'll remember me."

"Oh, trust me Frankie, I'll *never* forget you. *Or* Robert!" They all laughed.

Frankie sat with bated breath as Ruth carefully unwrapped her gift. She gently opened the lid and sat there with her mouth open. She looked at Frankie with tears in her eyes.

"Frankie! This is so beautiful! You shouldn't have done this!"

"Nonsense, Ruth. You deserve it."

"Oh, it's exquisite!" Ruth started to cry as she reached over to hug Frankie.

Frankie put the necklace around Ruth's neck, admiring it.

"It looks beautiful."

"It *is* beautiful, Frankie. I'll treasure it always. Thank you."

"You're welcome. I've also got something for Pete."

"I think he's out the back."

"I've gotta see this," said Robert.

They all went out into the yard where Pete was working on the cricket pitch.

"Hey Pete!" said Frankie

"Hi Frankie. Hi Robert."

"I've got something for you, Pete" said Frankie, handing him his present.

He shook it "It's not Fantales, is it?" he grinned.

He tore open the paper and opened the box to find the big silver whistle with his name engraved on it.

"Ooohhh! Thanks Frankie! I needed a new whistle!"

He quickly put it around his neck and began blowing it as loud as he could, grinning from ear to ear in between blows.

Ruth stood there with her hand over her mouth laughing and shaking her head.

Frankie looked at Ruth. "Sorry," she grinned. Ruth kept laughing.

"*And* Pete," Frankie waited to get his attention. "There's something else."

She held up the envelope. "*This* is for everyone here, but I thought because you're the president of the sports club, I'd give it to *you* to take care of."

Pete opened the envelope, a huge grin beaming on his face. He held the voucher up for everyone to see. "Five hundred dollars!"

"You can go and choose some new sports equipment, Pete. I'm sure you've got some good ideas how to spend it."

"Yeah, I do Frankie, I do!"

"Thank you!" Ruth mouthed to Frankie with teary eyes.

Robert stood there chuckling as Pete paraded back and forth holding up the voucher and his new whistle. "This'll be the best sports club in Ballarat, Pete!"

"I know! I might have to put up the membership fee!"

Frankie laughed. "Well, I better go and pack, I guess."

"Where are you going, Frankie?" asked Pete

"I'm going away for a while, Pete. Robert's mum's not well, so we're going to visit her."

"When are you coming back?"

"I don't know. But I promise we'll come back and visit. Or you can come and visit us."

"Okay. I'll bring my whistle." He grinned.

"So, what are you doing with this pitch, Pete?" Robert asked as they went out into the middle of the yard to share cricket banter.

"Thank you, Frankie," said Ruth. "For everything. It's very generous what you've done."

"This place has been my saving grace, Ruth. And so have you. It's the least I could do. Better go and pack my things. I won't be long."

Frankie ran upstairs to pack her belongings. Before she left her room for the last time, she sat down at the dressing table and looked in the mirror. She remembered her first day in this room, sitting in this very spot, applying concealer to hide her bruised face. It all felt like such a distant memory. So much had happened since that day and she wouldn't change any of it. It had all brought her to this moment.

She was about to start a new life, a life filled with hope and love and family and opportunity. She felt like the luckiest woman alive. Maybe she was. But one thing was for sure. She was grabbing it with both hands and *never* letting go.

Frankie made her way back downstairs, saying a quick goodbye to everyone she could find on the way. She went out the back where Robert, Ruth and Pete were working on the pitch under Pete's strict instructions.

She hugged Ruth. "Take care of yourself, Ruth. I'll see you soon, okay?"

"You take care too, Frankie. Good luck with everything. I know it'll all work out for you."

"Let me know what pops up too, okay?"

"You'll be the first to know!" Ruth laughed.

She went over and gave Pete a hug and a kiss.

"See you, Pete. Keep everyone under control won't you. I'll be looking forward to hearing what new equipment you've bought." Pete gave her a thumbs up.

Robert shook Pete's hand. "See ya, Pete. Take care mate. Good luck with the pitch. Catch you down the track."

He gave Ruth a hug and kissed her cheek.

"Don't worry, Ruth. I promise I'll take good care of our girl."

"Thank you, Robert. Look after yourselves. All the best with your mum too."

He smiled and squeezed her hand. "See you at the shack, hey?"

Ruth nodded, wiping a tear from her cheek.

Frankie quickly picked up her suitcase as Robert grabbed her hand and led her down the hallway and out the door.

As they drove away from Learmonth House for the last time, Frankie was filled with a multitude of emotions. But as much as she was going to miss Ruth and the wonderful bond they shared, she wouldn't change a single thing. She was ready. Ready to start her new life with Robert, whatever that may bring.

"You okay, beautiful?"

Frankie nodded, wiping her eyes.

Back at Robert's they started packing for their trip. Frankie read out the list while Robert laid everything on the bed.

"I think that's everything," said Robert, zipping up the suitcase and carrying it into the lounge room. He dragged out the duffle bag. "Better not forget this."

Frankie unzipped it. "Hey, where are the guns?"

Robert paused. "In safe hands."

"Okay then." She shrugged her shoulders. "Hope Tom's got a safe," she muttered to herself before zipping the bag back up.

Robert took some bottles of champagne and wine from the wine rack. "*This* is for the shack. To celebrate."

"Oh, I forgot to show you." Frankie pulled the envelope from her bag and handed the photos to him. "Isn't it beautiful?"

He nodded. "It sure is. Jesus, Ernie really *does* look like Neil Mason, doesn't he?"

Frankie laughed "Yeah, he was a good sort!"

"I'm not gonna have to fight Neil off as *well,* am I?"

"It'll probably be *me* fighting Neil off once you two start talking about vineyards!"

"Yeah, probably." Frankie glared at him. "I promise I'll be good!" he laughed, putting his hands in the air.

"You better be!"

"Oh yeah? Or else what?" He grinned and kissed her, before picking her up and carrying her into the bedroom.

After their lovemaking, Frankie laid there gently circling the grazes on Robert's chest with her fingers.

"Are you going to miss being here?"

"Not really. I'm just looking forward to our new life. And spending some time with Mum."

"Does she know we're coming?"

"Well, I told her I'm bringing you to meet her, but I thought we'd just turn up and surprise her."

"One of many surprises we'll plan for her." Frankie paused "I hope she likes me."

Robert kissed her forehead. "She'll *love* you. *Everyone* will."

A whole new world was about to open up for Frankie. She felt both nervous and excited about meeting everyone. She imagined herself at the farm, surrounded by Robert's entire family. One big, beautiful, noisy shemozzle. She daydreamed about having their own children, imagining what they'd look like. She started giggling.

Robert looked at her. "What?"

"I was just imagining what our kids would be like."

"They'll be bloody terrors no doubt, if they take after us!"

Frankie laughed. "I hope so."

"So do I."

CHAPTER THIRTY

The six-thirty alarm rang out. Finally. The day was here. The first day of the rest of their lives. "I can't believe it's finally here!" Frankie squealed with excitement, throwing her arms around Robert.

They sprang out of bed and after a very talkative shower, ate a quick breakfast before packing the car, ready for their trip.

Frankie read out the list one last time as Robert checked everything was there.

As they jumped in the car, Robert looked over at Frankie, grinning. "Ready?"

"Shit yeah! Woohoo!" Frankie leaned out the window as they drove off, waving goodbye to Robert's house.

They arrived at Golden Leaves.

"Right, let's load up Joan's twenty tonne of stuff." Robert patted the steering wheel. "I hope old Bessie can handle it."

Clare followed them into reception.

"Morning guys!" she chirped. "You look nice today, Frankie!"

"Thanks Clare, so do you!" Frankie smiled at her. "We're taking Joan on her holiday today. See you on our way out."

As expected, Joan's door was already open, her suitcases sitting at the doorway.

"Eureka!" shouted Frankie excitedly.

Joan appeared, her face beaming. Instead of her usual long flowing dresses, she was wearing a pair of white linen pants with a long colourful blouse and white loafers on her feet.

"Ciao Bella!" said Robert in an Italian accent, lifting her arm up to kiss her hand. "Bellisima Signora!"

'Wow Joan, look at you!" said Frankie. "Am I rubbing off on you?"

Joan laughed "This is my country attire, Frances. The shack's no place for a wheelchair! And it looks like I'm rubbing off on you. Is that a new dress?"

Frankie did a twirl. "Yes, actually. Robert bought it for me."

"It looks lovely. As I said, you should wear dresses more often."

"It's keeping them *on* that's the problem," laughed Robert.

"Wait till he sees the dress you'll be wearing *tomorrow* night!" she whispered to Frankie, winking at her.

Robert looked at Joan's suitcases. "Bloody hell Joan! Anyone'd think you're going for good!"

"Robert!" yelled Frankie, horrified.

Joan threw her head back laughing as Robert started wheeling her suitcases down the path.

Frankie took a quick look around the unit, trying to ignore the fact that this would be the last time she ever set foot here.

She knelt down in front of Joan. "Are you okay? Do you want to sit and have a cuppa before we go?"

"Oh God no!" said Joan, waving her hand. "I've been sitting in this place long enough!"

Frankie picked up the dresses hanging over the door as Robert returned.

"Haven't forgotten anything? Kitchen sink perhaps?"

Joan giggled as Robert whizzed her down the path. Frankie gently closed the door and followed them, dresses draped over her shoulder.

Maggie was waiting in reception, clipboard under her arm.

"All set?" She smiled at Joan, "Have a lovely holiday, Joan. Don't let these two lead you astray."

Robert laughed out loud "I think it's actually *us* you should be worried about Maggie!"

"Anyway, have a great time. And Rob, if you need anything, give me a call. I'll see you all in a few days." Maggie rushed out, giving them a wave as she left.

"Have a great holiday!" twittered Clare.

Frankie felt a sudden pang of guilt and sorrow, knowing this would be the last time she would ever hear Clare's cheery voice. She was going to miss that sound.

"We will. Take care, Clare." Frankie gave her a big hug and kissed her on the cheek before heading out the door.

Frankie sat in the middle as Robert helped Joan into the passenger side before folding away her wheelchair.

"Ready for lift off?" asked Robert as he started old Bessie.

"Ready!" squealed Joan with excitement.

Frankie nodded, tears in her eyes. Robert laughed and put his arm around her, kissing her head. "My little chocolate éclair."

"What?"

"Hard on the outside, but soft and gooey on the inside."

"Oh, fuck off Robert!" Frankie snapped as she wiped her eyes.

They all laughed as they drove away from Golden Leaves for the very last time.

Frankie felt like a kid again as they travelled along the highway, laughing and singing along with the music. Robert was in fine form, telling his corny jokes and making them play eye spy. She recalled the feeling of excitement as a child, stepping onto the train with her parents, bound for a wonderful adventure.

The butterflies were once again fluttering in her stomach as they headed into the great unknown, and it felt wonderful. She felt alive. A whole new life was waiting for her and Robert. And even though Joan's life was entering its final chapter, she couldn't help but also feel excited about the surprise that awaited her tomorrow. Frankie had planned everything to perfection and all she needed now was a perfect sunset to match.

As they drove towards the Dandenongs, Joan gave them a running commentary on her knowledge of the area, and entertained them with colourful stories of her times there with Ernie.

The quaint little towns and beautiful scenery were breathtaking; a far cry from the ugly, bustling concrete jungles of Melbourne. The air was clean and fresh, and the sounds of traffic were now replaced by the calling of birds ringing from the majestic rainforest trees. It felt magical, like they'd been transported to a hidden paradise.

As they pulled into the car park at the top of the mountain, Frankie gasped.

"It's wonderful, isn't it!" Joan smiled

Robert got out and took Joan's wheelchair from the back, opening the door to help them both out. They wandered over to the lookout and stared in amazement at the breathtaking view.

Robert put his arm around Frankie and pointed out Melbourne.

"I didn't realise how high up we are! It's amazing!"

Frankie pointed to the beautiful glass-sided building behind them. "Is this the place where you used to come with Ernie?"

Joan nodded "We used to haunt this place when we came to the shack," she laughed. "It's very romantic at night too Robert. You can have dinner and look out at all the city lights."

"Thanks Joan. I might bring her here, if she's good."

They slowly ambled around the pathways and bushland gardens which surrounded the entire restaurant. The views stretched as far as the eye could see in every direction.

"This is magnificent," said Robert. "You couldn't get a better view if you tried! Speaking of nice views, you two stand there."

He pulled out his phone and took a photo as Frankie bent down and put her arm around Joan.

Making their way into the restaurant, the waiter came over to greet them.

"Joan?"

She looked up and paused. "Phillip!"

"Oh, Joan how lovely to see you! It's been so long!" he chirped, hugging her and kissing her on both cheeks. "How are you?"

"I'm wonderful, Phillip!" Joan smiled at him. "I'm here with my friends. This is Frances and Robert."

He shook their hands with a huge smile. "Lovely to meet you. How long's it been, Joan? Where's Ernie?"

"Ernie passed away six years ago now."

"Oh, I'm so sorry Joan, I had no idea."

He put his hand up to his mouth, patting Joan's arm.

"Well, you still look as beautiful as ever! And that blouse is *amazing*!" He beamed at her.

"Are you staying at Olinda?"

"We're just passing through this time, on our way to Sorrento. But no doubt you'll be seeing more of Frances and Robert. They'll be looking after the place from now on."

"Ooh, how wonderful!" He gently patted Frankie's arm. "You'll absolutely love it. It's a beautiful part of the world up here."

"It sure is mate. Can't wait," said Robert

"Anyway, follow me, I'll show you to your table."

He led them to a table right next to the window overlooking the entire valley to Melbourne and beyond. He flicked each of their napkins open before placing them carefully on their laps.

"I'll leave you to look at the menu and I'll be back in a few jiffies." He smiled at them and flitted off.

Joan leant forward and whispered "If you ever want to know the gossip about *anything* or *anyone* around these parts, Phillip's your man. Has his finger in *lots* of pies."

"Well, his finger won't be going anywhere near *my* pie!" Robert chuckled as Frankie elbowed him, making Joan giggle.

As they sat enjoying the beautiful view and a delicious lunch washed down with a local Verdelho, Frankie felt like she was sitting on top of the world. Joan reminisced about her life with Ernie and Robert talked about his dreams and plans for their new vineyard.

As they were leaving, Phillip hugged Joan, kissing both cheeks. "It was so wonderful to *see* you, Joan! Make sure you come back again soon!"

"I'll try to duck in when I can," she winked at Frankie.

"And no doubt I'll see you two soon. It was lovely to meet you!"

He shook Robert's hand and kissed Frankie's cheek.

They all waved and made their way back to the car. As they sat in the car waiting to go, Robert took a deep breath.

"I want to savour this moment. We're about to see the shack."

"Well hurry up! I can't wait!" said Frankie, bouncing up and down in her seat.

"Yes, hurry up Robert. We haven't got all day!" Joan laughed, as Robert started the car and drove deliberately slowly out of the car park.

They meandered their way through the forest lined streets as Joan gave directions. Robert wound down his window to breathe in the crisp mountain air.

"There it is!" Joan pointed to the driveway, leaning forward with an excited look on her face. Robert pulled in and stopped next to the letter box, which was made from an old metal beer keg. The white paint had mostly peeled off, and a faded black number '21' was just visible on the front.

"Should I check the letterbox?" Robert looked at Joan as he opened his door and got out.

"You'll probably need a sack. And watch out for spiders," she laughed. He carefully opened the flap, pulled out the contents and jumped back into the car, dumping a mountain of papers onto Frankie's lap.

"There better not be spiders in here!" yelled Frankie, throwing them onto the floor.

They slowly followed the track through the trees until they came to a locked metal gate. Frankie reached over and pulled the set of keys from the glove box.

"From memory, I think it's *that* one," said Joan, pointing to the gold-coloured key. Robert got out and opened the gate before driving through and locking it behind them.

They slowly drove deeper and deeper into the rainforest. The vegetation was thick and lush, the two overgrown tyre tracks being the only sign of previous human habitation. Frankie sat in awe as they slowly made their way through the majestic forest, entirely surrounded by the vibrant calls of the abundant birdlife.

Eventually a clearing came into view and as they slowly emerged through the trees and into the sunlight, there it was. The Love Shack. Robert stopped the car as they all sat staring in silence. Frankie looked at Robert, tears rolling down her face. Joan had a huge smile on her face.

"Here we are!"

He opened his door, running around to open the passenger side.

"How's it looking, Joan?" asked Robert.

"Surprisingly good, actually. I thought it might have fallen down by now."

"Joan look!" Frankie ran over to the huge crepe myrtle at the front of the house which was covered in a beautiful mass of white flowers.

Joan's face beamed. "Oh, it's flourishing! Ernie would be so proud."

Frankie and Robert held Joan's arms as they made their way slowly over to the house. They climbed the stairs leading to a verandah which wrapped around the entire building. The house was painted dark green, with white windows and railings. The exterior was peeling and weather beaten but it still had all the romantic charm of a country cottage. A rambling overgrown garden surrounded the house, and a huge old water tank sat leaning against the side.

Frankie passed the keys to Joan and stood back in anticipation as Joan unlocked the front door. As the door creaked open, Joan stood in the doorway looking around, a huge smile on her face.

As they all slowly made their way inside, Frankie gasped, totally mesmerised. The house was lined with timber boards which were painted light green on the walls and stained dark on the floors. A wide hallway ran down the centre of the house, a bedroom leading off either side. Both bedrooms had big timber sash windows at the front, and were filled with antique furniture, including ornate cast iron beds.

"Oh my God! Look at this furniture!"

Frankie sat on the bed looking around, hardly able to believe her eyes.

"Yes, we bought all of this. Ernie loved cast iron furniture."

The hallway led onto an open living area, a huge, tiled fireplace sitting majestically in the centre. Antique furniture adorned the room, as well as a big woven rug which sat in front of the fireplace.

"Look at that fireplace!" Robert bent down in front of it, looking up the chimney.

"Yes, it works Robert. We used it last time we were here. We spent many a night in front of that fireplace."

"Yes, I think I remember you telling us that story," said Frankie laughing.

A doorway at the rear led to a small galley kitchen off to the left, complete with a wood fired oven and old timber benches with cast iron pots hanging from a ceiling rack. To the right was a bathroom with a white claw foot bath in the centre and white pedestal basin. An antique timber dresser sat below the window.

"Joan, it's gorgeous!" squealed Frankie. "It's nothing like a shack!"

"Well," said Joan, "compared to our other houses it is, but we always loved it." She stood in the centre of the living room looking around with a contented smile on her face.

They all made their way out the back door which led back onto the verandah. The house backed onto a huge clearing which was filled with overgrown fruit trees.

"That paddock's about four acres, Robert. Perfect for your vineyard. And down past there, where the trees start again, that takes you down to the creek. Let's go for a drive and I'll show you."

Frankie got out the video camera as Joan gave them a guided tour. They slowly made their way along the overgrown track, which was hardly visible in places.

As they drove past the clearing and back into the rainforest, the sound of running water got louder. Robert held Joan's arm as they slowly made their way down to the creek. It was exactly as it looked in the old photo. Beautiful huge gum trees and lush ferns framed the pristine, crystal-clear creek as it rushed its way down the gully.

"This is paradise!" said Frankie in amazement.

Robert bent down to take a drink. "This water will be perfect for my wine. Unbelievable."

They continued their tour, driving slowly through the beautiful rainforest, until they finally came to another clearing at the end of the property.

"Holy shit!" gasped Robert as they got out of the car. Appearing right in front of them was the edge of the mountain, with a breathtaking view overlooking the entire mist-covered valley.

Frankie stood there with her hand over her mouth, totally lost for words.

"It's beautiful, isn't it! I wanted to keep this last bit as a surprise. Ernie and I used to spend hours here, just sitting and taking in the view."

They all stood together in silence, watching as a pair of wedgetail eagles gracefully soared above the valley.

"That'll be you and Ernie soon," said Frankie with tears in her eyes.

Robert put his arms around them both, pulling them close as they all stared in awe at the absolute majesty of mother nature.

CHAPTER
THIRTY-ONE

They spent the rest of the day exploring the magnificent property from boundary to boundary, with Joan proudly leading the way.

Back at the shack in the late afternoon, they relaxed on the verandah, drinking champagne and listening to the symphony of wildlife preparing for bedtime. As the beautiful burnt orange sunset lit up the sky, Joan reminisced about her many afternoons with Ernie sitting on the same verandah surrounded by the same beautiful sights and sounds.

That evening they sat around the cosy fireplace laughing and telling stories as Robert threw together a casserole in an old cast iron pot over the fire.

"You *are* a good cook, Robert. This is delicious!" said Joan.

"Told you Joan, he's a man of many talents." Frankie grinned at Robert.

As the fire began to die down at the end of the night, a loud thump on the tin roof made Frankie jump. "Shit! What was that?"

Joan laughed. "It's just the possums dear. You'll get used to it. I remember when I first heard them, I thought there was a prowler outside. They make the most horrible growling noises. I'm surprised they're not running through the house to be honest."

"We *are* in the rainforest, Frankie. Critters *everywhere*! What was *that*?" Robert gasped, wide eyed, pretending to be scared.

"Stop it!" she slapped him.

"We had a snake in here once."

"*What?*" said Frankie, horrified.

"Yes. It was curled up in the firewood."

"Fuck!" Frankie jumped up as Robert laughed hysterically.

Joan giggled. "It was only a python. Ernie took it outside. He never hurt anything, loved *all* animals. Even the ones that could bite you."

"Oh great, now I'm going to have nightmares."

Robert put his arm around her. "Don't worry, I'll protect you from the big bad scary monsters."

"Like you?" she laughed.

They wandered up the hallway with Joan as she went into her bedroom carrying her candle.

"Today's been wonderful. Thank you both for bringing me back here. See you in the morning."

Frankie kissed Joan on the cheek. "It *has* been wonderful."

Robert led Frankie into their room as they got undressed, sliding under the covers. Robert blew out the candle and the room instantly turned pitch black. Not a single shred of light could be seen from anywhere.

He pulled Frankie close. "I think there's a snake in the bed," he whispered.

"Really?" giggled Frankie

"Yep. But don't worry. It's only a python."

He gently kissed her as they slowly and quietly christened the first room of their new Love Shack.

At the first sign of light, Frankie woke to the chorus of birds greeting the beginning of the new day. She laid there listening to all the different calls, most of which she'd never heard before. She couldn't imagine a more beautiful thing to wake up to. Except for Robert.

She kissed his chest, smiling at him as he opened his eyes.

"Morning. Feel like a walk?"

Quietly they got dressed and crept out the front door.

The dappled sunlight glistened on the dewy undergrowth as they walked hand in hand along the track, breathing in the beautiful crisp clean air, quietly watching the myriad of birds busily flitting among the trees.

As they reached the gate, Robert gave Frankie a big bearhug. "Can you believe this place Frankie? I had no idea it would be this amazing!"

"It's pretty overwhelming, isn't it? It just doesn't feel real!"

Frankie hung her head as she felt a sudden sharp pain inside her. "I just can't believe that tomorrow she'll be gone."

"I know," Robert sighed. "But just remember this is exactly what she wanted. *And* imagine the look on her face when Neil turns up tonight!"

Frankie couldn't help but smile thinking about it.

As they got back and walked through the front door, Joan was sitting on the edge of her bed in her dressing gown, quietly singing to herself and brushing her long grey hair.

"Morning Joan," Frankie sat on the bed next to her. "It's a beautiful day out there!"

Robert stood in the doorway. "How are *you* feeling today?"

Joan smiled with a faraway look. "I'm fine, Robert. I'm ready."

"Not dressed like *that* you're not!" joked Robert. "Come on, I'm taking you two out for breakfast."

As they packed up and waved goodbye to the shack before slowly driving away, Frankie looked over at Joan.

"Did you like coming back?"

Joan's eyes started to water. "Yes dear, but it's just not the same. Not without Ernie." They drove in silence to the café for breakfast.

"I want to put a bench at the lookout," announced Frankie out of the blue as she drank the last of her coffee. "It'll be the love seat. And we'll even plant a love tree there as well."

Joan's face lit up. "Oh, that sounds wonderful Frances!"

"Sorry, I know I'm just a man, but what the hell is a love tree?"

"A crepe myrtle, Robert" Frankie rolled her eyes at him sarcastically. "Like the white one out the front. It was the tree of Aphrodite, Goddess of Love. It's a symbol of love and good fortune."

"Very good, Frances!" Joan clapped her hands together.

"Okay. Stupid me. Should've known that."

"You can be in charge of the bench," Frankie laughed.

They finished their breakfast and got back into the car.

"What's that noise?" said Robert, holding his hand up to his ear.

"What?" said Frankie.

"Shhh. Listen. Can you hear it? I think it's, yes, it's Sorrento! It's calling us!"

Frankie elbowed him as they all laughed and headed off down the highway.

As they made their way closer and closer to Sorrento, Frankie felt a sense of dread growing inside her. This was it. Today was the day. The day Joan would be leaving this world behind. Yet no-one was talking about it.

Like it wasn't happening. Like they were all on a happy little road trip. But it wasn't a happy little road trip. It was Joan's one way ticket to her own death. This was all just a bullshit charade. Thoughts started swirling around and around in Frankie's head until she felt like she was going to explode.

"Joan, are you ready?" Frankie blurted loudly.

Everyone went quiet.

"I'm sorry, but I need to talk about it!"

Joan put her hand gently on Frankie's arm and smiled at her.

"Yes Frances. I'm ready. You don't need to worry dear. I heard Ernie's voice at the shack. I know he's close. He's waiting for me."

Frankie started getting teary.

"So, you're not scared?"

"Oh no dear, far from it. The thought of living without him is what scares me the most. It's time to go home."

"So where *is* Ernie? Is he buried somewhere?"

"He's actually in Sydney Harbour. Daniel and I scattered his ashes there. He loved being on the water."

"Well, you can join him there. Maybe we should look out for *two* ducks!"

"Floating right outside Daniel's house." Joan giggled.

"You two quack me up!" joked Robert, making them laugh.

Frankie felt a huge sense of relief knowing that Joan was more than ready to leave this world behind. All she needed to focus on now was making this night spectacular.

As they drove over the headland, Frankie gasped as the magnificent coastline came into view. Robert pulled into the car park at the top of the escarpment, and they all got out to soak up the breathtaking scenery. Frankie took some footage of them all overlooking the ocean.

"There it is!" said Joan, pointing into the distance at the majestic white building perched high on the cliff face. "The Bella Donna!"

"Let's go check in!" said Robert, jumping into the car.

They slowly drove along the foreshore, the white sandy beaches contrasting perfectly against the shimmering, clear blue water. A warm sea breeze gently drifted through the pine trees lining the esplanade as happy people wandered their way along the street, past the many shops and cafes, the smell of coffee and saltwater filling the air.

Joan's face was beaming. "It hasn't changed much since we were here last. A few new shops maybe, but it's pretty much how I remember it."

"It's beautiful!" Frankie looked at Robert. "Have you been here before?"

"I think we came here as kids once, but I don't really remember it. Michael and Adam probably would."

"Maybe we could bring your mum here?"

"If you do, make sure you stay at the Bella Donna," said Joan. "Wait till you see it."

Climbing up the hill, the magnificent view once again appeared, overlooking the entire coastline. The entrance to the hotel came into view, a tall stone archway surrounded by lush tropical gardens.

"We're here!" squealed Frankie.

The stone fenced driveway swept around to the entrance of the hotel where men in crisp white suits and hats stood waiting to greet the incoming visitors.

"Good morning, sir" said the valet as Robert pulled up at the entrance. "Are you staying at the hotel?"

"Yes, we sure are" said Robert as they all got out of the car.

The porter appeared immediately with his shiny brass luggage trolley as Robert took out their bags and Joan's wheelchair, leaving the duffle bag for last.

"I'll carry this one," he said quietly to Frankie.

After being courteously greeted by the hotel's concierge, they were ushered through the huge glass doors into the grandiose marble-floored lobby with towering carved archways, ornate ceilings and crystal chandeliers framing the entire area.

An enormous marble fountain dominated the centre of the lobby, the bubbling water cascading over the breasts of a barely clad statue, with vibrant bouquets of flowers fanning from either side. Red velvet covered antique lounges sat below imposing gilt edged mirrors and artworks hanging above.

"Holy crap. This is amazing!" whispered Frankie.

Robert nodded in agreement as they glided their way across the polished floor to the reception desk, which was tastefully decorated with bankers' lamps and huge bright bunches of sunflowers.

"Good morning, folks. Welcome to the Bella Donna Hotel. Are you checking in?"

"Yes, we've got a booking in the name of Hadfield."

Frankie whispered in Robert's ear, and he wheeled Joan away.

"Ah yes, here we are. The Executive Ocean View Suite."

"I've also booked the outdoor dining area for tonight, so I'd like to confirm all the details. I think it was Kristen that I spoke to?"

"Yes, that would be Kristen, our Functions Manager. I can call her and arrange for you to speak with her. One moment."

Frankie looked over, smiling as she watched Joan and Robert admiring the fountain.

"Kristen can meet with you in twenty minutes in the fourth floor lobby, if that suits you?"

"Perfect."

Frankie waved Robert over and they made their way into the gold mirrored lift. As Frankie pressed button three, a sudden flashback to Christian's apartment lift sent a cold shiver down her spine.

"Three twenty-one. This is us!" As they walked through the door, Frankie looked around stunned. She'd never seen anything like it. The suite was pure luxury, with exquisite antique furniture, high ornate ceilings, crystal chandeliers and beautiful gold-plated fittings. Each bedroom had its own marble bathroom complete with gold tapware.

"This is insane!" yelled Robert as he checked out every room.

"Hey, look at this!" he yelled from the bathroom. Frankie went in to find him pointing at the bidet. "It's got its own remote!"

Frankie slid open the heavy glass doors which led out onto the marble tiled balcony. Huge white pillars adorned each corner, with beautiful hanging flower gardens trailing over every edge. The uninterrupted ocean view stretched off into the distance as far as the eye could see. She stood breathing in the warm salt air. It was even more breathtakingly beautiful than she could have ever imagined from Joan's stories.

Joan came out onto the balcony and put her arm around Frankie. "This is exactly how I remember it."

"My God Joan, it's *so* beautiful."

Robert came out to join them. They all stood there together in silence, once again mesmerised by the flawless beauty of mother nature.

A knock at the door interrupted their silence. Robert helped the porter unload their luggage.

"I have to go and talk to them about tonight. I won't be long," Frankie whispered to Robert. "I'll be back in a minute!" she yelled to Joan.

Frankie arrived back twenty minutes later, and they all ventured out to explore Sorrento.

They strolled down the promenade, soaking in the warm sunshine and gentle sea breeze. Following the waterline, they made their way to the end of the pier, where they sat and watched kids jumping off into the water. After teasing them by yelling out scores after each jump, the kids heckled Robert into showing them how it was done. Stripping down to his undies, he announced he would be performing his famous double somersault dive, which turned into a double somersault bellyflop, causing a huge uproar of riotous laughter and booing. Frankie was laughing so hard she had tears running down her face.

After barrages of back-and-forth banter and laughter, Robert got dressed and they wandered back down the pier, the kids' taunts still trailing off behind them, Frankie and Joan still giggling.

"That hurt!" said Robert, finally far enough away from the kids to rub his red stomach.

Frankie stopped dead, crouching over with uncontrollable laughter again as she recalled Robert's dive. "Oh, *very funny*!"

Frankie was still having random bursts of laughter as they walked back along the promenade.

"I haven't seen anything that funny for a long time. But luckily, I got it on video. You should've heard the noise it made!" She burst out laughing again.

"Glad I'm of *some* use then! See what I have to put up with Joan?"

"It *was* pretty entertaining Robert!" Joan started giggling again.

As they made their way along the street chatting and browsing in the shops, they came across a quaint little Italian outdoor café, filled with big earthenware pots of flowers, brightly painted metal furniture and colourful umbrellas.

Joan's face lit up. "Let's have lunch here."

They spent a relaxing afternoon sitting in the warm breeze, eating delicious Italian food and sharing a bottle of lambrusco.

"So, Robert, what type of grapes are you going to grow at the shack?" asked Joan as she sipped from her glass.

He paused, twirling the wine around in his glass.

"Probably Pinot Noir I'm thinking, or maybe even a Chardonnay. I'll have to do some research and see what grows best around there." His face lit up. "Tonight, I'll be able to pick…"

Frankie kicked him under the table, glaring at him. "I'll be able to pick… something nice from the wine list."

"Here's to a wonderful night" said Frankie, raising her glass. "And us. Cheers." They all clinked their glasses together.

CHAPTER THIRTY-TWO

Back at their suite, Joan sat on the balcony admiring the view.

Frankie led Robert into the bedroom. "Neil's supposed to get here about five, so would you be able to have a drink with him while we get ready?"

"Sure! We can talk vineyards."

"And then we'll meet you in the bar on the fourth floor at six, okay?" Frankie jumped up and down with excitement. "I can't wait to see the look on her face!"

"So, what does Neil know about this whole thing?"

Frankie shrugged her shoulders. "I have no idea. That can be your job."

"Leave it up to me!" Robert saluted before picking Frankie up and throwing her on the bed, kissing her. "Do you reckon Joan would hear us if we…"

"You'll have to wait! You need to get ready," said Frankie as she jumped up and threw a towel over Robert's head. Robert groaned and rolled over, hugging the pillow.

Frankie was sitting on the balcony painting Joan's nails when Robert strutted out in his black tuxedo, spinning around in front of them.

"Woah!" said Frankie, staring. "You look *hot*!"

"*Very* handsome, Robert! You could get *married* in that suit!"

Joan winked at Frankie.

"Thank you, ladies" he said, polishing his fingernails on his jacket. "I'll leave you two to make yourselves beautiful, well, *more* beautiful, while I go and entertain myself for a while."

He looked at Frankie "And I'll see you both *in* the bar, *on* the fourth floor, at six o'clock *precisely*."

He kissed Joan's hand before giving Frankie a long kiss. "Ciao Bellas!"

Frankie watched Robert leave with a big smile on her face. She couldn't wait to blow his mind.

They ordered some champagne from room service and sat chatting and laughing on the balcony, finishing their nails. "I'm going to miss doing all this with you."

Joan patted her hand. "Me too, Frances. Maybe we'll meet again down the track sometime. You never know. Anyway, let's just make the most of our last night together."

She picked up her champagne. "Let's go out with a *bang*!"

"Cheers!" Frankie clinked her glass. "Let's go knock 'em dead!"

As they sat in their plush hotel robes in Joan's bedroom, Frankie watched in amazement as Joan once again magically transformed her into a vision of beauty. "I hope I remember how to do this!"

"It's just practice, Frances. I'm sure you'll get the hang of it." Frankie then watched as Joan effortlessly transformed herself as well.

She helped Joan into her gorgeous blue dress, zipping it up before standing back to admire her.

"Oh my God Joan, you look absolutely stunning." Joan turned from side to side as she looked in the mirror.

"Not bad for an old girl, Frances," she laughed.

Frankie put on her black dress and stood in front of the mirror, a huge smile on her face.

"Oh, Frances look at you. You are an absolute picture." Joan's face was beaming as she looked at Frankie.

"Oh, jewellery!" Joan opened the case and took out their jewellery, laying it on the bed. "I've brought along some extra jewellery for you too, Frances, and please don't argue with me. It's just a few pieces that I want you to have. Special pieces."

"Joan, I…" Joan glared at her and Frankie pretended to zip her lips.

"Thank you, Frances"

They both put on their shoes and stood side by side looking in the mirror.

Frankie took a selfie of them both before picking up their bags and the video camera.

"Ready to break some hearts?"

"Let's go get 'em!" giggled Joan.

"No," said Joan as Frankie went to get her wheelchair. "I'm walking tonight. I've loaded up on anti-inflammatories. I want to remember tonight like it was when I was here with Ernie."

"Good for you, Joan."

Frankie took her arm as they made their way to the lift. Her heart was racing with nervous excitement. This was the final moment. The big finale.

Please, please, please God let everything go to plan.

As the gold doors opened, Frankie spotted Robert sitting at the bar. Her heart skipped a beat, but then she sighed with relief as Robert leant forward to reveal Neil sitting next to him.

As they got out of the lift, Robert looked up and saw them, a huge grin lighting up face. He nudged Neil as they both looked over and stood up.

Robert came over to meet them.

"Look at you two! Frankie! Oh my God!"

Robert escorted them both to the bar, staring at Frankie the whole way.

Joan's face froze as she saw Neil standing there. Robert introduced them.

"Joan, this is Neil Mason. Neil, this is the lovely Joan Middleton."

Neil took her hand, kissing it gently. "It's a pleasure to meet you, Joan. May I say you look very beautiful this evening. Would you do me the honour of letting me join you for dinner?"

Joan stood there nodding and smiling with her mouth open, unable to utter a word.

"And this is my beautiful partner, Frankie Hadfield" said Robert, putting his arm around her.

"Hello Frankie." He kissed her hand. "It's a pleasure to meet you. Robert's already told me a lot about you."

Frankie was also gobsmacked to meet Neil in person. He was even more handsome in real life with his rugged good looks and piercing blue eyes. She understood why Joan was so flustered. Even though he was an older man, he had a charming and sexy presence about him. She could feel herself blushing and hoped she had enough makeup on to hide it.

"Right, let's sit and have a drink, shall we?" said Robert as he herded the starstruck girls over to the red velvet lounges. "Ladies, what would you like?"

Joan sat there smiling, staring at Neil. "Champagne perhaps?" said Robert.

"Champagne sounds good," said Frankie as she squeezed Joan's hand.

"Same again Neil?"

"Please."

Robert went to the bar as Frankie's nervousness skyrocketed.

"So, Joan, Robert tells me that you used to come here with your husband?"

"Yes," she smiled.

"It certainly is beautiful here. I've never been to Sorrento before."

"Me either," blurted Frankie. "Thanks for coming Neil."
What the fuck am I saying?

She wished the ground would open up and swallow her. *Hurry up with the drinks Robert! A triple vodka would be good about now.*

"My pleasure, Frankie. I'm sure it'll be a great night."

Robert returned with the champagne and beer.

"Cheers," he said as they all clinked their glasses together. "Here's to a wonderful night."

After a couple of champagnes, Joan finally relaxed, chatting to Neil like she'd known him for years. They talked about everything showbiz; they even knew a lot of the same people. Joan was clearly relishing every minute of Neil's company, and he seemed to be enjoying it as well.

Robert leaned over to whisper to Frankie "You look *so* scorching hot tonight; I don't know how I'm going to be able to keep my hands off you."

She grinned at him. "So, you like the dress?"

"It's magnificent Frankie. *You're* magnificent. I can't believe you're mine." He kissed her.

The Maître d' walked over to them with a friendly smile.

"Good evening, ladies and gentlemen. Your table is ready, if you'd like to make your way onto the balcony."

"Ooh!" said Joan with excitement.

Neil took hold of Joan's arm to escort her as they all made their way outside.

Their table was stunning. Elegant gold candelabras decorated the centre, along with flower arrangements, sparkling crystal glasses and shining silver cutlery. A classical string quartet serenaded them as the waiters showed them to their seats.

Beyond the balcony the beautiful blue ocean stretched out into the distance as the sun slowly edged towards the horizon.

Frankie felt like crying with happiness. Everything was perfect.

They sat enjoying each other's company, laughing and telling stories.

Neil was a wonderful storyteller and had everyone spellbound one minute, and in fits of laughter the next.

As the sun began to set, the sky lit up in beautiful pink and orange hues, with scattered purple and blue highlights.

"Joan, would you care to dance?" asked Neil, holding out his hand to her.

"I'd love to."

He led her to the front of the balcony, putting his arm around her waist as they swayed to the slow romantic music of the string quartet.

"Frankie?" Robert put out his hand.

The four of them danced on the balcony as mother nature adorned the sky with a kaleidoscope of colours, the soft music ringing out into the beautiful warm night air.

"Tonight couldn't be any more perfect" Frankie said, putting her head on Robert's shoulder.

"You could be naked."

She threw her head back and laughed. "That's true. So could you."

"What a beautiful night this is!" beamed Joan as Neil led her back to her seat.

"There's nothing like a beautiful sunset over the ocean," said Neil. "Monet himself couldn't have done a better job!"

The waiters brought out platter after platter of food, including lots of sumptuous local seafood. They grazed for hours as they sat drinking wine and sharing stories.

Neil talked about his winery, much to Robert's delight, even agreeing to visit the shack once Robert had his vineyard up and running. Joan reminisced about her night at the Bella Donna with Ernie, mentioning for the fifth time how much Neil reminded her of Ernie and how handsome he was.

Robert tapped his wineglass with his knife to get everyone's attention.

"I'd like to thank you Neil, for being our guest tonight. It's been so great to meet you, and I hope we see you at the shack one day. And to our beautiful Joan, tonight's guest of honour, Frankie has something for you."

Frankie handed Joan an envelope. As she opened it and unfolded the paper, tears started to well in her eyes. Frankie leant over and hugged her.

"Oh, Frances thank you. This is wonderful!"

"Don't thank me, thank Daniel."

Joan held it up to show Neil. "It's a foundation in my name. It's going to raise money for Alzheimer's research."

"That's wonderful, Joan!" Neil smiled. "I'll definitely make a donation."

"Oh, *would* you? There's also going to be fundraisers each year."

Neil nodded "Count me in!"

Joan hugged him.

The waiters arrived with a decadent selection of desserts which they all managed to somehow fit into their already full stomachs, followed by freshly brewed coffee.

"You know it's always fascinated me," said Neil "why they serve coffee at the end of the night when all you want to do is go to sleep."

"Speak for yourself!" said Robert, putting his arm around Frankie and squeezing her.

They all laughed, Neil nodding in agreement, pushing his coffee cup towards Robert.

"This has been an amazing night." Neil smiled at Joan, kissing her hand. "With amazing people."

He looked over at the driver sitting waiting for him at the bar.

"Thank you for inviting me." Neil stood up. "Frances," he kissed Frankie's hand. "Robert." He shook Robert's hand as Robert gave him a quick hug, slapping his back.

"See you in the Dandenongs"

"Look forward to it."

Neil smiled at Joan before hugging her. "This has been an honour, Joan. I just wish I'd met you sooner. Maybe Ernie would've had a fight on his hands."

Joan giggled. "It's been wonderful to meet you, Neil." He kissed her cheek before making his way out of the lobby with his driver, turning to bow and blow a kiss to them.

They slowly made their way back to their suite, laughing and chattering about what a lovely man Neil was.

Joan took her shoes off and laid on the bed. "Oh Frances, tonight was wonderful. It was like a dream come true. You went to so much trouble to make it perfect. Thank you."

"You're welcome, Joan. I'm glad you enjoyed it. I can't believe we also jagged a perfect sunset!"

"It was beautiful. See, Ernie's smiling down at us."

"Not sure he would've been smiling at Neil," joked Robert "trying to steal his woman."

Joan laughed, waving her hand. "Oh no, Ernie was never the jealous type. He knew he was the only man for me."

She looked up at them both.

"I don't know how I'll ever thank you two enough for everything you've done for me. I'm so blessed to have met you."

They both sat on the bed next to her. Joan closed her eyes.

"I'm ready now."

Frankie stared at Robert, the colour draining from her face. Robert hugged Frankie before going into the bathroom, returning with a glass of water and two tablets.

"Joan, these tablets will make you drowsy. You'll simply drift off to sleep."

"Thank you, Robert" she sat up and swallowed them, washing them down with water before lying back down.

"Here Joan, I'll show you the footage from today."

Frankie laid down next to her, Robert on the other side as they watched the video, smiling and laughing together.

Frankie held Joan's hand. "I love you, Joan."

"I love you too, Frances. I'll see you again dear."

As the video continued to play, tears filled Frankie's eyes as Joan slowly drifted off to sleep. She hugged her, rocking her back and forth, kissing her face and sobbing uncontrollably. Robert put his arms around them both, tears also streaming down his face.

Robert moved next to Frankie, holding her close while she cried.

"It's okay beautiful. This is what she wanted. You made everything absolutely *perfect* for her."

"I'm going to miss her so *much* Robert!" blubbered Frankie.

"I know," he hugged her tight, kissing her head. "I know."

They laid with Joan for an hour while she slept peacefully. Robert took Frankie by the hand and led her into their bedroom, sitting her on the bed.

"I'm going to give her the morphine now. Why don't you stay here?" She nodded.

Robert returned several minutes later, sitting next to Frankie and putting his arm around her.

"She's gone," he whispered, hugging her and stroking her hair as she cried.

The next morning Robert rang the ambulance to report Joan's death, before ringing Maggie.

"What happened?" asked Maggie.

"She must have passed away in her sleep," said Robert. "We all had a lovely night last night, and we sat up talking until around midnight. Then we found her this morning. I've checked her over. There's no sign of distress. It looks like she passed peacefully."

"Oh, that's so sad," said Maggie. "I better ring her son."

"I can do that Maggie. It's probably more appropriate. We *were* the last ones with her."

"Okay then. Have you rung a doctor?"

"I've called the ambulance. They should be here soon."

Maggie sighed. "Well, at least she got to have a holiday I guess."

"She had a fantastic time, Maggie. I'm just glad we got to share it with her."

"Okay Rob. Can you tell her son to ring me please, we'll need to sort out all the details." Maggie paused. "How's Frankie?"

"She's devastated. Her and Joan were pretty close."

"Yes, I thought that. Well, look after her Rob and keep me in the loop. Enjoy your time with your mum and the rest of your family. Take care, okay, and I'll see you when you get back. Stay in touch."

"Thanks Maggie. I'll talk to you soon. Bye."

"How did that go?" asked Frankie

"Yeah, it went well. She didn't seem too surprised. I told her I'd ring Daniel."

"Do you want me to ring him?"

"It might be best if I do it. I can give him all the medical jargon."

Robert answered the knock at the door, ushering in the two paramedics.

Robert led the way into the bedroom, repeating the story he'd told Maggie. He also filled them in on Joan's background of rapidly deteriorating Alzheimer's and their quest to take her on a holiday before her relegation to the nursing home. One paramedic remarked what a beautiful environment it was to spend your final hours, before taking all the details down.

They wheeled Joan's body out on a stretcher as Frankie watched on with tears in her red, puffy eyes.

"Better ring Daniel," said Robert, picking up his phone.

"I want to speak to him as well."

Robert looked puzzled. "Okay."

Frankie watched as Robert stood on the balcony speaking to Daniel. From Robert's body language the conversation seemed calm. He eventually walked back inside, handing her the phone.

"Hi Daniel."

"Hello Frankie." Daniel had clearly been crying.

"Daniel, I'm so sorry about your mum. I know I've been such a bitch to you, but I want you to know I really loved your mum. She had a wonderful time last night, and you should've seen her face when she saw Neil! She was so happy." Frankie started to get teary. "And when she saw the foundation certificate, she was over the moon. I just wanted to say thank you Daniel. For everything." She started to cry.

Daniel was also crying. "Okay Frankie. Well, I'm glad she had a good time. Thanks for going to so much trouble for her. Robert told me all about it."

"I'm going to send you all her memoirs, Daniel. And I've also got some videos from last night. You'll love them. Oh, and Neil said he'll be happy to support your foundation."

"Oh really? Okay, great."

"I hope that we get to meet you one day. Maybe we could help out with your fundraisers."

"Yeah, maybe."

"Okay Daniel, take care."

"You too, Frankie. Bye."

Frankie looked at Robert. "What did you say to him?"

He wrapped his arms around her. "I told him that you were a godsend to his mum and that you brought her joy and happiness and friendship and laughter. All of which is true. I told him how much you loved her, and she loved you. Also, which is true. I simply told him the truth."

Frankie smiled at him. "I really *do* love her."

"And *I* love *you*!" Robert picked her up and carried her into the bedroom.

As they drove away from the hotel, Frankie felt a strange sense of freedom. Like a giant weight had been lifted from her. She thought about the night before. It couldn't have been more perfect. Joan's final night had been everything she wished for, and thanks to the foundation, her memory would live on. The world would know about the vibrant Joan Middleton, Broadway dancer and beautiful bombshell who loved with such passion it could inspire even the Greek gods. Frankie smiled to herself as she heard Joan's voice in her head.

Robert pulled into the car park at the lookout on top of the escarpment and ran around to open Frankie's door. He led her over to the railing which overlooked the rugged cliff face and out into the beautiful endless blue ocean.

He grabbed both her hands, staring at her with a huge smile on his face.

"What!" she laughed.

He reached into his pocket. "Joan gave me this last night. She wanted me to give it to you." He slowly opened his hand to reveal a beautiful gold band encrusted with diamonds. "It's the eternity ring Ernie gave her." He slid it onto her finger and wrapped his arms around her, swinging her around.

Frankie cried tears of joy as they stood on the cliff, hugging and kissing each other.

"Let's go beautiful. I can't wait to tell my family." Frankie looked at him. "I finally found the one! *Eureka!*"

"*Eureka!*" screamed Frankie, jumping into Robert's arms.

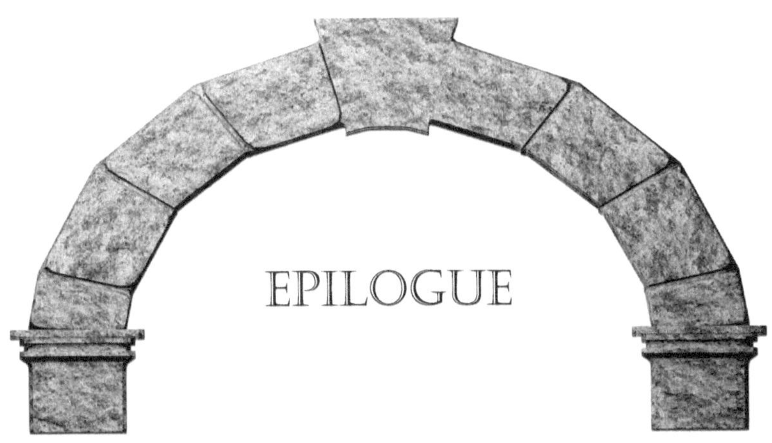

EPILOGUE

Jackie Hooper shook her wet umbrella before carefully navigating her way through the glass carousel door, her briefcase and takeaway coffee in the other hand.

As she made her way to the lifts, the heavy-set suited man sitting in the lobby stood up to follow her.

"Jackie."

She stopped to look around. "George. Look, I've already *told* you, my client's whereabouts are strictly confidential!"

He stood arrogantly smirking at her. "Is that so?"

"*Yes,* George it *is!*" she said sternly. "It's none of your *business!*"

"*Well,* Jackie, I've just come from visiting *my* client. He's lying in St Vincent's. Just woke up actually. From a *coma.*"

He moved closer, menacingly staring her in the face. "And from what he just told *me*, your client's whereabouts are very *much* my business."

Jackie paused. "*Shit!*"

George shadowed her as she bustled her way into the lift, elbowing button twenty-three.

THE AUTHOR THANKS

Writing this book has been an amazing and rewarding challenge. I've had a lot of help along the way.

To my wonderful family and friends: Thank you for being my sounding board, my advisors, my proof readers and my cheer squad. Having you in my corner means a lot to me and has made this journey so much easier.

To the Lake Macquarie Fellowship of Australian Writers: You welcomed me as a novice and made me feel instantly at home. Thank you for your support and guidance from your wealth of combined knowledge.

To Lea: Thank you for all your talented work on my cover design. You managed to capture the essence of my story instantly – you are brilliant.

And to Sandi – My publisher, friend and mentor. Without all your hard work, enthusiasm and encouragement I would have been lost. I can't thank you enough for all the time you have spent helping me to achieve my dream. You are an amazing woman!

ABOUT THE AUTHOR

Kayla Spain was raised in Newcastle, surrounded by siblings, friends, and pets of all types: a dog, a cat, budgies, a galah, silkworms, mice, and even a sheep. Her childhood was spent playing outside; a true gift she will never take for granted.

Today, she still adores nature and animals, and has many feathered friends who visit her yard daily to sing to her – and maybe get a treat in return.

Her family are her world, and she has recently become a grandma to "the most beautiful little girl".

Kayla is a passionate advocate of the random and ridiculous and believes that laughter really is the best medicine for any ailment this modern life throws at us.

She has always enjoyed creative pursuits and, one morning, she woke with an idea. "I might write a novel". A few months later it became a reality.

She believes that anyone can create magic, no matter who they are. Just sit still and listen. Kayla encourages other artists to follow their dreams: "If you are passionate about something, you will achieve it, no matter how hard it is, or however long it takes".